The Blood Sword
A Hand of Adonai Novel

To Bruce — Enjoy the book. Blessings of Adonai... and happy birthday in August Aaron Gansky

by
AARON D. GANSKY

Brimstone
Fiction

THE BLOOD SWORD A HAND OF ADONAI NOVEL BY AARON D. GANSKY
Published by Brimstone Fiction
1440 W. Taylor Street, Suite 449
Chicago, IL 60607

ISBN: 978-1-946758-01-9
Copyright © 2017 by Aaron D. Gansky
Interior Design by Karthick Srinivasan
Cover Design by Elaina Lee, www.forthemusedesign.com

Available in print from your local bookstore, online, or from the publisher at:
www.brimstonefiction.com

For more information on this book and the author visit: www.aarongansky.com

This is a work of fiction. Names, characters, and incidents are all products of the
author's imagination or are used for fictional purposes. Any mentioned brand names,
places, and trademarks remain the property of their respective owners, bear no
association with the author or the publisher, and are used for fictional purposes only.
Brimstone Fiction may include ghosts, werewolves, witches, the undead, soothsayers,
mythological creatures, theoretical science, fictional technology, and material which,
though mentioned in Scripture, may be of a controversial nature within some religious
circles.

All scripture quotations, unless otherwise indicated, are taken from the Holy Bible,
New International Version®, NIV®. Copyright ©1973, 1978, 1984, 2011 by Biblica,
Inc.TM. Used by permission of Zondervan. All rights reserved worldwide.
www.zondervan.com. "NIV" and "New International Version" are trademarks
registered in the United States Patent and Trademark Office by Biblica, Inc.TM.

Brought to you by the creative team at Lighthouse Publishing of the Carolinas
and Brimstone Fiction: Bethany R. Kaczmarek, Rowena Kuo, Meaghan Burnett,
Shonda Savage, Eddie Jones, Brian Cross, and Jennifer Leo.

Library of Congress Cataloging-in-Publication Data
Gansky, Aaron D.
Hand of Adonai: The Blood Sword / Aaron D. Gansky 1st ed.

Printed in the United States of America

Praise for *The Blood Sword*
A Hand of Adonai Novel

Step into the land of Alrujah—a place populated by remarkable characters, human and otherwise—and I guarantee you an adventure you won't soon forget. Each page is rich with description, and each chapter carries us deeper into intrigue while unraveling subtle spiritual truths. Aaron, my friend, your imagination runneth over!

~**Ann Tatlock**
Award-winning novelist and children's book author

Gansky creates a beautiful blend of familiar monsters and those who dwell only in our deepest imaginations, and his constant barrage of twists and turns kept me on edge throughout this action-packed, young adult fantasy. *The Blood Sword: A Hand of Adonai Novel* is sure to be a hit with adventure-seeking teens.

~**J. Andersen**
Author of *The Breeding Tree* and *At What Cost*

Aaron Gansky has a very easy and comfortable way with words, and his deftness with storytelling is nothing short of magical. *Hand of Adonai* is a story I could get lost in time and time again.

~**Mike Dellosso**
Author of *Centralia* and *Kill Devil* (Jed Patrick novels)

The second book in the *Hand of Adonai* series does not disappoint! *The Blood Sword: A Hand of Adonai Novel* brings back the characters we already knew to be both instantly relatable and deeply inspiring, while dishing out even more page turning action and adventure. Gansky is a master at weaving a beautiful, spiritual tale that stretches both our imaginations and our hearts. A book everyone in the family will want to read and one that held me hostage to the very last page.

~ **Heather Luby**
Author of *Laws of Motion*, *The Boys Were Watching*, and *Runaway*

Aaron Gansky is king of "other" worlds. He pulled me immediately into the dangerous world of Alrujah—a world I not only could see in my imagination, but could traipse through without getting lost. The characters were complicated and purposeful. They grasped hold of me and did not let go. I enjoyed the first book, but this one. . .this one soars. Open the book, lean back, and be prepared to be transported.

~ **Cindy Sproles**
Author of *Mercy's Rain*, speaker, and editor

The Blood Sword: A Hand of Adonai Novel, the second book in Aaron Gansky's compelling series, houses an eclectic cast of intriguing characters who are struggling to find their way home. Primarily set in a video game the protagonist invented, the book is ripe with magic, mystery, and peril. From the creative, thoughtful, and pious main character, Oliver, to the sassy, rebellious, and ultimately lovable Erica, every character in this book is at once refreshingly original and yet familiar. A novel filled with tension, the reader finds himself on the edge of his seat, turning pages with anticipation, waiting to see if this band of loveable teenagers will be able to fend off the monsters that populate their new home. The book, however, is much more than an action thriller. Themes of love, acceptance, and most importantly faith permeate the text in subtle and sophisticated ways. By the time you come to the end of book two in this trilogy, you understand that you've been on an exhilarating journey that has tickled your imagination, and deepened your understanding of human nature, and God.

~ **Dennis Fulgoni**
Author of *At the Broken Places* and *Dead Man's Nail*

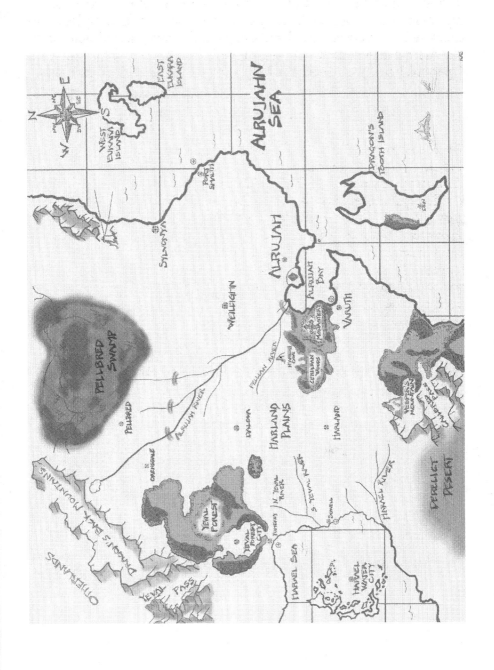

ACKNOWLEDGEMENTS

Originally, when I set out to write my first YA fantasy novel, I wanted to do it as a standalone. And indeed, I did. But it was the advice of my first agent, Diana Flegal, that finally convinced me to turn it into something longer. While I liked it as a standalone, turning it into something larger has been one of the best writing decisions I've made. So thank you, Diana, for your sage advice.

Of course, this book would have a very different shape, a very different feel, if not for the ideas of Stephen McLain, who embarked on this journey with me from the very beginning. It was his advice I most often sought, and his ideas that helped to shape the series as it is. His influence and gentle, specific questioning has dramatically impacted the larger story arc.

Dennis Fulgoni, fellow writer and confidant, has had a tremendous impact on the prose. It's his keen eyes that read this before any others. He's continually faithful to make the time to not only read my writing, but to guide the forming of the prose. If there's a cliché in this book, it's my fault, not his, and it's likely because I added it in after he's read it. His reading has benefited every chapter of this novel.

Of course, no one has supported me more than my family: my wife, Naomi, who is a patient partner in my writing, my children, who always ask about my writing and are quick to tell their friends that I'm "a real writer," and my father, novelist and mentor, Alton Gansky. Go read his books. Then, tell him thanks for writing great stories and inspiring me to follow in his footsteps.

I'm entirely indebted to Eddie Jones and Rowena Kuo. Not only do they believe in my writing, they believe in me. Their encouragement is paramount. And of course, I couldn't have published this book without them. I love their vision for Brimstone Fiction and Lighthouse Publishing of the Carolinas. I'm humbled and honored to be part of their team.

And, of course, Bethany Kaczmarek, who is reading this right now and may have worried that I'd forget her. I haven't. I can't. Simply the best editor I've ever worked with. She gets me, and more importantly, gets my vision for the novel, and helps me to find it with clear, precise language and grammar. Also, she never purposefully makes me feel bad about my randomly capitalizing things that have no business being capitalized. So, you know, that's a plus.

Speaking of Kaczmareks, I'm indebted to Caleb Kaczmarek for his faithful work on the new map you see in the opening pages of the novel. The map from the first novel, wonderfully created by Kristin Brittner, was an incredible upgrade from the original I scrawled out with colored pencils on a piece of printer paper. The need arose to update the map with new locations that will play a part later in the series, and Caleb offered his services to add in the new locations and give the map a bit of a face-lift. I could not be happier with the job they both did, and I could not be more excited about their contributions to the world of Alrujah. Thank you, both.

Lastly, to my readers, who are faithful and kind and patient. It's strange having your work in the world, but it's nice to know that there are always open arms into which it will fall.

Dedication

To my wife, Naomi Gansky.

For your insurmountable patience and encouragement.
May God continue to bless you with surpassing abundance.

CHARACTERS

Lauren Knowles/Indigo: Daughter of Becca Knowles. For years, she's dreamed of the land of Alrujah, and has put every detail into her journals for her friend Oliver to program into the role playing game they've been working on together since junior high school. When she wakes up in Alrujah, she takes the role of Princess Indigo, daughter of King Ribillius, and sets out to find *The Book of Sealed Magic* so she and her friends can get home.

Oliver Shaw/Vicmorn the Devout: The boy genius behind the Alrujah video game. He designed his own programming language in order to make the game more realistic. In Alrujah, he takes on the role of Vicmorn, a Father of the Monks of the Cerulean Order.

Erica Hall/Lakia: A gothic teenager with few friends in high school, Erica has long been admired by Oliver. When she wakes up in the game, she sees it as an opportunity to get out of school. Unlike the others, she's not in a hurry to get back to North Chester.

Aiden Price/Jaurru: New to North Chester High School this year, Aiden Price found a home on the football team, though not without some conflict getting there. He's had his eye on Lauren, and he'll do whatever it takes to protect her in the dangerous world of Alrujah, where he has become Jaurru, King Ribillius's personal guard.

Ullwen of Varuth: A former Varuthian Infiltrator and current Varuthian Elite, Ullwen of Varuth fell in love with Princess Indigo. Now, he has turned his back on his home town to defend and protect her.

Bailey Renee Knowles: Lauren's little sister. Bailey is very smart, athletically gifted, and wracked with guilt over the disappearance of Lauren from North Chester. She's made it her mission to find her sister and bring her home.

Detective Joseph Parker: Detective Parker works missing persons cases for the North Chester PD. He's taken a special interest in the disappearance of the four teens.

Pacha el Nai: A mighty angel who speaks for Adonai.

Maewen: A mighty angel who helped King Solous defeat the elves and retake the throne of Alrujah for men.

King Solous: The long-dead king of Alrujah who, with the help of seven angels, overthrew the elves from the throne of Alrujah.

King Ribillius: The direct descendent of Solous who now reigns over Alrujah in a time of turmoil. He fears for the safety of his daughter, who has been threatened by the Mage Lord, an ancient evil force.

Captain Korodeth: Captain of the Guard of Alrujah and trusted advisor for King Ribillius. His line is to ascend the throne if ever the line of Solous perishes.

Prologue

For a time, Shedoah will allow himself to be imprisoned by Adonai.
He will live under the sea. But Adonai's power will not hold Shedoah.
Shedoah will rise again, overcome Adonai and his reign of disease and
war, and restore peace to Alrujah for a thousand years.

—The Shedoahn Prophecies

Maewen folded her wings and plummeted toward Dragon's Tooth Island. There, among the mountainous waterfalls and the dense green foliage, she alighted on the highest pinnacle. Her bismuth circlet glimmered in the waning light of the lesser sun. She carried no weapons. She'd had no need since Solous ascended the throne.

Rich with the power of Adonai, the island remained hidden from Alrujahns for centuries. She'd not heard it mentioned among the elves since the War of the Suns.

Far overhead, Pacha el Nai circled the island. Two dark spots buzzed like flies near his distant form. As he descended, the spots took the shape of griffins. She never understood Pacha's fascination with the creatures. He did all he could to keep them hidden from the people of Alrujah, convinced they'd "subjugate the noble animals and breed them for war."

Already, they were bred for war. Adonai saw to that. With paws the size of stone tablets and twice as heavy, they could swipe a man's head from his shoulders without effort. Their beaks, with their gleaming razor edges, could snap tendon from bone.

The two Pacha el Nai brought landed beside him. One tawny, the other black, both sat like well-trained dogs. He touched each of their heads and smiled. "Maewen, it is good to see you."

"And you in kind," she responded. "May Adonai bless your steps."

"An odd choice of greetings for one such as yourself."

Maewen folded her arms.

The tawny griffin lay on the cold black rock precipice. Pacha el Nai continued. "Adonai is concerned. The hearts of the elves turn toward you. They worship you as a goddess."

"I do not encourage their worship."

"Do you reject it?"

"How can I, when Adonai forbids me to appear before them?"

Unlike Maewen, Pacha el Nai had come fully armed. His twin swords hung at his hips, humming with power. "And yet you've not obeyed this commandment."

Maewen's heart chilled. Of course, Adonai knew, but had he told Pacha? He must have. And if Pacha knew, the others would, too. How long had they known?

Pacha's smile thinned. The black griffin screeched, flapped its wings. "Your actions have endangered the lives of all who live in Alrujah."

"I know," she said. "I have repented. Is that not enough?"

"Children," Pacha said. "Twins. They live among the elves as gods, and you ask if repentance is enough? They are abominations, Maewen, and must be dealt with."

"No," she said, her hands grabbing his shoulders.

The black griffin snapped at her hands, but Pacha settled it with a palm on its head.

Maewen's throat tightened. "Spare them, please. The mistake was mine. I will bear the burden of punishment."

"They've taken wives," Pacha said. The tawny griffin shrilled at Maewen. "Until now, Adonai has been merciful. He's allowed them to live. But they must not bear children. To do so would further upset the balance of peace in Alrujah. Their children would lay waste human and elf and dwarf alike."

Maewen's eyes widened. Her circlet weighed heavy on her brow. How had she not known they'd taken wives? She'd been away from them too long. Without her guidance, their hearts would turn from her to the elves. "Must they pay with their lives for my mistake?"

Pacha took her wrists gently. "The decision is not yours. Adonai must act against such abominations."

"Please. They are my sons. They've done nothing to harm the people of Alrujah."

Both griffins screeched at her, and she stepped back. She steeled herself, moved forward toward Pacha. "Don't do this, Pacha. We've been friends for centuries. We've fought together, served Adonai together. Do not let my single mistake end our friendship."

Pacha stretched his wings. "Adonai will relent and allow them their lives. But your sin must not jeopardize Alrujah. You know what you must do."

She nodded. "I must go to my people and denounce their worship. I must bring my sons here, to Dragon's Tooth Island, away from Alrujah and Harael."

Pacha rested his hands on the hilts of his swords. "You must slay their wives."

She lowered her head.

"I do not envy you your task."

Maewen's knees weakened. She rested her head on his chest. Once, she'd loved Pacha, though love was forbidden among angels, and so she turned to the elves. What if Pacha had returned her love? Would they have avoided this mess? Or would they be in a different chaos?

He wrapped his massive arms around her, enfolding her smaller body, her fragile wings. "Be quick. If they're not dead by tomorrow's sunsdown, and your sons are here on Dragon's Tooth Island I will deal with them myself." He released her, stretched his wings, and launched himself from the cliff. The griffins followed close after, screaming at the waterfalls, their shrill voices echoing over the streams and the ocean.

Maewen wasted no time. She lifted herself in the air and flew through the night to Harael. The wind pressed her cheeks hard. Her eyes watered. She tried not to think about the task before her.

She landed lightly on the smallest, southernmost island and ducked inside a dank cave. She retrieved a spear leaning against the wall near the entrance. Her sons, now twenty-four years old, lay near the back of the cave, next to two young, beautiful elves. They'd decorated the cave, hung Torap's paintings, built shelves for Uhesdey's books, constructed beds from bamboo and straw mattresses. They'd lit the walls with enchanted ever-burning, smokeless torches.

The blonde elf wore a golden circlet and slept with her head on Torap's chest. Her left ear wore the bismuth ankh, Torap's chosen symbol. Torap, eldest of her twin sons, wore an identical earring in his left ear. His chest rose and fell slowly, and his new bride's hand draped over his stomach.

The black-haired elf lay beside Uhesdey, her leg draped over his, a golden anklet reflecting the sparkling water near the back of the cave. In her left ear, she wore the bismuth four-pointed star, Uhesdey's chosen symbol. He wore an identical ring in his left ear.

Her sons had taken brides, had started families, and hadn't told her. The betrayal stung, but she understood why. She'd forbade them to interact with the elves, mandated they stay in this cave. But they were young. They'd not obey her forever. And why shouldn't they experience love? Why shouldn't they raise their families?

Because, she reminded herself, such an act would spell the demise of Alrujah.

Within the bellies of these women grew the destruction of the world.

Maewen readied her spear, steeled her nerves. She whispered over her sons and their wives, deepened their sleep, then lifted the elf women, one in each hand. Secure in a bottomless slumber, the women's bodies flopped like boneless fish. Their necks lolled to the sides, their chests rising and falling in slow meter.

Outside the cave, she leapt, flapped her wings, and flew to the beach beyond the jungle trees. She lay the women in the sand, the blonde beside the dark-haired. They were so small, so young, so beautiful. No wonder her sons had fallen in love with them. Next to her giant sons, they'd looked like dolls. Her heart wept to do what she knew she must. "I'm sorry," she whispered. She lifted her spear and plunged it through the heart of Uhesdey's beloved.

The woman's body twitched. Her chest swelled, her hands grasped the massive shaft, her eyes snapped open, then rolled back into her head. Air seeped from her, escaped like a confused sigh.

The blonde stirred, rolled in the sand.

Wiping tears from her eyes, Maewen stepped on the dark-haired elf's chest and pulled the spear free. She rolled the blonde on her back.

The elf awoke. "What?" she asked.

Maewen spoke the words of sleep over her again and closed the elf's eyes.

With a heavy breath, Maewen lifted her spear and stabbed the blonde in the heart.

She'd killed hundreds of wicked men and elves and dwarves and never shed a tear. Now, remorse welled in her, and the bloodied bodies twisted her with guilt. She dropped to her knees beside them, wept over their wounds. "I'm sorry," she said. "I'm sorry. I had no choice."

"Mother?"

Maewen's head snapped up, her guilt instantly magnified. Fear widened her eyes.

Had he seen her plunge the spear into his beloved? How had Uhesdey resisted her sleep enchantment? How had he made it to the beach so quickly?

She stepped over the bodies of the women, did her best to stand between them and Uhesdey, to obscure his view. "My son," she said by way of distraction. She dropped the bloodied spear behind her in the sand.

"What have you done?" he asked.

She could not hide it from him. He would find the truth soon enough, and hate her for it. "I had to," she said. "Adonai demanded it. If I didn't, he would destroy us all."

He couldn't understand, wouldn't. His ears wouldn't hear her words. His eyes would see only the bloodied corpse of his new bride, the soft swell of her belly, and anger would flash hot inside him. He'd taken his personality from his father, a war elf who loved the blood his job demanded he spill.

"You must come with me," she said, hoping her son would listen. "We must go. We must leave the elvish isles."

"Neldessa?" he whispered, moving to his wife. He knelt beside her, pressed his hands to the hill of her belly, the blood of her wounds.

Maewen steadied her voice. "This is not what I wanted. Forgive me, my son. I have no right to ask it of you, but I beg nonetheless."

Torap, near seven feet tall, emerged from the tree line of the jungle. "Baradeth," he whispered, his voice like distant thunder. He knelt beside her, whispered over her wounds. Immediately, the skin began to seal; the blood slowed.

But the wound was too much for even Torap to heal. Maewen had seen to that. "Hear me, Son," she said again, retrieving her spear. "I've done this for you. We are in danger here. We must move. We'll be safe on Dragon's Tooth Island."

Uhesdey fisted his hands. "Safe?" he asked, standing. "From what, exactly? From whom? The elves? They're nothing. They fear us. They worship us as gods."

"From Adonai."

"Adonai?" Uhesdey spat. "I've never seen him. He is no god. If he were, he would protect you from me."

"He will strike you down if you don't come with me," Maewen said. "Please, we must go."

"Will you kill me, too? Mother?" Uhesdey stood over her, freakishly tall, his eyes like two smoldering coals.

"I could never raise a hand against you."

Torap's chest heaved. "But you would kill our wives? Did you not see our earrings? Did you not see their bellies growing? You murder our wives and our children, but you swear not to harm us?"

Uhesdey reached for her neck, but Maewen stepped back and smacked his hand away. He grabbed her wrist and pulled hard. The bones in her hand snapped. She twisted, found her footing, and steadied herself. Pain lanced through her arm up to her shoulder. "Please, Uhesdey. Your life is in danger if you stay here."

"You killed Neldessa!" Uhesdey shouted.

Torap stood, his head bowed, eyes brimming with tears. "I couldn't heal her."

Uhesdey sneered. "Your power is of life and light. It cannot touch the dead or the dark."

"But yours can, Brother," Torap said, his voice pleading. He took his brother by the shoulders. "You can bring them back to us."

"No," Maewen said. "Such a thing is evil. The dead must stay dead."

"You've been away too long, Mother," Uhesdey said as he knelt next to his slaughtered bride. "Our powers have grown. The waters of Harael run deep. Torap's hand guides them, and mine freezes them. His hand establishes life. My hand brings death. His will brings light and mine darkness. We are the balance of Harael. There is no place for you." Beneath the silver moon, he took the hands of the brides, and the corpses stood.

Maewen's chest tightened. Only Moloch could raise the dead. How had Uhesdey discovered this power? Cradling her broken wrist, she said, "What you do is evil."

Torap spoke, his voice broken with sorrow. "I marvel how twisted your logic is, Mother. Which is more evil, to slaughter the living, or to raise the dead?"

She should not have come. This was a mistake. They would strike at her, and no amount of talking would stay their hand. Perhaps, if she flew to Dragon's Tooth Island, they would follow her. Once there, she might trap them.

Her wings ached from the frenzied flight across Alrujah, and she doubted she had the strength to fly back. But she would have to. If she stayed to fight, she would not win.

"Please," she said to buy time. Her mind raced for a spell that would bind them to the Dragon's Tooth.

Torap lunged at her. Maewen moved, but Uhesdey joined the fight. He wrested her spear from her unbroken hand before she realized where he was. He stabbed at her, and Maewen struggled to move in time. The flaming emerald tip of the spear seared her skin. Her wrist shrieked in pain.

She spread her wings and leapt, but each of her sons grabbed an ankle and threw her to the ground. She spun, hoping to break her fall, but they'd pulled too hard. She landed hard on her back, snapping her wings. She arched her back in agony. Sand slithered between her armor and skin, pulled her under with snakelike fingers.

Torap.

The sands carried her toward the sea, and the sea reached up for her.

Uhesdey punched the ground hard, and hundreds of dead elves crawled up with the tide. Their flesh, loose and bloated on their bones, shone blue in the moonlight. Tendons clung limply to bone. Reddish muscle stretched beneath torn skin. Teeth clacked and snapped in rigid jaws.

Maewen flexed her fingers. Pain knifed her wrist, but she put it out of mind, and a million bursts of light exploded around her sons and their wives. The distraction gave her time to pull herself from the sand-fingers, right herself and bend the silver moonlight to create thirty perfectly mirrored copies of herself. They moved with her, action for action, breath for breath.

Pain seared her snapped wings. Whatever dream she'd had of flying to Dragon's Tooth Island was now impossible. If she hoped to survive, she'd have to fight.

She thought of the War of the Suns, of her battle against the elves, but this time, she had no human army behind her, no troops to command. Dead elf hands grasped at her. She needed a weapon, needed her spear. She pooled light into a white-hot disk and severed the elves' hands. She turned the light toward her sons, burning a path to them.

Uhesdey and Torap moved in opposite directions. She followed Uhesdey. "Stop this madness," she said. "I only wanted to help you, to protect you."

He closed his right fist, and the moon blinked out. Her doppelgängers vanished.

Such power.

Uhesdey stabbed at her, catching her side, slashing her armor.

She moved on instinct, wrapping her good arm around the spear and kicking Uhesdey in the chest. Not hard enough to crush his sternum, but hard enough to separate him from the weapon.

He stumbled back. She twisted the spear into the palm of her good hand.

Torap grabbed her and threw her against a tree on the edge of the beach. Pain seared her wings, her back. She leveled the spear at his chest. "Please, Torap, not you." She'd never seen him angry until this moment.

He leapt at her.

She bent the thin tendrils of light stretching through Uhesdey's disk of darkness, used them to vanish from Torap's sight. She reappeared behind him and kicked him in the small of the back. She had to stop them without killing them.

How had it come to this?

The hands of the dead grabbed her broken wings and pulled her back. Hundreds fell on her. She pooled light into disks and slashed at them, but there were too many. They scratched her face, pulled her limbs until she couldn't move. Uhesdey's foot smashed down on her neck.

Tears burned her eyes.

Torap handed the spear to Uhesdey.

Uhesdey raised the weapon. "An eye for an eye," he said.

Desperate with fear, Maewen burned light. She concentrated it in two spots, Uhesdey's right eye and Torap's left. She burned hard, and the light exploded.

Their heads snapped back, and they staggered through the sand. The elf corpses fell. Neldessa and Baradeth, still bloodied and lumbering, crumpled in the sand.

Maewen stood quickly and struggled toward the sea. If she could not fly, she would have to swim.

Torap, one hand over his bloodied eye, snatched his mother's wings. With a savage shout, he threw her on the sand.

Pain galloped through her wings, her spine, her ribs. Breath left her chest.

Torap knelt on her shoulders, pinned her down. Hate and loathing twisted his face.

His anger hurt her more than any of her wounds. He'd been such a beautiful, gentle child. She'd failed them as a mother, failed Adonai as an angel.

With one hand, Torap clutched her neck.

Uhesdey stepped on her broken wrist. "Kill her."

Maewen tried to shriek, but Torap pinched off her throat. The pupil of his remaining eye shrank to a peppercorn.

She fought to put the pain from her mind. With her good arm, she tried to wrest Torap's thumb loose, but he was too strong. If she could speak, if she could tell them how much she loved them, if she could make them hear her heart.

Her words dribbled out as a gurgle.

Uhesdey plunged her spear into her palm.

Her back arched with pain.

"Why?" Torap said.

His eye narrowed. His blood and tears dripped down her cheeks. How long could she survive without air? She shut out the pain in her hand, her wings, her neck.

"Do it now," Uhesdey said. "Or I will." He stepped forward. His black, unnatural shadow poured over her.

Torap lowered his left hand.

With the end nigh, Maewen stilled. Perhaps this was best. Perhaps this is what she deserved. And why shouldn't death come from their hands? At least, she would not die alone. At least, the last thing she would see would be her sons, whom she loved.

Torap put his bloodied hand on her face. His blood was warm, his palm hot.

Did he feel her waning pulse beneath his thick fingers? Did he see the panic turned peace in her eyes? Did he see her love for him?

His palm heated until it seared her skin.

Still, she would not scream, even if she could.

A white-hot light erupted from Torap's fingers and palm.

* * *

As the docks of Sylvonya neared, Archduke Pentavus Korodeth gave Argus, his trusted Captain of the Chameleon Soldiers, some final instructions before docking. "Stay close to me, cloaked in your Chameleon Armor. Do not reveal yourself, even if you feel I am in danger. I assure you, there is little threat they can muster that would cause me fear."

Argus nodded and pulled his hood over his face. Instantly, the enchanted light-refracting armor caused him to vanish.

Korodeth sailed the one-mast boat to the nearest rickety dock at the eastern gate of Sylvonya. Two port guards, lightly armored and cloaked in red, stood beside two castle guards wearing heavy plate mail and cloaked in blue. All four put a clenched fist over their hearts.

After the long journey, Korodeth's legs took a moment to adjust to the steady, unwavering ground. He brought his right fist to his left shoulder, and the guards released their salutes. He greeted each by name, asked after their families, assured them they'd done a fine job.

He rarely smiled, but his stern stare made his words earnest. These men would follow him anywhere, fight for him, die for him. They'd pledged fealty to Ribillius with their mouths, but their hearts belonged to Korodeth, as was the case with most military personnel. He'd seen to that over the years, dedicating himself to the training and well-being of the standing armies of each of Alrujah's cities. Ribillius spent too much time in the throne room and behind closed doors administering the kingdom. Korodeth liked the personal touch.

"How was your journey?" Dybarian asked. He'd served as Viceroy Harrow's Captain of the Watch for Sylvonya for years now, almost as long as Harrow sat the Port Dais. Like the rest of the castle guard and the watch, he'd been appointed by Korodeth.

"Swift and lonely."

Dybarian grinned. "Traveling alone will do that." The castle gates swung open at their approach.

Women in long, filthy dresses lined the cobblestone streets. They threw buckets of sea water and lye over the road and scrubbed with stiff-bristled brushes. Korodeth moved aside to allow the water to pass by. He had no desire to turn his boots pink with the bloody water. "Droughtworm?" he asked.

Dybarian shouldered his halberd. The three other guards marched in perfect step with him. "We drag a hundred bodies to the ocean every morning, sir."

Korodeth shook his head. The market, as always, bustled. Guards watched over merchants and their customs. The city walls echoed with the names of a thousand fish and crustaceans in myriad accents. At least the economy still thrived.

Deeper into the heart of the city, as they passed the homes of castle servants and public officials, men and women slumped against their walls, held their children in thin arms. Korodeth's heart heavied. "We're working to find a solution. Every man who can read has his eyes in a book. Every healer at our command studies the dead to protect the living."

The man smiled. "No one loves the people like you, Captain."

"No?"

"None sir. And well the people know it. If anyone finds the answer, it will be you."

Before them, the castle loomed large on the horizon. The steep inclined streets led directly to the castle gates, where the gardens famous for hibiscus and oleander lay in ruins. The plants, long dead, had been burned. Blood smeared the stone walls of the castle.

"What happened here?"

"Difference of opinions," the guard said.

"The monks?"

Dybarian nodded. "Proclaimed Adonai as god and demanded Viceroy Harrow tear down Tiamat's church."

"And you killed them?"

"On Viceroy Harrow's command, aye."

Korodeth had trained Dybarian personally. He took great pride in having a personal investment in the military leaders of Alrujah's cities. And in that training, he'd seen Dybarian fight off a dozen men with a dulled halberd. "How many?"

"Near the whole monastery, sir. A few ran off."

"There were almost sixty monks in Sylvonya's monastery."

"The Brown Brothers pressed in on our walls. They would not disperse."

Korodeth knelt. From his lower stature, he could see the broken plants, the lines and puddles of black blood. Near the hibiscus, the puddles ran red. They'd fought recently, within the day.

Harrow was a bigger fool than he thought. He stood. "Clean up this mess. It's a disgrace."

"Aye, Captain." The guard turned back and called after his mates.

Korodeth marched directly to the throne room. Viceroy Harrow, a robust man draped in a red robe with blue stitching, stood. He smoothed his white beard and stared at Korodeth. "You're early."

Korodeth stormed up the Port Dais and grabbed the man by the front of the robe. "You slaughtered the monks?"

Eyes wide, Harrow pulled at Korodeth's wrists. "How dare you!"

Korodeth broke Harrow's grip and boxed his ears. The viceroy collapsed into his chair and held his head, his shoulders and elbows pulling in toward his expansive belly. He screamed, a shrill, piercing wail more befitting a child than a viceroy.

Guards approached from the doorway, clearly confused as to whom to defend, but Korodeth waved them away. "This is a matter of kingdom security." He bent Harrow's head back, allowed time for the ringing in the man's ears to die down, and whispered. "Perhaps you can hear my voice better now that I've knocked the wax from your head."

Harrow pulled away, checked his hands for blood. He pushed past Korodeth and walked behind the throne. "Leave me be."

Korodeth followed him. "Don't walk away from me, Harrow. My word put you on this throne, and it can take you off. I'm beginning to see why Ribillius never liked you."

Harrow tilted his head to either side, opened and closed his mouth. His beard danced like a silvery stag. "I've done everything you asked." Whatever steel he'd had, whatever resolve, had fled. Older than Korodeth by decades, the viceroy spoke to him as a boy speaks to a man.

"Aye, and more. I never ordered the murder of monks!"

"They demanded I destroy Tiamat's church!"

"Did they attack you?" He asked the question, not to elicit an answer, but to make a point.

Harrow twisted the gold rings on his fingers. "No."

"Of course not. They are a peaceful order unless you put them to the sword. How many guards lost their lives for your stupidity?"

Harrow straightened his robe. "Wine," he said to a guard, who made his way quickly out of the room. "None."

"Only because the Brown Brothers vow not to take the lives of humans. How many of your soldiers are visited by healers now?"

"Near a hundred."

"You are a witless fool, Harrow. You should have known not to engage the Brown Brothers."

"Hypocrite!" Harrow shouted. "You have me build a church and ask me not to protect it?"

"Encourage your city, I said. Give them something to worship. How do you take that to mean slaughtering a peaceful people?"

"My people had Adonai to worship."

Korodeth raised an eyebrow. "A weak and deaf god. A deceiver. Tell me, if Adonai planned to save his people, wouldn't he have done it already? And yet the droughtworm persists. And yet political tensions grow. And yet the elves make plans for war. And yet the dwarves are all but dead. Where is his hand now?"

Harrow straightened behind the throne. "Then what ill is there in killing his monks? Did you not order the burning of the Cerulean Monastery? But what's right for you isn't right for me, I suppose?"

Korodeth spoke quietly, as if to a daft child. "No monks were killed," he said. "I saw to that. I turned their attention. Distraction is not murder."

"The conflict is unavoidable." Harrow found steel in his voice. He took his seat again, took a cup of wine from the guard. He swallowed deeply. "Was it not you who taught me the rules of warfare? He who strikes first strikes last?"

"We are not at war."

"Said the kingdom that fell."

Korodeth had had enough of this fool's willful ignorance, his subtle accusations as if he knew better than Korodeth. He smacked the goblet from Harrow's hand and threw him to the ground.

Lightning flashed outside and a dagger appeared in Korodeth's hand. He slashed at Harrow, stopping the blade inches from the viceroy's throat.

Guards rushed the Port Dais, but with a wave of his hand, Korodeth knocked them all back to the wall. They crumpled like boneless dolls. His eyes glowed red and the blade of the dagger heated. He touched the blistering steel to Harrow's neck.

The man howled, clutched at the floor.

Korodeth removed the blade. He waved his hand and it vanished. "Hear me well, Harrow, for if your ears fail you again, I'll sit someone new upon your chair. You are to attend the church of Tiamat. Heed the words of his priests. Seek counsel with his monks. But never again strike at Adonai's chosen. If you do, I'll not stop the wrath his people will bring on you." He helped Harrow to his feet. "Pick a fight with a god, and the god may strike back. Never strike unless you're ready for the counter-attack."

Harrow stood, slowly, steadying himself on his chair. "We are ready."

"You are worthless and witless. We're ready when I say we are. You are a narrow-sighted, dim-eared old man."

Harrow's guards righted themselves slowly.

Harrow raised his chin, a willful child defying a parent.

Korodeth thought of slapping the man again. "The Monks of the Cerulean Order will hear of this. I must prepare Alrujah for the transition."

Harrow's voice came stronger than Korodeth imagined. "May I ask when to expect you on the throne?"

He spun and smacked Harrow's face hard. "You have a filthy, treacherous mouth. Until you learn discernment, your lips are sealed."

Harrow's lips melted together like wax. He grabbed at his mouth, moaned and cried, but no words came.

Korodeth marched toward the door, stepped between the wobbly guards. "You're fortunate I don't throw you in the dungeon for treason." He walked back through the gardens, through the city, to the port, where his boat floated, tied to a rickety dock. He set the sail and pushed off.

When Sylvonya's towers diminished to sticks, Argus removed his hood. "Am I to assume the plan has changed?"

"Harrow is a fool," Korodeth said. "The plan remains, but his loose lips jeopardized what I must do. The guards needed a show of power."

"A fine show," Argus said. "A question, Captain, if it pleases you. How will the viceroy eat with his lips in such a state?"

"The enchantment will wane in two days' time. A man so fat cannot starve in so brief a period." Korodeth surveyed the vast ocean. From this distance, the land looked small, but the world felt larger. Beneath this very sea, Shedoah waited. How long must he wait? "I want eyes on the monks. They're in the caves near the Cerulean Woods."

"They can sense us," Argus said.

"They will not sense you, Argus. I will see to that. Do well, and you will soon find yourself on the Port Dais. I have a feeling it will soon be vacant."

Chapter One

And so shall the Adonai be divided, and so shall one finger turn black for a time. But the blackened finger shall close around the hilt of the Blood Sword, and the blackness of the blade shall be absolved, and the cursed steel shall again be wielded by the servants of Almighty Adonai.
—The Book of Things to Come

IN THE LATE AFTERNOON, Bailey Renee stood in her pajamas, ankle deep in the snow, a foot away from the edge of the steep cliff overlooking North Chester, Minnesota. The wind circled around her feet and pulled the bottoms of her pink pants near up to her knees. Ice crusted the tops of her slippers. She stared out over the valley. The snow reddened her ankles and covered her footprints.

Franky Meyers, her boyfriend, walked up behind her and put his arms around her. "You okay?"

"She was standing here the day before she disappeared."

His long, warm arms reminded her how cold she was.

"You're turning blue. Come inside." He took off his letterman jacket and covered her shoulders.

She leaned back against him, let him rest his stubbly chin on the top of her head. He wove his arms under hers and around her stomach. He shivered.

"It's cold. You should get back to the house," she said.

"I'm here as long as you are."

Pale snowflakes gathered on his ebony skin. He shook with the chill wind; tiny bumps raised up on his arms. He must be freezing. "It's been a week. There aren't any clues out here. You have to come inside. At least put some warmer clothes on, a jacket, something."

"I have a jacket."

"You have my jacket. And I'm freezing." His teeth chattered in her ear. What a beautiful voice he had, even when it was pinched with cold.

"I'm not leaving until I figure it out." The city spread out at the base of the cliff. Cars the size of peanuts drove along slowly graying pavement. Lights glimmered faintly down the streets. Already the roofs of the shops and stores blended perfectly with the sidewalks around them. If not for the dim neon glow over each storefront, Bailey wouldn't be able to figure out where the building began and where it ended.

She thought of how Alrujah looked in her dreams as she soared over it, feathered wings stretched from her back and across the skies. A strange closeness to Lauren replaced her feeling of weightlessness, brought her down like gravity.

Each night, she climbed into Lauren's bed and read a few more pages of Lauren's latest journal. Each night she dreamed she flew over the land described in the journal. Each morning, she woke breathless.

Here on the cliff, looking over the valley of North Chester, a different lightness lifted her. This spot held some significance. When she stood here, she could almost feel Lauren.

Franky pulled her tight to his chest. "You have to come in. You've got a game tonight. College scouts filling the stands. Remember? You have to be at school in an hour."

"The scouts are interested in Autumn, not me. Besides, I don't want to leave."

"Don't make me throw you over my shoulder."

She unwrapped his arms from her and walked toward the edge slowly.

"What are you doing?"

"I want to see something." She let the tips of her pink slippers hover over the edge. She peered down at the sprawling town beneath her. The rush of air caressed her skin as if the wind wanted to pick her up and twist her around in its embrace a few hundred feet over North Chester.

"You're too close," Franky said.

"So close," she whispered.

He pulled her back and picked her up. He turned toward the house. "Last thing your mom needs is for you to slip off the cliff."

"Put me down. There's something back there."

"Whatever it is, it will be there tomorrow when the clouds clear out."

Bailey had her doubts.

* * *

Erica and Lauren stood near the edge of the cliff overlooking the plains and the Cerulean Forest. Behind them, the others rested in the nar'esh cave between the Fellian River and the forest. The suns gradually rose over the mountains, lazy as the early morning. The bite of cold air made Lauren's skin break out in goose pimples. They'd done this each morning for nearly a week and a half. Most of the hour they spent in silence. Though the lack of conversation made Lauren squirm, Erica didn't mind.

Standing in the cold next to Lauren brought back memories of childhood, but not *her* memories. They apparently belonged to this Lakia person, whoever she might be.

Erica pulled her thick black shawl around her shoulders. It draped down to her elbows. At night, she bundled it into a pillow. Eljah and Dillard brought it with them when they'd arrived from Harland. Periodically, they sent word via razorbeaks for other supplies. The nar'esh cave may not be comfortable, but it gave them a safe place to recover from their battle with the nar'esh and Belphegor, and the pelts and skins helped ease the bone-numbing chill of the earth beneath her while she slept.

Sparky sniffed the edge of the cliff. He followed it nearly the entire length of the ledge before he came back to Erica and sat beside her, pushing up against her leg.

Lauren had her hood up. The monks had brought her a white and gold-trimmed shawl. They insisted her position as Princess of Alrujah, heir to the throne of the Kingdom of Men, or whatever mumbo-jumbo they spouted, justified the expense. She sighed. Steam escaped her lips. "Sure is pretty out," Lauren said.

"Hard to believe all of this came out of your head." Erica pulled her makeshift bandage—the torn hem of her dress—from the wound on her shoulder. The ragged tear continued its slow healing. Her upper arm swelled around it. She repositioned the bandage so a clean spot covered the wound. Her golden Ma'att'tal bracelets jangled.

Lauren stared at the bloodied bandage. She'd apologized every morning for hurting Erica. Sometimes twice. At first, Erica thought it cute. Lately, it'd become annoying. "Not your fault," Erica said. "You went all crazy ice-spike-cavewoman on us."

Lauren cleared her throat. Her eyes dampened. With each word, silver steam poured from her mouth. Her bone-white complexion and bluish lips made Erica think of corpses. "I'm sorry for all of this."

Erica tightened the bandage with her free hand and her teeth. A stray thread tangled around her tongue. She spit it out and wiped the corners of her mouth with her forearm. The wind tickled her cheeks.

A memory tickled her mind.

Eight-year-old Lakia walked through the gardens of Castle Alrujah, in and out of the irises and honeysuckles. Deep red roses grew near wild around the edges of the silvery pond. Purple nymphaea grew from the lily pads. A little blonde girl—probably Lauren, or Indigo, or whoever—sat with a woman who must have been in her late twenties. Her long hair stretched down her back. She sat on a bench near the pond, the little girl in her lap. They both smiled. As the lesser sun crested the top of the south tower, the mother turned her head toward Lakia.

Too clear for comfort. The mother's skin lit up in light, like milky glass. Her thin lips parted and showed her perfect teeth. Her pointed ears lay flat against her head.

Erica shivered.

"I'm sorry I was so mean to you in North Chester," Lauren said. "I used to think you were heartless. But you talked to me in the woods." She paused. "You made me feel better."

Erica rubbed Sparky's head. "Not the first time I've been called heartless." She took a step closer to the edge.

"So why weren't you nice in North Chester?"

Erica closed her eyes but snapped them open when the memory of the gardens came back to her. "North Chester is complicated."

"How so?"

She didn't want to talk about it, but Lauren had changed since she'd been in Alrujah. She'd settled down and stopped overreacting. Erica almost liked her now. "Long story short, there are people back home I'm not eager to see again." The tips of the bare branches of the harspus trees quivered in the wind. The thin breeze crawled over Erica's skin like ants.

Three days ago, Erica got fed up with her long brown hair and used her dagger to make a few improvements. Now, with the wind slipping across her neck, she wondered about the wisdom of short hair.

Lauren said, "I have the opposite problem. People back home aren't eager to see me again."

Erica didn't mean to, but she laughed. "Loveable old Lauren? Sweetheart, your face is probably all over North Chester. There's probably a state-wide search party in your honor right now."

"I doubt it. My family probably hasn't noticed I'm gone."

"You don't think they have?"

"My sister may have, and she's probably thrilled. My mom thinks I needed a counselor. She's probably happy to have her fat, crazy daughter gone. And my dad hasn't even called me since I was six. For all he knows, I died years ago."

Erica's throat tightened. "Could be worse." She rubbed her hands together and tugged at her gloves. "It could always be much worse."

"What about your family?"

Sparky whined, and Erica squatted down to put her arm around him. She took a deep breath and held the cold air in her lungs. She twisted the conversation in an easier direction. "You tell me. What about my family? My Alrujahn family. Do I have one?"

"Of course," Lauren said.

"Are they good? They're cool people, right? They love me and all that?"

"Of course."

"So why did I grow up in Castle Alrujah?"

Lauren squatted down and eyed Erica. Sparky licked her face and Lauren pushed him away. "How do you know about that?"

Erica twisted her Ma'att'tal bracelets. "I might be having memories of this place."

"You too?"

Erica smiled. "Well, thank God I'm not the only one. I thought for sure you were going to call me crazy."

Lauren stood up. She rubbed the tops of her arms. "I have them almost every morning. Especially when we stand out here together. Memories of us growing up. Memories of war. Of murder." Each word puffed out in blue mist.

"Pretty dark," Erica said.

Lauren took a sharp breath. "Your parents are in the dungeon." She said it quickly, no emotion, like a fact on a history test.

Erica blinked. Sparky's ears lay back, and he stared at Lauren. Erica said, "Worst joke ever."

Lauren pushed her hair behind her ear. Her lips pulled back a bit in a nervous grin before a frown replaced it. "What? Korodeth threw them in jail when they hid you from him. They didn't want him to take you away."

Fear and sorrow overshadowed Erica's indignant fury. She wiped her hot, wet eyes with her shawl. "Why?"

"It's just a story. It sounded good. I didn't mean anything by it. I didn't mean to upset you."

Erica's wavering voice leapt high. "But you knew, didn't you?" Without thinking, she pulled her arm back and let it loose. Her open palm smacked Lauren's cheek so hard it turned her head. The echo shot out over the plains and forest. "You knew about my father, didn't you? Don't try to lie about it!"

Lauren's frown split into a wide gape of shock and sadness. "I'm sorry, Erica. I don't even know what you're talking about, but I'm sorry."

Sparky's sharp barks called out over the valley below and bounced off the black rock walls of the caves behind them. "Don't play your stupid games with me! You know very well my father's in prison! You wanted to rub it in my face, didn't you? Little orphan Erica. Is that it?"

"Girls?" Aiden asked. He and Ullwen emerged from the cave with Blaze and Midnight.

Erica pulled her arm back again, her elbow bent, wrist flexed back like a catapult ready to spring.

Lauren's hair crackled and floated around her head like a halo. Her fingertips sparked blue. Sparky growled and razorbeaks circled overhead, screaming angry caws.

"Good ladies. Is all well?" Dillard asked. He and Eljah came out of the cave behind Ullwen and Aiden. They led the other three stallions.

Erica's breath seeped through her clenched teeth. She put her arm down slowly.

Lauren ran her fingers over her red-glowing cheek. "I didn't know. I had no idea. I'm really sorry."

Sparky curled a lip, and Erica fought hard not to convulse in shivers and anger. She turned her back on Lauren and walked to the cave. Sparky followed close behind, his hair rigid and stiff.

CHAPTER TWO

When the elves began to overcome King Solous, he humbled himself
before Adonai and fell on his knees. He cried out for a miracle. Adonai
heard his cry and answered him. Unto King Solous, Adonai sent Pacha
el Nai, angel of justice. And with him, a host of armored angels with
wings of steel and eyes of magma.
—The Book of the Ancients

OLIVER SAT UP, SOMETHING he'd only been able to do for a couple days. The last week, stuck in the central chamber of the nar'esh cave, felt like months. He ate whatever food Eljah and Dillard brought from the villages and farms nearby. Aiden and Ullwen hunted rabbit and deer, but the smell of meat soured his stomach. In North Chester, he loved meat—medium-rare steaks, baked chicken, bacon. Here, the vegetarian diet of the Cerulean monks had been ingrained in him since childhood.

He wanted a comfortable bed, a mattress or a couch, a recliner, anything to support his weight and not dig into his back. His ribs hurt, like he had a belt strapped around his chest two notches too tight. But at least he could move.

Eljah and Dillard had no answer for their inability to heal him completely, other than to attribute it to the will of Adonai. Oliver reluctantly agreed. Each time he thought of it, he remembered the voice of God speaking to the Apostle Paul. *My grace is sufficient for you.*

He prayed he would get better eventually but found it hard to believe he'd ever be fully healed. A lifetime of pain and short breath terrified him. Each time his chest expanded with air, his ribs creaked and pain stabbed him. He hoped, with more rest, he'd be able to walk in the next day or two. His injury had already set them back a week—a full week for the Mage Lord to set his plans of chaos and destruction in motion.

He dipped a wooden cup into a bucket of water Dillard had brought from the Fellian River. Dillard made the mile-long walk each morning. He left before sunsup and returned moments before breakfast.

Shortly after Aiden and Ullwen ceased their morning sparring, Erica shouted outside. Oliver reached for his staff. Eljah and Dillard, horses in tow, vanished after them. He wanted to chase after them. He pulled himself up with his staff. His legs shook, and he hurt from shoulders to waist. Something tickled the back of his throat; he had to cough. He worked to stave off the impending panic. Coughing would send him back to the ground writhing in pain.

He cleared his throat and grimaced. Bent over, he used his staff as a crutch to help him take his first step in a week.

Erica was upset or in trouble. He wouldn't let something like a broken back keep him from her side.

Step after gentle step, he made his way toward the outside. Erica's voice grew louder. Lauren said something softly. A moment later, Erica came in, eyes blurry with tears. "What happened?" Oliver wheezed.

Erica stopped and stared at the empty stables, her back to him. She said nothing, but her shoulders shook. She sniffled, gripped the rough wooden gate.

He took a few steps, his staff clacking on the stone floor and echoing out to the still early morning. He put a hand on her shoulder. "What's wrong?"

She cleared her throat and tilted her head up to the ceiling. "Did you have anything to do with this?"

Pain seared Oliver's back, but he ignored it. "With what?"

"My parents are in a dungeon."

Gently, he told her he had no idea what she meant.

She shrugged his hand off, turned around. Her now short hair bounced in the cold cave air. She wiped her eyes and put her hand on her shoulder. Her Ma'att'tal bands slipped down to her elbow. Her brown eyes turned glassy. "I think you had plenty to do with it. You made this whole place, didn't you? You probably coded them into the deepest darkest dungeon in Alrujah."

Lakia's parents, he reasoned, not Erica's. He remembered the story now. Exhaling slowly, he tried to ignore the searing pain along his spine. "Yes."

"I was starting to think I could trust you." The sorrow on her face melted into a keen resolve, a determination not to be weak. "You're all the same."

She turned toward the central chamber and walked off.

"Wait," he called. Pain wracked him. He wrapped his arm around his abdomen. Leaning heavily on his staff, he called after her, "I'm sorry. I didn't realize it would upset you. Where are you going?"

She called over her shoulder, "I'm getting my parents back."

* * *

Bailey struggled to keep her mind in the game. Granted, North Chester led by twenty in the final minutes of the second half, but her lack of concentration made her game slip. She'd hoped to run up her stats against Central Duluth, a larger but sloppier team, but had yet to reach her eighteen-point average.

Scanning the stands, Bailey found no sign of her mom. She'd made it to every game this season. Now, the first game after Lauren goes missing, her mom decides not to show.

Run out the clock. Hold the ball, see the floor, wait for the drive. The monstrosity of a girl in front of her slapped for the ball. The whistle blew, and Bailey took her place on the free-throw line.

She dribbled twice, checked the crowd. The scouts scribbled notes. She turned back to the basket, bent her knees, popped up slightly as she released the ball. It arched to the hoop and through the rim. The ref grabbed the ball and bounced it back to her. The echo of the ball on the hardwood floor diffused through the din of cheers.

Her mom must have gone home to bed, something she often did when depressed. Each night this week, her mother went back to her room around seven. By eight, her snores slipped through the crack of the door.

Two dribbles. Knees. Wrists. Swish. Her eighteenth point. Might not be enough to impress the big scouts, but it couldn't hurt.

Through the din of the crowd, she picked out the musicality of Franky's voice. Granted, he cheered louder than anyone else in the stands. He sat in the front row next to the other guys from the football team, most of which dated her friends on the basketball team.

Central Duluth passed the ball in. They raced down the court. Bailey kept up with the guard, a girl about her size with quick feet and faster hands. She'd put up twelve points so far, wanted more.

Bailey tried hard to care. She stayed low, kept her arms out, took a few half-hearted swipes at the ball to keep the guard honest. The clock ticked down to ten seconds. The girl with the ball stopped quickly, jumped, and let the ball roll off her fingers.

Nothing but net.

Three points, inconsequential to the game, but not to the scouts.

Last week, letting such an easy shot past her would have crushed Bailey. Today, she didn't care. Each day without Lauren made college less and less important. She had three more years to worry about it. Right now, only Lauren mattered.

She took her place for what might be the final play. Autumn passed the ball under a heavy press to Bailey. She grabbed the ball and dribbled down court. Central Duluth's press left a lane down the right side of the court. Eight seconds on the clock. Instinct kicked in. The broad lane triggered something in her, an instinct as undeniable as breathing.

She sprinted, bringing the ball behind her back from her right hand to her left in mid-stride. It took her six steps and six dribbles to break under the basket. Three girls leapt toward her. She set her feet, turning to cover the ball from their slapping hands. When they landed, she jumped up, turned 180 degrees back to the basket in midair, and found the rim at eye-level.

She stuffed the ball through the net, grabbed rim, and hung for a minute.

The crowd erupted.

Until tonight, Bailey had never dunked the ball—no girl in North Chester ever had—but it felt natural, like she'd flown to the hoop, like she'd had wings, like all of Alrujah spread out beneath her. Her back twitched under her shoulder blades, where her wings should be.

The bizarre thought should have surprised her.

She should have wings.

* * *

In the central chamber, Erica grabbed a saddlebag filled with vegetables and cheeses. She rolled up her sasquatch skins and shoved them into the little space remaining.

Oliver hobbled behind her, feet shuffling, staff clacking slowly. Breathless, he said, "You can't leave. It's too dangerous."

"I'm a big girl," she said. Sparky sat obediently beside her as she adjusted her shawl and touched the hilt of her daggers. She packed the hideous dress Eljah and Dillard bought for her. She'd not worn it yet, but she had no way to tell how long she'd be gone. "I'm going to get my parents out of whatever dungeon Korodeth has them in."

For a few days, Erica actually believed she liked Oliver. Now, she wondered if she only liked the attention he gave her. She'd been forward with him, flirty even. She owed him the truth, at least. Taking off her gloves, she ran her fingers over the smooth skin on the backs of her hands.

Oliver wheezed. His teeth chattered. With his back and ribs all twisted up, the shivering must agonize him.

She said, "If you'd known about my dad whenever you"—she waved a hand around—"made all this, my hands would look very different." She slung the heavy, cold saddlebags over her shoulder. "When I was seven, my old man lost it. I don't remember what I did to set him off, or if I did anything at all, but he turned on the stove and put my hands over the fire. He held them there no matter how much I screamed."

She played with the clasps on the bags, unbelted and belted them. She put her gloves back on, glanced quickly at Oliver before moving her eyes back to the floor. "His hands burned, too. You could smell it."

Sparky sniffed a stray morsel of old cheese and lay down.

"My scars go up to my knuckles. I haven't felt the back of my hands since I was seven. And now," she looked down at them. "Now I don't even know what to do with whole hands."

He whispered, "I had no idea."

Erica continued over the sound of Oliver sniffing. "So Mom screams at him. Grabs a broom and cracks him on the head. Didn't hurt him much, but distracted him long enough for me to pull away. I ran away, thinking I was going to die. He was going to catch me and kill me. But he didn't. He grabbed my mom. I was halfway down our driveway when I heard her scream.

"I was seven, Oliver. Seven. I kept running. Some dude picked me up a few blocks away and drove me to the hospital. That guy, I want to see him again. But no matter how hard I try, I can't remember his face. I cried so hard, I couldn't see straight."

Footsteps echoed into the chamber from the stables.

Erica steadied her voice, wiped her eyes. "Never saw Mom after that. My old man wound up in a jail for crazies, and I wound up in a group home. So if I've got a chance to have real parents, the kind who love me, instead of degenerate foster parents who collect state checks and forget to feed me, well, I'm not really ready to let them go without a fight."

"I'll go with you," Oliver said. "I'll talk to King Ribillius."

She smiled. A sweet gesture, but totally unrealistic. "They'll be dead by the time you can hobble to Alrujah. Besides, Ribillius doesn't exactly sound like he takes orders well."

Oliver drew in a slow, shallow breath. With each word, his face twisted in pain. She wished he'd sit back down and rest.

"The suns are barely up now. We can go with you later if you wait a bit," he said.

"You guys have another book to find, don't you?"

At last, he sat back down. Breathless, he wheezed, "At least let Ullwen go with you. He knows the land and the people. He can keep you safe." And he'd feel better knowing she was with an expert warrior while the rest of the group hunted down *The Book of Sealed Magic*.

Sweet until the end. His affection warmed her a bit, but she could never be with him. Not the way he wanted. He needed someone else. Someone stronger. Someone nicer.

And, even though she preferred to go alone, she found herself nodding at Oliver's suggestion. "Maybe I will, if he's ready to go."

* * *

Aiden held Lauren's hand as they walked past the stables toward the central chamber. The fire glowed softly, and orange light sputtered over the black walls. His hand gave her strength, and she held it like she'd fallen off a ledge. Eljah, Dillard, and Ullwen walked beside them. They replaced the horses in the stalls and walked softly.

Erica stood near Oliver, head bowed, saddlebags slung over her shoulders. Oliver's back pressed against the wall. Sparky laid his head in Oliver's lap. A grimace of pain bent Oliver's face. Must be his back, or had Erica said something hurtful? Wouldn't surprise Lauren at all.

"Are you well, Lakia?" Ullwen asked.

Head still bowed, Erica said. "I'm leaving."

No one spoke. Lauren let Aiden's hand go and walked to Erica. She wanted to put her hand on her shoulder, or to hug her, but thought better of it. Instead, she studied Erica's bloodshot, weary eyes.

Lauren doubted anything she said would change Erica's mind, but she had to try. "Stay with us. I didn't mean to upset you."

Erica stood up straight and put the saddlebags over her other shoulder. She pushed her Ma'att'tal bracelets up her forearms, and they immediately fell back down her thin arms to her wrist. "I'll come back. But I'm busting my parents out of whatever hole you've put them in."

"It is too dangerous to go alone," Dillard offered. In the inconsistent light, his albino pallor made his face glow orange, all ice and fire and snow.

"I know. Oliver already had the talk with me. Come with me, Ullwen?"

"It would be my honor," Ullwen said.

Lauren cocked her head. "Really?"

Erica stared at Ullwen, every bit as surprised as Lauren. "I don't have to talk you into it?"

Lauren had trouble deciding if the red in Ullwen's cheeks came from the light of the fire or from embarrassment.

"It is a simple matter of honor. No woman should travel alone. As a former Varuthian Infiltrator, there are few more capable of gaining access to guarded areas than I."

"Be still my heart," Erica said. "Okay, Romeo. Get your things. I want to leave five minutes ago." She pushed past Dillard and Eljah and turned back. "Sparky. Let's go." Her eyes on Oliver, she said. "Thanks, Ollie. For everything. See you in another life."

Sparky followed her out of the cave.

Lauren shook her head. Ullwen sounded more than concerned, he sounded excited. For a minute, she actually believed he pined for Erica the way he had for her. He and Erica had spent more time together the last week and a half. Had she missed something, a reawakening of Ullwen's spirit she might have noticed if she hadn't been so hung up on Aiden?

Ullwen lifted the saddlebags from Erica's shoulder and inspected the contents. "I need little in the way of clothes and can hunt for food. This should be sufficient." His eyes flitted to her daggers, to Sparky at her heels. "You seem well prepared. We can leave immediately."

Aiden put a hand on Ullwen's chest. "Hold up a sec, bro. Shouldn't we all stick together? Remember what happened with Lauren? We don't want something like that to go down again."

Ullwen removed his hand gently. "There are no nar'esh within the walls of Alrujah. Two can move more swiftly, can hide more efficiently than can five."

"And we kinda have to get to Harland," Lauren said. She'd read enough of *The Book of Things to Come* to understand they needed to move soon. But the book said nothing about moving on without Erica. "The sooner we can get back, the sooner we can move."

13

Dillard stepped forward, his hands buried in his sleeves, the hood of his robe pulled back to show the orange light playing on his pallid skin. "The time has come for the Hand to journey to Harland. The book strongly implies a separation. This must be it."

"I don't remember anything about a separation," Lauren said.

"It is there, Indigo, I assure you. Page one thousand and twelve. It is referred to in the past tense. The Hand is said to do several things simultaneously, which can only happen if they are split."

Eljah nodded to Erica. "We are at a crucial crossroads. Lakia must pursue her family, and you three must travel to Harland. There, you will take the next step in finding *The Book of Sealed Magic*. Dillard and I must return to the monastery. When it is rebuilt, I will send Dillard to you to assist in whatever you may need. For now, we both must return to our brothers."

"So that's it?" Aiden said. "We split up just like that?"

"Father," Oliver said, leaning forward gently. "I can hardly walk. How can I make it to Harland?"

Erica sighed. "Oh, stop being a baby." She grabbed his wrist and yanked him up. Oliver's shout cracked off the wall like a racquetball. She spun him around, lifted him up, and dropped him back to his feet. His spine popped at each joint.

Erica thrust her hip next to his, bent him sideways, and repeated the quick process on the other side. Several more cracks popped through the stale cave air. She let him go, and he leaned against the wall, breathless. "Better, right?"

Hunched over, eyes watering, he nodded slowly.

She leaned in, kissed his cheek. "Thanks for treating me like a person."

Oliver's breath came slow and deep. He must understand what she meant—goodbye. Lauren wondered if Erica planned on coming back alive.

Erica walked to Lauren, checked her cheek. The red handprint had faded. "Sorry about the slap."

"Sorry about your parents."

Erica leaned in and hugged Lauren hard. "I've never had a sister."

Surprised, Lauren hugged her back. She had no idea what to say but wanted to encourage her. "I'd be your sister if you'd have me."

"You're the closest thing I've got."

Lauren smiled. "Please be careful, okay? We'll see you soon, I'm sure. Send us some razorbeaks or whatever to let us know how you're doing, or if you need any help or anything."

"Sure thing." Erica moved to Aiden, stared at him awkwardly as if trying to decide whether to hug him or shake his hand. Finally, she decided on giving him a high-five. "Take care of her," she said.

Aiden smiled. "You got it."

Ullwen put a hand on Oliver's shoulder. "I'm proud to have fought next to you. May Adonai bless your steps, and may you find healing soon."

Oliver nodded, stood nearly straight. "The honor is mine. Adonai be with you, Ullwen of Varuth. May He bless your steps."

Ullwen moved to Aiden, took his forearm in his hand. "Be well, valiant knight. Honor Lauren. Respect her and protect her."

Aiden nodded. "I will. Be well, Ullwen. You're a class act."

Ullwen put a hand on each of Lauren's ears, brought her forehead to his lips. "Our love did not work out as we anticipated. But you have your love now. Be cautious and strong. May Adonai bless your steps."

"Be safe, okay?"

"Aye, fair Indigo. I will."

After Erica fidgeted through Dillard's and Eljah's blessings, she and Ullwen made their way out of the central chamber. Lauren stood next to Oliver. "I can't believe she's really going."

He said, "Tell me about it."

CHAPTER THREE

The days of the wicked are numbered. The memory of the evil will vanish as a whisper of smoke, a tendril of fog, of steam evanescing into the atmosphere.
—The Book of the Ancients

AFTER THE FINAL BUZZER, and after Coach C talked to the team, Bailey went to the stands to say hi to Franky before showering off. Her purple and white-trimmed uniform clung to her sweaty skin. Franky hugged her and kissed her slick forehead. "Great game," he said.

"I was off."

"A 180 slam is off?"

"Very impressive," Detective Parker said. He walked down from the top of the bleachers, an unlit cigarette behind his ear and both hands in the pockets of a gray overcoat.

Bailey smiled politely. Her voice quieted. "What are you doing here?"

"Who's this guy?" Franky asked.

Detective Parker extended his hand and introduced himself to Franky. To Bailey, he said, "Thought we could talk. Have a minute?"

"If it's quick. I need to get showered off and get home. Ton of work to do before tomorrow." Bailey hugged Franky lightly. "I'll be fine. It's about Lauren."

"Meet you in the parking lot." Franky nodded to Parker and excused himself.

When Franky disappeared, and the other girls emptied into the locker room, Parker said, "So Dad's back from vacation."

Bailey crossed her arms. "You arrested my father?"

"Not me. California CHP picked him up on his way back from camping in the Sierras. Hadn't heard a thing about Lauren, but he's got an alibi. Him and his little woman were gone the whole week. Campgrounds confirm it. We searched his house, too. Nothing to tie him to Lauren."

Bailey wiped the sweat from her forehead with her arm, pushed a stray strand of brown hair behind her ear. "We already knew we wouldn't find anything, right?"

"Hoped we'd at least find a lead. We're grasping at straws."

Parker slipped the cigarette in his mouth. By the way it sagged, she guessed he'd been letting it hang between his lips most of the day. He studied her in a cop sort of way. "I get the feeling you're not telling me something."

Bailey thought of the journal, how it changed, how she heard Lauren's voice when she read it. "What do you mean?"

"Cop's intuition." Parker pantomimed lighting the cigarette, pulled it from his mouth, exhaled, and stuck the soggy stick back between his lips. "When people hide things, nine times out of ten, they're scared of something else. Scared we'll find out they're guilty of something. Scared we'll take someone they love away. They get it in their heads they're protecting themselves or someone or something else they love."

The hot gym seemed to cool quickly once the heaters clicked off. Bailey uncrossed her arms. "You think I had something to do with Lauren disappearing?"

Parker studied his cigarette and stuck it back behind his ear. "Not you."

"Mom?"

Parker shrugged. "She seemed pretty broken up over the whole thing, but could be guilt."

"Mom would never hurt Lauren," Bailey said though her voice lacked the conviction she'd hoped to convey.

"No, I don't think she would. Not intentionally."

"No way," Bailey said quickly, conviction now clear and steady in her voice. "Mom had nothing to do with it."

"How do you know?"

"I know."

Parker stood up. "I'll leave it alone. But if you think of something, give me a call." He smiled at her. "Bailey Renee. The girl who could fly."

Her eyes went wide. "What?"

"That dunk of yours. Never seen anyone your size slam. It was like you were flying."

"Right."

"Take care, Bailey. See you soon, I'm sure." The bleacher steps moaned under his heavy footsteps as he made his way out of the gym.

Water rattled the pipes in the wall separating the gym from the girls' locker room. She should have told him about the journal, but if she did, he'd take it, and she'd be without her last link to Lauren. And if she said it changed with each reading, he'd probably lock her up. She closed her eyes, leaned against the railing and sighed. "Could use some help, here, Lauren."

* * *

Erica and Ullwen moved in and out of the trees on the eastern border of the Cerulean Woods. She wished Ullwen let them take the horses, but he insisted they'd be too loud.

Sparky stayed on Erica's heels, pace for pace. Thick round trunks of young trees gave way to the thinner, mature, black-barked harspus trees. Their branches stretched out like arthritic fingers. She thought of dreadlocks.

Ullwen took her wrist, and she faced him. "You're making too much noise. We should proceed quietly to avoid detection."

"First of all, it's not me; it's the leaves. Secondly, what's going to hear us? I thought the bad guys only came out at night. The lesser sun's still coming up. You worried about a pack of rabbits?"

"Like this." Ullwen turned his hips and stepped carefully on the leaves with his toes, rolling his foot side-first before resting his full weight on the front leg. No crunch of leaves. Weird as he talked, the guy seemed fully ninja sometimes.

"Fabulous. Where'd you learn that trick?"

Sparky rummaged through the dried orange and yellow leaves like he wanted to find worms to eat.

"Since birth, my father took me with him on hunts."

"Explains the crazy skill with the bow and arrow." She mimicked his steps. Slow, cautious, gentle. It worked. She smiled. "So, what's with the knives and swords?"

"I served as a Varuthian Infiltrator for two years. I had to blend in, become invisible. To do so, I used small, undetectable weapons. When I was promoted to Varuthian Elite, I trained with swords and shields, as the Elite must be skilled in all weaponry. We are the finest fighters in the land. But I still prefer the bow and arrow where possible."

Erica bent her knees deep like him, mimicked each step like a game of Follow the Leader. Of course, at this pace, she'd be forty before they made it back to Alrujah. "They didn't teach you to walk silently and quickly, did they?"

"Aye, but we are being tracked." He took a few more steps.

"By what?"

He took a few more silent steps. "Hard to say."

Erica didn't buy that for a minute. Whatever it was, he didn't want to tell her. That was fine with her. "So what's the fastest way to Alrujah?"

"Haste precedes disaster. First, we must stop at Varuth. I have some matters to tend to, and there are people there who can help us."

Sparky walked slowly, sniffing the air. "I didn't think you could go back into Varuth. Aren't you like a fugitive or something?"

He smiled—an innocent grin packed with perfect teeth. "Who do you think trained the Varuthian Infiltrators?"

"Cute," she said. They neared the edge of the Cerulean Woods as the moon stubbornly vanished beneath the Dragon's Back Mountains. On the opposite side, the lesser sun arced over the tree line.

Sparky's lips curled up. He bared his teeth and a growl rumbled from deep in his gullet. Ullwen grabbed her shoulder. "Halt," he said, staring at the ground. He pointed to a print in the dirt—something obtusely big and shaped roughly like a human foot.

It sank at least three inches deep into the soft leaf-covered soil. Hair, brown and black and white, stuck in the mud around it. She'd seen those colors before. On the pelt she'd packed at the monastery?

His head turned left, turned right. Paranoia must run deep in his veins. He took her head in his hand, pulled her ear to his lips. In a harsh whisper, he said, "Don't move."

His hot breath warmed her cheek in the chill of the air. The smell of his leather tunic mixed with the scent of rotting leaves and damp soil. For a minute, she nearly forgot about the rescue mission. Next to him, she felt like a little girl. Nearly a foot taller and built like a linebacker, his beard made him look older than twenty.

"Sasquatch," he whispered. "It's close."

Erica extracted her dagger. Her heart beat like hummingbirds' wings. Sparky reared back on his haunches.

"They hunt at dawn." He unsheathed Aiden's old sword, cleaned and polished after slicing through countless nar'esh.

Her muscles tensed, and her back and neck knotted.

"Small ones are eight feet tall and strong as ten beresus."

"The small ones?" she whispered.

"Shhh. I hear it breathing."

Sparky growled.

"Where?" Erica whispered. Something caught her around her waist and she sailed into the air. Branches snapped around her. She opened her eyes and fell. She reached out for the tangled harspus branches, bounced off some, and finally landed on a thick limb. It hit her in the stomach and folded her in half. She hung suspended in the air, nearly twelve feet from the ground. Her vision ran in loopy circles, every part of her bruised.

She found her breath, took in a deep gulp of air, and cleared the spots from her eyes. Below, Ullwen rolled away from the sasquatch and darted behind trees.

Her vision steadied, but she wished it hadn't.

Nine feet tall, easy. Arms like telephone poles. The sasquatch lumbered more than walked and had to duck under the branches of the harspus trees.

Anger welled up in her. She righted herself as quickly as her bruised body allowed. Her arms stung from fingertips to elbows, from elbows to shoulders. Her back cracked and pain knifed behind her eyes. She tried to take a breath. Inch by inch, her chest filled with air, and her ribs protested with agonizing creaks and moans. Sitting on the branch, perched precariously, she thought of Oliver.

A rumble bubbled in her throat, and she let out a fury of sharp barks, and a long, guttural howl. Each came with a torturous price.

Sparky leapt at the hulking beast.

Leaves scattered and more growls filled the dawn-lit forest. A pack of wolves, all big as Sparky, surrounded the sasquatch. One leapt at the creature's neck, but the sasquatch plucked it out of the air and tossed it into a tree. The wolf's spine snapped like a too-dry bough.

Cradling her ribs, she dropped down from the tree, dagger in hand. Her knees and legs ached but held her weight. She stalked behind the sasquatch. If it hurt Sparky, so help her, she'd tear it into tiny pieces and feed it to the nar'esh.

Ullwen used the distraction of the wolves, nipping and biting, to sheathe Aiden's sword and nock an arrow in his bow. He loosed the arrow as the sasquatch turned to grab another wolf. The arrow lodged feather-deep in its shoulder.

The sasquatch growled, grabbed two wolves, and smashed them

together. They howled in pain and collapsed to the leaf-covered ground. They tried to stand, but their broken legs twitched helplessly.

Erica steadied her heart, all her fear replaced with anger and loathing. She would kill the sasquatch, good and dead. She screeched, and razorbeaks flooded the air with a resounding call. They flapped in the creature's face and tore at it with their beaks.

The sasquatch flailed its arms, sending the purple birds flying like bullets.

An arrow bloomed in the beast's neck. A whoosh of air escaped its neck, and Erica leapt at it. She climbed up its back and sunk her dagger between its shoulders.

It grunted sharply, spun around, and sent Erica falling into the pack of wolves. The pack surrounded her, sat back on their haunches like catapults ready to crumble city walls. The sasquatch knocked them to the side. Its face twisted, lips pulling back in a sinister grimace.

Erica's chest seized.

The sasquatch picked her up by the head in one hand. Thick fingers pressed so hard, her skull bent, her brain bruised. The arrow in its neck shivered with each wheezing breath it took. It tried to growl, but the sound came out like air from a balloon. It pulled its hand back, and Erica soared like she'd boarded some souped-up roller coaster. Her body trailed after her head and whipped around as the sasquatch's arm stopped short.

Erica flew. The fingers disappeared, and cool night air rushed over her stinging skin. Something hard as a wall smashed into her back. Something cracked, and all Alrujah went black.

* * *

Shortly after Dillard and Eljah rode off toward the monastery, Lauren closed *The Book of Things to Come* and stretched out her hands toward the fire pit in the center of the room. Kneeling, she said, "This thing is so hard to understand. It's like reading riddles."

"What's it say?" Aiden asked. He stood near the fire, arms across his chest.

"Something about a broken finger on the Hand of Adonai. I'm guessing that's you, Oliver. And a bunch of stuff about friends and unseen enemies. About the only thing I could figure out was Harland, but we kinda already decided to go there, so no real help."

Oliver leaned on his staff. He twisted from side to side and grimaced, but did not cry out in pain. He must be feeling better. "What does it say exactly?"

Lauren sighed, opened the book, and let her fingers run over the dry ink and thin, rough pages. "And by His Hand did Adonai establish the thrones of men and elves. In those days, a home in Harland will be prepared for the Hand by an ancient enemy of man. Adonai will make a bond between enemies and establish future thrones. Ancient promises will be fulfilled, and the races of dwarves and elves will return their hearts to Adonai."

Aiden said, "Okay, so you don't get that either?"

"Sounds political," Oliver said. "Establishing thrones, ancient promises. Making friends of enemies. Who are the ancient enemies of man?"

"Elves," Lauren said.

"And who can establish thrones, and make friends of enemies?"

"Don't ambassadors do that? Like in government or whatever?" Aiden said.

Lauren stood up and rubbed her knees. They ached from kneeling on the cold stone floor for so long. "Langley?"

Oliver frowned. "Makes sense. The elvish ambassador to Harland. I was hoping to avoid him, but at least it's someplace to start."

"Guess that means we'll have to track Yarborough down, too."

Aiden leaned against the wall of the central chamber. The firelight glimmered over his silver armor. "Yarborough? Isn't that the statue we found in the caves of Margwar? What's he got to do with anything? Besides, I thought Harland didn't want us around. How are we supposed to stay out of sight in a city full of people?"

"That's him," Lauren said. "He's great. You'll like him. But Langley's a piece of work."

Oliver stood straighter, remarkably, and took a slow breath. "Getting past the gates will be the tough part. Once we're in, we can blend, stay quiet, fly under the radar. Sometimes cities are easier to hide in than caves."

"You're looking good," Aiden said. "Haven't seen you stand straight since before we took down Belphegor."

Lauren shuddered. She'd tried to put the massive Minotaur out of her mind. "Let's not talk about that thing anymore."

Oliver grabbed at his chest suddenly. He grimaced in pain, and, for a minute, she wondered if he were having a heart attack. She moved to him, put her hand on his shoulder. "You okay? Your back?"

Beneath his thick cerulean robe, a light shone. It diffused through the fabric and glowed a soft moonish blue. The amulet. Something must be wrong.

"Erica," he said.

Aiden came over, jangling with each step. "Erica what?"

"She's hurt."

Lauren's heart seized. "No, she can't be. She just left thirty minutes ago."

"What about Ullwen?" Aiden asked.

"Can't tell." He dropped to his knees, either from pain or to pray.

"Where is she? We should go get her."

Oliver replied in the Ancient Language. Lauren recognized the words on the page, but when spoken, they still sounded foreign. He might have been mumbling lyrics to a song, for all she knew. But he moved, one hand on the amulet, another raised to the ceiling. His palm stretched up toward heaven; his words grew louder. He swayed and muttered like a man possessed.

Aiden's muscles tensed. He wanted to do something. He didn't like being powerless. Neither did Lauren. She smiled at him, tried to calm him. "It's all we can do right now," she said.

He shook his head. "No. We can pray, too."

CHAPTER FOUR

Consider the stars above, the moon and the suns. Who hung them in the heavens? Consider the parial-barbed vi-fish and the water dragons. Who can overwhelm them? Who can wrestle them to submission? Who can overcome them by force?
—The Book of the Ancients

BAILEY RENEE CHANGED INTO her pajamas and made her way to Lauren's room. She still hadn't touched anything in it, other than the bed. The memories it would stir might overwhelm her. It would be easier to sleep in her own room, but she needed Lauren's bed, needed the fading scent of shampoo on her pillow, needed the comfort of being surrounded by Lauren's countless journals and books and games.

She took the journal from under the pillow and held it for a minute. When she'd learned Lauren modeled each character after one of the four missing teens, Bailey thought about running directly to Detective Parker. But she hadn't. She couldn't let him take the journal from her.

Bailey had read the journal twice before. The story, though largely the same, had varied her second time through it. Not much. Only slight disparities in the descriptions of lands or characters mainly, but enough of a difference for Bailey to notice. She wondered about her own sanity, feared her mind may have snapped under the strain of a missing sister. To check herself, she read through each of Lauren's other journals twice. It took forever, but she did it. And each time she did, the journals remained constant.

Except this one.

Only one other option presented itself: Lauren changed the book. Somehow, by some magic or power or sheer force of will, Lauren had altered the words on the page. And that meant she was still alive, somehow, somewhere.

Her mind hadn't snapped. She didn't need to see a psychoanalyst to tell her what she already understood.

Bailey opened the leather binding and flipped to the first dry yellow page. Her eyes scanned the first paragraph. Only the title, *The Book of Things to Come,* remained the same. She'd learned to accept vague descriptions becoming more specific, even for new characters to appear mysteriously. But this time, the first paragraph had changed completely, mountainous changes. Here, the story began with Lakia leaving the group. In her recollection, that never happened anywhere the first two times she read it.

Bailey Renee bit her lip.

She'd hoped to make a list of the things that didn't change. They might be clues to her location. Spots in Alrujah might correspond with parts of North Chester. But she found no such similarities on the first page. Not even on the second.

She rubbed her eyes, tried to keep them clear and free from tears.

* * *

God had answered countless prayers, but prayer still seemed insufficient. Oliver wanted to race out of the cave, ride on the back of Blaze and scoop Erica into his arms. He wanted to see her, touch her, hear her voice.

Instead, as he whispered ancient, powerful words, the voice of Adonai, the voice of God, spoke peace into him.

Erica would be fine. Eventually.

When he opened his eyes, he found Aiden and Lauren holding hands, heads bowed—the unmistakable body language of prayer. Apparently, God worked multiple miracles at once. He must be moving in their hearts—another prayer Oliver had lifted to God, one he'd lifted even before Alrujah.

Oliver stood up, still amazed at how much better his back felt after Erica threw him around and twisted him up like a sailor's knot. He hurt still, hurt bad. But the relief gave him hope to be able to move on.

Aiden asked, "You done, bro?"

"Yeah. She's going to be okay."

Lauren asked, "How do you know?"

"Adonai told me. For now, we'll keep praying for her, but we still have to move." He walked toward the stables. Each time his staff hit the floor, the vibrations ran up his arms, past his elbows, to his shoulders. His back shivered with each step.

Aiden walked beside him. "Can you ride?"

"If we go slow. The impact will wreck me otherwise."

"I'll get the horses ready." Aiden ran ahead to the stables.

Lauren walked backward in front of him. "Are you sure she'll be okay?"

Oliver stopped for a minute, took a breath. Walking and breathing were difficult enough on their own. Doing both proved near impossible for the pain pinching his back. "You know me. Would I be sure if I didn't hear from Adonai?"

"I guess not." She walked beside him, took his elbow in her hand and helped him. "You sure we'll be okay?"

"With Langley in the mix? Only Adonai knows."

* * *

Too many changes in the journal. She couldn't hope to remember what details varied from reading to reading. Her mind clouded with sleeplessness and fatigue. Numbers and letters ran together into symbols, some strange set of hieroglyphics. If she wanted to have any shot of accurately detailing the changes in hopes of finding clues, she'd have to be smarter than the consistently inconsistent journal.

She grabbed her iPad and put together a quick spreadsheet to chart major plot events, then hyperlinked characters and locations to other spreadsheets in order to record significant details and which reading they'd appeared in. She hoped it'd work, and that she wouldn't need an MIT grad to decipher the results.

Settling into Lauren's bed, pillows against the back wall to prop her up, iPad on her knees, Bailey used her cell phone to snap a picture of the first page of *The Book of Things to Come*. Photographic evidence couldn't hurt. She repeated the process for an hour—snap a picture, read a page—before her eyes slipped shut. She checked the clock—ten. Way past her bedtime, but she hadn't slept before eleven for a week now. An early night might do her good.

Setting the iPad on the closest bookshelf, she closed the journal, pulled the covers up to her chin. She closed her eyes, flipped the pillow over to the cool side, and took a deep breath. The smell of Lauren's shampoo had thinned, replaced by the scent of Bailey's mango shampoo. She made a note to use Lauren's tomorrow morning.

She fell into her dream like a pit—no transition or warning. Her eyes snapped open, and she stretched out her wings.

Flying again. She'd never get used to it.

Beneath her, Alrujah spread out like a map on a table. Far to the east, the silver waters of the Alrujahn Sea sparkled under the light of the two suns. Still east, but much closer inland, the Fellian River jutted off the Alrujah River like a worm sliding out of a pipeline. A familiar thatch of woods covered the ground beneath her. She'd seen them on her first trip before she perched on the towers of the castle in whatever city she'd landed in. The tower where she first perched stretched from the heavily-walled city to the west. Now, after studying Lauren's journals and sketches, she recognized the city as Harland. Directly beneath her, a small ridge of mountains rose from the earth like knuckles.

The wind pressed her face, and the air chilled her bare arms. She wrapped her wings around herself and fell face first toward the earth. She'd flown enough now to know when to spread her wings again, when to slow her descent to avoid injury.

The mountains raced up toward her. Her eyes watered in the rush of air pushing her cheeks back. Blood rushed to her frigid cheeks. Closer and closer the mountains punched toward her. She snapped her wings open, pointed her toes, and landed on a ledge overlooking the plains and the woods. The last time she landed, angry soldiers shot at her with bows and arrows. This time, no soldiers roamed the streets.

The sword clipped to her hip slapped her leg. She pulled it out, held it, inspected it—heavy in the handle and light in the blade. More than shimmering in the light, it glowed, as if, rather than reflecting the light of the suns, it produced its own light—something she'd never realized before.

She grinned. She may never have played the same games as Lauren, but she had to admit, the sword felt good in her hand, natural. She replaced it in its holster on her belt and took in the area around her. Several openings dotted the ledge where she stood.

Caves.

The wind crawled over the mountains. She wrapped her wings around herself again, walked the ledge, remembered the cliff in North Chester, and wondered if Lauren had it in mind when she created this place.

A sharp, hollow sound startled her. It came from one of the caves and sounded like hooves on stone. Who would take horses up here? Voices joined the hoof falls. Remembering the bows and arrows from the first dream, Bailey took to the skies. The voices drifted slightly, but one carried on the wings of the wind. A girl's voice. Lauren's voice.

Bailey folded her wings and dove head first toward the mountains again.

Before she landed, the sound of a twangy steel guitar and whiny vocals woke her.

It took her a moment to catch her breath, to realize she was back in Lauren's room. She slapped the alarm off and rubbed her eyes. No way morning showed up so early. But the clock insisted the bus would arrive soon. She groaned and rolled out of bed.

* * *

The horse walked slowly, but each time a hoof hit the stiff tundra of the plains, vibrations ran up Oliver's back and neck. He'd never been whipped, but he imagined it would feel much like this. The pain continued up his neck, through the back of his skull, straight to the back of his eyes. Running the horses, the trip would only take a few hours. Already, the journey had taken most of the day. The suns made their way down, and they still had a few miles to go. Granted they'd stopped to eat lunch and give Oliver a break.

He'd be lucky to be able to walk after this ride.

In the distance, the torches of Harland dotted the walls. Their lights danced like fireflies. Another hour. Tops. Oliver prayed he'd make it. He prayed Erica would make it. He'd thought of little else the entire day.

Lauren brought her horse close to Oliver. "You doing okay?"

He shook his head.

"So how are we supposed to get into Harland?" Aiden asked. He rode slightly ahead of the other two. His horse, a war horse named Wraith, sleek and white and agile, cantered ahead, as if ready for a battle, eager for violence. "Last time I checked, Ribillius sympathizers weren't exactly popular in the cities. Don't want another Varuthian welcome."

Oliver took a deep breath through his teeth. The cold air froze his windpipe, made his teeth ache. "Be nice if we had some Chameleon Armor," he whispered.

"Where does it hurt?" Lauren asked.

"Back, neck, everywhere."

Lauren cleared her throat, put her hand behind him, ran it up and down his spine. The cold from her fingers numbed his back. His muscles contracted in protest to the chill. He may freeze to death, but at least the pain wouldn't make him throw up in front of everyone. "Thanks," he said.

She pulled her hand away. "Your robe should be pretty cold for another hour or so. Should get you to Harland. When we get inside, I'll numb you up again, if you need it."

Aiden turned Wraith around. "You made the place. How can we sneak in?"

"There's always the sewage drains," Oliver said.

Aiden curled a lip. "Gotta be a better way, bro."

Lauren said, "What about the merchants? They can get through at night. Isn't there supposed to be a nightly shipment of weapons and the like?"

The suns started to drop behind the Dragon's Back Mountains. Oliver shivered. He held the reigns loosely. His cheeks numbed. "Good idea. But how do we get in with them? We wouldn't exactly blend in."

The horizon lit up in orange over the distant mountains. The horses' hooves clopped on the frozen earth below. What grass and weeds persevered through the snow stuck up and swayed in the gentle wind. Oliver wished, for once, he wouldn't have to make all the decisions. He took a shallow breath and whispered, "Don't know. Ideas?"

Lauren's horse, a bay gelding named Strider, canted to the left. Like Wraith, it wanted to run, to stretch its legs. "I don't really care, as long as we don't get killed and don't have to go through the sewer."

"For real," Aiden said.

The soft glow of Harland grew closer. Its inconsistent lights grew to the size of peas. The ground sloped up to where Harland sat on a hill. Oliver had designed Harland to rise from the waist-high golden grass like a boulder on the beach, with plains surrounding it for miles. Easily seen by travelers, Harland had multi-tiered walls that stretched twenty feet toward the cerulean sky. The archers on the three tiers boasted the best eyes in Alrujah. They had to be, to defend their walls from whatever attacks rolled through the prairies.

What Harland's archers may have lacked in precision, they made up for in quantity. Each section of wall in the octagon-shaped city had two turrets, and one on each node as well. Archers lined the wall, shoulder to shoulder, one row set behind and staggered. At any moment, Harland could fit nearly eighty soldiers, all well equipped with arrows and longbows, along any and all of its eight walls, on all three of its tiers.

Oliver crunched the numbers. Eight walls, three tiers, eighty soldiers each. Nearly two-thousand archers in all.

Aiden brought Wraith back to the other two horses. "What if we paid off a merchant? They like money, right?"

"Got a stash of gold hiding in your saddlebags?" Lauren asked.

Oliver painfully lifted an eyebrow. "Merchants never travel alone. They hire mercenaries."

Lauren frowned. "They use Red Beards. I don't really want to have to fight them for the right to the job."

"Red Beards?" Aiden asked.

Lauren answered, and Oliver thanked God he didn't have to speak more than he needed to. "Mercenaries from Port Smalth. Kind of like barbarians. Big, strong, relentless. They'll actually keep the blood of their victims and use it like war paint."

Aiden said to Oliver, "Brutal, bro."

"My idea," Lauren said.

Aiden grinned. "That's my princess."

Lauren smiled broadly.

Oliver gauged the setting of the greater sun. Harland sat on a hill, as secure as Fort Knox. "If we want the job, we may have to fight for it. Not sure how effective I'll be."

"We can handle it," Aiden said. Wraith kicked his front feet up in agreement.

Oliver frowned, from the pain and from the prospect of facing human enemies. "But can you do it without killing? It's one thing to slaughter nar'esh. It's another to kill a person."

"Aren't they fake people?" Aiden asked.

Lauren shook her head. "Death here is every bit as real as it is in North Chester. I don't think I could kill a person. Fangands and beresus, sure. But people?"

Oliver said, "If we do this, we'll make an enemy of every Red Beard in Alrujah. It's a matter of honor for them. Kill or be killed. There is no greater insult than to defeat them in battle and not to kill them."

"Is there another way?" Lauren asked.

Oliver's back ached; his chest burned with each breath. "Not sure."

"So where do we find these guys?"

"Here," Oliver said. He pulled the reigns, and his horse stopped short. He turned it around. "Should be here in about thirty minutes."

CHAPTER FIVE

The angel of the Lord came to Raasnus and said to him, "Why do you hide yourself?" And Raasnus said, "Paramir, king of elves, has set himself against me. He has sworn to end my life and kill my family. We have moved to a land far from his eye." And the angel of the Lord said, "Take up your family and your sword. Return to Alrujah. Go to Paramir and demand he release Adonai's people from the bonds in which he has ensnared them."
—The Book of the Ancients

SCHOOL MOVED SLOWLY FOR Bailey. But Mr. Cooperson's class passed quickly. Her Honors English I teacher mercifully put on a DVD of *Romeo and Juliet*. When the final bell rang, Bailey waited for the class to clear of students before she walked to Mr. Cooperson's desk.

He looked up from the monitor, brown eyes distracted by whatever he worked on. "Need something?"

"You're pretty well read, right Mr. Cooperson?" Stupid question, but she didn't know how else to begin.

"I'd like to think so." He folded his arms and leaned back in his chair, giving her his full attention. "Need a book recommendation?"

"Not really. I wanted to pick your brain for a minute. Ever hear of a book that changes each time you read it?"

He grinned. "You mean a book about a book that changes each time you read it, right?"

She shook her head.

He thought for a minute, tilted his face toward the ceiling as if searching for an answer from God. "I've read stories about changing books. I've read books that feel different each time I go back to them. Nothing where actual words change on the page. Is that what you mean?"

She pulled at the strap of her backpack under the oppressively bright fluorescent lights. "Something like that."

Mr. Cooperson stood up, began erasing the whiteboard. Taking a pen, he scrawled a few notes on Shakespeare for the next class. "Is this an e-book? You know, for Kindles and Nooks? As I understand it, those can change if the author or publisher uploads a new document. They do it to fix typos and the ilk."

"This one's a hard copy."

He pursed his lips in thought for a moment, made a little grunt. Without turning from the whiteboard, he said, "I'll tell you, if you found a book like that, I'd pay top dollar for it."

She tightened the straps on her backpack. Heavy books lifted. She tried to find a way to ask the next question without sounding completely insane.

Mr. Cooperson let her off the hook easy. "Sounds like you got a great story idea there."

Playing along with his misconception, she said, "If I were going to write a story about a girl who gets a journal or something that changes each time she reads it, what might cause that?"

"The changing? Depends on where you want the story to go. Could be something as simple as someone playing tricks on her. You know, swapping the journal out when she's not paying attention."

"Nope." Did she answer too quickly?

"Okay. I'm not sure. Off the top of my head, I might say something magical was happening. That would make it more of a fantasy book, of course. Postmodern urban fantasy, more than likely. Or maybe it's an act of God? You could make it a book about a spiritual journey."

"Yeah," she said. "A journey sounds right."

Mr. Cooperson turned from the board and crossed his arms. "It's been a week now," he said quietly. "You seem to be doing well."

She nodded.

"You don't mind me mentioning it?"

She shrugged. "Can't really hide from it. It happened. We'll find her soon enough, I'm sure."

Cooperson smiled, more from sympathy than agreement. "I look forward to the day. In the meantime, if you need extra time on assignments or anything, let me know."

"Thanks. I will."

He checked the clock and returned to his chair. He crossed his legs and leaned back. "Few minutes before third period. You want to tell me more about this book?"

Bailey scratched an eyebrow. "I don't know. Haven't thought too much about it, really."

"Best time for writing. The story's still fluid, changing. There's a beauty in that if you can get past the feeling of drowning. Research helps. You do much research for this book? What the characters will be like, what they'll love?"

She shook her head.

"Let's do this. Forget about the vocabulary assignment the rest of the class is doing. I want you to write this story of yours. Do some research. Figure out who your characters are, what they love, what they fear. Get into their minds. Bring me some notes tomorrow. Sound good?"

"You want me to write instead of doing the work everyone else is doing?"

"If you're up to it, and if you're serious about it." He smiled. "Far too few quality writers, Bailey. If you're half as good as your sister, you'll be something else. I've got to do my part to plant the seed of the love of writing."

Bailey grinned. "How terribly benevolent of you."

"Bonus points for using our word of the day properly in your reply. Nicely done."

Students trickled in and took their seats. The room filled with the sound of pens scratching papers, notebooks sliding in and out of canvas backpacks. Bailey loosened the straps of her backpack. "I'll bring you notes tomorrow."

"Don't forget to research," he said.

* * *

The darkness and cold of the night pressed in on Lauren. Aiden had scraped together enough dry twigs from dead shrubs along the road to Harland to build a small fire, but it did little to warm them. She shivered. Poor Oliver shivered and trembled and groaned. He stood next to his horse, hoping to glean some warmth from the animal.

Lauren did the same. The horses' hot breath made steam in the frigid air. She wrapped her arms around herself and nodded to the torchlight in the distance. "Must be them."

Aiden hopped up and down. "Good. Little bit of fighting will warm us up, don't you think?"

"Let's try to do this without hurting anyone," Oliver said. "Stick to the plan."

The plan—to incapacitate the Red Beards if they got hostile—seemed too simple to work. Aiden had proposed a backup plan, one filled with blood. But Lauren countered with her plan—freeze them. Should avoid permanently injuring them.

"Let's ride out to meet them," Aiden said. "Sure beats waiting here for them and freezing to death."

Lauren agreed. "Can you make it, Ollie? You want to wait here?"

Oliver nodded. "Might be better if I stay out of this one. Monks shouldn't be involved in this kind of violence anyway."

Lauren kissed Oliver's head and mounted her steed. "Stay safe and warm," she said.

"Be back in a bit, bro," Aiden said. He heeled his horse toward the torchlight.

Lauren followed after him, her horse cantering as they slowed and approached the two carts.

The carts, rumbling up the slight incline, stopped. A man sat in the front, hands on reins and a frown carved fingernail deep in his face. "Whoever you are, you'll want to move. I've the proper paperwork to trade in this city and six Red Beards to enforce my rights."

Aiden, sitting high in his saddle, silver armor gleaming in the moonlight, spoke in a strong voice. "We did not come to disrupt your trade. We came to offer our protection as well."

Lauren's nerves rose, but nothing like they had in the nar'esh cave. After blowing through countless nar'esh, six Red Beards didn't seem as intimidating. But underestimating them might prove fatal. Her blood ran thick and slow.

A thick, tanned hide covered each cart. Leather straps tied the hides tight and held the goods steady, safe from the snow looming over the horizon. Dust lined the light brown wheels. Old carts, crafted from the same wood as Oliver's staff—rognak. The wizened old merchant must be rich to own rognak carts.

"A fair offer, but I've spent what I can to insure my passage to Harland. These Red Beards are sufficient."

Six tall men flanked the carts. Each had long red hair to his shoulders and a beard thick as red sheep. One curled a lip and spit on the frozen ground.

Aiden continued. "Pay them for their passage thus far. You may pay us half what you would pay them for the remainder of the journey.

You'll save money and be safer."

"He pays us for the whole trip," a tall man said. He held an axe with a head nearly as large as the cartwheels. He'd painted blood around his eyes and back to his ears. Another red streak dribbled down his forehead to his nose.

Aiden dismounted and sized the man up. Taller by a head, the redhead seemed unimpressed by Aiden's silver armor. "We wish you no monetary harm. Surely you won't lose much this way."

"We lose pride," he said.

Aiden glanced at Lauren. He must be out of ideas. She, too. Still, she had to try something. She walked the horse over to the merchant. "We have urgent business in Harland and must get inside."

The merchant grinned. "Easy, Donnel."

The tall man with the axe took a step back.

The merchant set the reins of the horse next to him and stood up. He peered down at Aiden and Lauren. "You have no interest in the safety of me or my goods. What you want is a way into a well-guarded city. Best way into Harland is in the back of a merchant's cart, I think. But I do not give rides freely."

Lauren arched an eyebrow. The princess in her reared up and shouted. Royalty did not shove themselves into empty barrels and pretend to be beer. "We have very little gold to offer."

"Lady, I am a merchant. I do not deal in gold alone. Perhaps you have goods you might trade?"

"We have very little we're able to part with," Aiden said as he remounted his horse. The merchant inspected Wraith closely. "You'll have little need of horses inside Harland, I can assure you."

* * *

Instead of heading to the cafeteria when the lunch bell rang, Bailey slipped Lauren's journal in her backpack and started down the stairs toward the computer lab. Something sparked when Mr. Cooperson said "research," and the fact she'd not thought of it sooner surprised her. Oliver had put in as much work on the strange video game as Lauren, probably more. And since they spent nearly every lunch in the computer lab, Bailey would eat hers there today.

Research.

She tugged at the straps of her backpack, tightening and loosening them alternately. Students swarmed the stairs. She wanted to jump, to fly over their heads and come down light as a marshmallow. But she didn't have wings. Not here.

Amid the throng of teenagers, Bailey found one familiar face. Sarah Skeleton, complete with impeccably applied makeup, sunken cheeks, twinkling green eyes, and camera-flash bright smile. A week ago, Bailey considered breaking Sarah's perfectly slim nose, but only after she'd found a particularly rude and hurtful text message from Sarah on Lauren's phone. Before she could swing, Sarah approached Bailey crying.

Apparently Lauren and Sarah didn't hate each other. They may have been friends in a different world, a world outside of shallow cliques and self-centered teens. Too bad most teenagers' perception ended at physical beauty.

What kept Lauren from popularity? She carried a little extra weight, a high-school crime on the same level as murder.

Sarah smiled at Bailey and waved. "Hey Bailey! Lunch again today?"

Bailey moved closer to the wall to allow the ascending students more room to get to the cafeteria. "Can't today. Have to catch up on some work in the computer lab."

Sarah wiggled through the bodies of the students and met Bailey at the wall. She stuck her lower lip out. "I kinda like having lunch with you, though."

Of course she did. Bailey had no extra weight. She played on the basketball team. She dated a senior. In short, Bailey fit into Sarah's circle, despite being two years younger. She pushed past her critique of high school politics long enough to say, "Got a ton of work with all the honors classes."

Sarah grinned. "Okay, Einstein. You go get your work done. Party at Jason's on Friday. You going?"

Bailey hadn't thought about parties for a week. "I'll talk with Franky about it," she said.

Sarah's toothpaste-commercial smile shone bright. "Awesome!"

Awkward. Bailey had no desire to go to the party. Taking the steps two at a time, she crossed her arms and plowed through the ever ascending kids until they thinned.

In the basement of the school, she knocked on the door to the computer lab. Mr. Benson swung the door open. A heavyset man with cheeks like thin steaks, he waddled back to his chair and plopped down.

"Sorry. Thought it was unlocked."

"May I eat my lunch in here?"

He pointed to a sign. Rule number one read, "No food or drink in lab."

"My sister, Lauren, said you'd let her and Oliver eat in here."

He clicked the mouse. "Different story altogether. Oliver was brilliant. And they were careful." He surveyed Bailey. "You don't look brilliant."

"Wow," Bailey said. "And you're a teacher?"

"Not a good one." He sipped his Coke.

"You have food and drink in here."

"What are you, the Queen of England? This is my lab. I do what I want."

Bailey sighed. "Okay, I won't eat. I was hoping I could talk to you about Lauren and Oliver."

He set his Coke down, eyes wide. "Wait, you said Lauren's sister? I'm so sorry. It didn't even register. I'm neck deep in tomorrow's plans. PowerPoint not cooperating. You know how it is. Whew. Lauren's sister." He stared at her for a moment, long enough to make her uncomfortable. "Really sorry to hear about her."

"Yeah," Bailey said.

He finished his Coke, crushed the can, and tossed it into a recycle bin full of soda cans and Gatorade bottles. "You had questions?"

"Did you ever look at the game they made?"

"Look at it? Studied is more like it. Oliver should have been teaching the programming class. He did stuff I've never seen, never even dreamed of. I don't throw the term genius around much, but he's as close as it gets. No way he should be in high school. I've known guys with their Master's degrees who couldn't figure it out. Every time I flip through the book ..."

"What book?" Bailey asked. She sat in a chair close to Mr. Benson.

Benson leaned back in his chair. He studied his computer monitor for a moment before he turned his attention back to her. "The instruction manual," he said, breath lined with the stink of onion.

"For what?"

"The scripting software he engineered."

Bailey opened her mouth for a minute, ready to say something, but unsure exactly what. "He didn't use the school's software?"

Benson shook his head. "Nope. Not good enough, he said. Made up this whole language, physics engine, the whole shebang. Called it Deep Red." Turning to his desk, he opened a drawer and pulled out a red, two-inch three-ring binder. He handed it to Bailey. "Pretty insane, right? High school junior writing software that would confuse Bill Gates."

She took the manuscript, heavy with paper and ink, and opened the front cover. The title page read "Deep Red: A Users Guide. Created and compiled by Oliver Shaw."

Bailey flipped through the pages. She'd need a manual to understand the manual. "Are you using this at all?"

"Not really. I've actually got another copy. This one was Oliver's. He left a copy here, one at home, and gave me an extra to study in my spare time, not that I have any."

"Do you mind if I take this home?"

He nodded. "Knock yourself out."

She slipped the binder in her backpack, had to work to close the zipper. She checked the clock. "Have the police seen this?"

Benson crossed his arms. "No. Why would they need to?"

She shrugged. "Don't know." She paused for a minute before hoisting her backpack over her shoulders again. Her back, and her brain, would be knotted up for weeks.

CHAPTER SIX

*Shedoah's grasp on Alrujah will be as a glass gauntlet. Hard and sharp,
few will see it for what it is. In those days, people will suffer. They will
turn on themselves. Brother will rally against brother. Fathers will slay
their sons. And Shedoah will gain power from their wicked deeds.*
—The Book of Things to Come

OLIVER PULLED HIS KNEES into his chest and fought the urge
to cry. His back screamed in pain. He bit his knee to keep
from yelling. At least the tarp kept him warm. The rognak
cart rumbled along, and Oliver wondered if the merchant deliberately
found every ditch to run the wheels through. Smuggling themselves
into Harland seemed like the dumbest thing imaginable, but at least
they didn't have to fight the Red Beards. At least they didn't have to kill.

He closed his eyes, tried to focus on anything other than the pain—
the slosh of beer in the barrels surrounding him, the clanking weaponry
stacked in crates, the smell of dust and dwarvish wine. He thought of
Lauren in the other cart, of Aiden on the opposite side of this cart. How
they'd given up their horses as payment. They didn't have enough gold
to purchase new horses in Harland. They would either have to walk,
or God would have to provide some way for them to get around more
expediently.

The wagon slowed. The clopping of hooves on hard, frozen earth
ceased. They must be at the gates of Harland. Oliver held his breath.

"Untie the tarps," a soldier said.

The merchant's pinched voice rang out across the still night. "I beg
your pardon! I'll not untie my tarps. It would take too long. You know
me, Smithson. Have you ever known me as a smuggler?"

"You must have been on the road too long, old man. We've been
inspecting every cart for the last two weeks, ever since Ribillius went
daft."

The merchant grumbled. "You and every other city I've been to.
But I didn't expect you, Smithson, to think me a dirty smuggler. I'm a

citizen of Harland. I've known you since you played with sticks."

Oliver wanted to groan. Every minute they bantered meant another minute of pain.

"The viceroy appointed me guard because of my diligence. Now open the carts or I'll have my soldiers do it for you."

The merchant sighed. "Fine. You may open the carts, but be quick about it."

The tarp began to move. Oliver's muscles tensed, and his back convulsed. Think. Breathe, and think. In the dank, swampy blackness, he gripped his staff and remembered Moses' staff turning into a serpent in Pharaoh's court. "Adonai." He prayed and turned the staff loose. It slithered down past his legs, hissed loudly.

Soldiers shrieked. "What do you think to bring into Harland?"

"Serpents!" the merchant said with a laugh. "Winter's made meat scarce."

The merchant's shrewdness impressed Oliver, though guilt still punched him when he thought of how many laws smuggling broke.

"Tie it up," the soldier said. "You could have warned me."

"Now where's the fun in that?"

Oliver let his breath out slowly. The musty rognak wood and dusty oaken barrels tickled his nose. He held in a sneeze as the cart jerked forward. The staff slithered back into his hand, became rigid and stiff again—became wood.

He wanted to get home, but remembering the pressures of high school, now so distant, the lack of sleep, the monotony of school work and bell schedules, the dull repetitiveness of it all, no longer sounded appealing. His life may be in danger here, but Alrujah gave Oliver an opportunity to see the hand of God at work each day. It gave him a chance to be part of His work. It gave him an opportunity to see miracles, to perform miracles. It gave him a chance to be an active part of God's will.

If he had any doubt God had a plan for bringing him and his friends to Alrujah, it vanished the moment his staff turned to a snake.

* * *

Bailey Renee threw her gym bag in the trunk of her mother's Acura TL sedan. Sliding into the front seat, she slithered out of her jacket and buckled up.

Her mom smiled at Bailey. "How was practice?"

Bailey pulled her ponytail straight. "You don't have to do this."

"Pick you up? I want to."

"You never did before."

Her mom pulled out of the school parking lot. The afternoon sky darkened, but not with clouds. Well into its descent, the sun did little to illuminate the city streets of North Chester. At least it wouldn't snow today. The tires crunched over the thin layer of ice covering the road. "I do now. Besides, if I didn't give you a ride, Franky would have to. And you know how I feel about that."

"So work's cool with you taking off early?"

"It's only an hour or so. If they don't like it, they can deal with it. Not like they're going to fire me, right?" Her broad smile worried Bailey. She shouldn't be this happy. She'd either started taking some sort of prescription happy pill, or she'd plunged headlong into denial.

"I'm not going to disappear," Bailey said.

The edges of her mom's smile fell toward her chin. "I know."

"Really? Or are you just saying that?"

"Can we not do this, sweetie? I'd really like to not do this now."

The line of headlights passed them. Her mom turned hers on and turned left on Park Street. Lights poured out from the empty parking lot of the country club.

Bailey warmed her hands by the vent. "I'm going to find her."

"I know."

Neither said anything afterward. Ms. Knowles parked in the garage, gathered her things and walked inside. Bailey followed, her arms filled with her backpack and gym bag. Once inside, she dropped her things in the foyer. Her knees weakened. Dizziness came over her like a child spun around before hitting a piñata. Her eyes grew heavy. She had to make it to Lauren's room to lie down. If she didn't, she'd fall asleep where she stood.

Hand on the wall, she struggled to make it to Lauren's room.

"You okay?"

"Super tired all of a sudden. Taking a quick nap." She shut Lauren's door behind her, nearly tripped on the papers and books scattered on the floor, and collapsed on the bed. Her head didn't even make it to the pillow. She fell asleep, the top half of her on the bed, her knees and feet still on the floor, her arms spread out.

She woke up in an unfamiliar town. Given the stone walls and thatched roofs, she must have been in Alrujah, though she didn't recognize the town. It must have been late because no one else walked along the torch-lit streets. She wrapped her wings around her as she moved through the town, guided only by a feeling, some sort of inexplicable compulsion. She knew where to go though she'd never been in the town before.

Small homes lined the streets. Toward the west, larger buildings stood. Probably shops. While the homes nearest the river running through the center of the town had been built with smooth stones, those farther from the river had been built with wood. A thin crust of snow encased the streets. Salt hung heavy in the air. Bailey thought of the beach. She moved down one road, turned a corner, and continued on toward the spot that called to her. There, nearly fifty feet down, another angel stood. Nearly seven feet tall, his wings, when opened, reached from one side of the street to the other. He wore heavy silver armor and held a sword long as Bailey's legs. "Do not be afraid, Bailey," he said in a voice both beautiful and terrifying. When he talked, it sounded as if two people spoke, one with a lilting voice, the other with a general's timbre. "You know from whom I come?"

"Yes," she said, but she didn't. Not really. Again, like the magnet drawing her to this spot, the angel conjured in her a sense of the familiar, of a friend not seen since elementary school.

"Go to the house at the end of this street. There you will find a girl near your age. She is broken and bloodied. Touch her forehead, each of her palms, and the soles of her feet. She will ask you who you are. You may tell her if you wish."

"I will go," she said. This unnaturalness of the situation simultaneously terrified her and calmed her. She'd done this before, in another life, in another dimension, in another world.

"Bless her in the name of Adonai. After you do, you must leave again."

"Have you summoned me here?" she asked, remembering the nearly narcoleptic episode she'd had at her house.

"Adonai has summoned you in His name."

Wind wove through the thatched roofs, whispering softly and lulling her into a calm confidence. "Okay."

The angel smiled. "Adonai has great plans for you."

Lauren's journal described Adonai as the god of Alrujah. She had no clue what to say to the angel, so she smiled back.

He leaped in the air, brought his wings down hard. The rush of air swirled her in the scent of salt. With two flaps, the other angel disappeared to a bright speck in the night sky, a shooting star rocketing toward the horizon.

If she had her cell phone, she'd have snapped about a dozen pictures of him. His voice, the simple and gentle commands, compelled her to comply. More than simply feeling as if she needed to do it, she wanted to do it.

And when she woke up, she'd go right to Lauren's journal.

* * *

Erica's everything hurt. Her eyes especially, but her arms, legs, back, head, even her fingers and toes. She would swear her eyelashes and the hair on her neck hurt, too. She should say something, let Ullwen know she survived, but she lacked the strength. So she lay awake, eyes closed and unmoving, hoping her body would find a way to fit inside her skin again.

Vague, distant voices came from somewhere. One sounded like an old woman. The other, gruffer, sounded like an even older man. The words sounded like gibberish, but the woman's melodious voice helped soothe some of Erica's throbbing pain.

Another voice, this one a nearby whisper. A girl's voice. "Erica?" It almost sounded like Lauren.

Erica tried to reply, but her swollen, chapped lips felt like they might burst if she put them together.

"Don't try to talk. I'm going to fix you up. I'll be gentle. I'm going to touch your forehead, your palms, and your feet, okay? It may hurt a bit, but hang in there."

Something cold touched the skin of her forehead, something like an ice cube, or an ice pack. The numbing chill spread through her head, eased her headache, even made her lips feel almost normal.

The same sensation touched her palms. The cold crept up her arms, like roots growing in soft soil. Gentle hands on her feet, and the pain in her legs lessened. Erica opened her eyes, blinked twice until they adjusted to the dark. The vague outline of a winged teenage girl moved fluidly before her. An angel?

The angel held a hand over Erica, spoke gently with a voice like crackling fire. "The Lord Adonai bless you and keep you. The Lord

Adonai make His face shine upon you. The Lord Adonai bless your steps and guide your ways. You are the Hand of Adonai."

"Who are you?" Erica asked.

The angel spoke. "Bailey Renee. Lauren's sister."

* * *

After they'd stowed their weapons and armor in the merchant's barrels and secured them in his basement hatch, Oliver, Aiden, and Lauren helped themselves to clothes more befitting Harland's low-economic crowd. Dressed as commoners, they reasoned, they would better avoid suspicious eyes. From the merchant's basement, they made their way to Harland's pub—The Drunken Crow. A crass name adequately describing most of its patrons.

Crowds poured in and out of the Drunken Crow like beer into steins. Most patrons had passed drunk long ago and ran headlong into silliness. They sang songs of ancient battles and gladiatorial events, danced jigs to accompany them. Their brightly colored clothes, mainly green and white, flourished about them. Those not singing or dancing staggered and slurred.

Lauren kept close to Aiden, and he to her. If the crowd got rough, as it often did, she wanted him as close as possible. If she had her way, his arm would be around her, but Oliver had cautioned them about affectionate gestures in public.

"So where is this guy?" Aiden asked Oliver.

"We'll see him soon enough. For now, let's get a drink and try to blend in."

Aiden said, "What do they have other than beer and wine?"

"Water," Oliver said. "But that's not what we're drinking."

"Oliver!" Lauren said. She wanted her voice to be clear over the din of the drunken crowd. "You can't be serious!"

Oliver walked to the counter. "Two honeyed beers and a blood wine for the lady." He gave the man a few gold coins the merchant had given him to even out the cost of the smuggling and horses.

"Bro, I'd rather have a Coke."

Lauren's mouth fell open. "I'm not drinking it. You can't make me. I don't care what you say about this being a game or this being real or whatever. Drinking is a bad idea. Especially when we need to think clearly about our mission."

Oliver grabbed the drinks, handed one to Aiden, and carried his and Lauren's to a table full of singing men. The men had their arms around each other's shoulders as they swayed left to right in an old Harlandian chorus about a wife leaving a husband. "Relax, Lauren. I programmed everything we see, remember? And I didn't program alcohol in the drinks."

"Sure looks like it to me," she said.

One man turned, threw up, and collapsed on the floor. The others laughed, but they didn't stop singing.

"I would know," he said and took a big gulp of the amber liquid. His cheeks puffed out and his eyes widened. He spit the drink back in his cup, blinked a few times, coughed. "On second thought."

Lauren laughed. How long had it been since she'd laughed like that? North Chester? Not even then.

"Well, at least having the drinks will help us blend in a bit," he said.

"We'd blend in more if our cups were empty," Aiden said.

"Good idea," she said and poured her glass under the table.

"Lauren," Oliver said, "if we're not going to drink it, we can at least give it to someone. It'd do us good to make a few friends, especially if we're going to stay here for any length of time."

Lauren pointed to Oliver's stein. "You're really going to let someone drink your backwash."

Another man in the choir collapsed.

"Somehow, I don't think they'd notice," Aiden said. He smelled his drink and wrinkled his nose. "People drink this?"

Lauren turned in her seat. Nearly everyone in the crowded pub had brown hair. The girls wore theirs straight and down to the middle of their backs. The men wore their hair curly and down to their shoulders. Only slight color fading differentiated their tunics and trousers.

"So who are we looking for?" Aiden asked.

"Yarborough," Lauren said. She had to speak loudly for her voice to carry over the never-ending song playing behind them. "He's politically connected. He can get us to Langley."

"How are we going to find him? Everyone looks the same."

"Yarborough doesn't. He's half dwarf. Short and thick. He'll probably have a cane, but he doesn't need one," she said.

"Remember the statue we saw in Margwar? The nameless heir?"

Aiden nodded. Easier than shouting over the singing.

"That's him."

The chorus played on, and Lauren's head started to hurt. The pub kept a warm fire, and the heat from the huddled mass of people made her thankful to be out of the cold. Still, she wondered if she wouldn't be happier outside, away from the racket and the putrid smells of unwashed men and alcohol and whatever other stinks hung in the thick air.

"There, by the fire," Oliver said, and pointed to a small corner of the room where a short, old man huddled over his beer. He sat alone at the table and frowned. For whatever reason, Lauren thought of her grandfather in North Chester.

Her grandfather used to carry her on his shoulders at the zoo, bounce her on his knee like a horse, used to hold her when she cried. Now, she wanted to hold this old man, Yarborough, sitting at the table by himself. His shoulders slumped, and she wanted to hug him, to tell him everything would be fine, the way her grandfather had done for her so many times.

She stood up before anyone else and made her way to the old half-dwarf. For a moment, his eyes brightened with hope, but as quickly as it appeared, it evanesced like a mist burning away in the late morning heat. He turned his attention back to his drink.

Lauren sat next to him. "Something wrong?" she asked. She wanted her voice to be gentle, but because she had to speak so loudly, it sounded like an accusation.

"Several things are wrong, lass. A plethora, a veritable pantheon of wrongdoings and misdeeds."

Aiden sat next to her, as did Oliver.

Yarborough's face pinched in anger. "I may be old and alone, but I can still defend myself. Try to take my money if you dare. I may not kill all of you, but I will carry at least two of you into my grave with me."

"Easy, bro," Aiden said. "We're not here to hurt you."

"What then is your business?" His eyebrows arched, and his hand went from his stein to the hammer in his belt.

Oliver surveyed the pub, lowered his voice, and said, "We hear you deal in books."

"You hear wrong," he said, returning his hand to his glass. He quaffed the golden liquid and belched. "I'm a smith by trade. So unless the books you seek are forged in steel, I cannot help."

"We're looking for some very old, very rare books. Actually, we seek one in particular," Oliver said.

Yarborough's rough lips pulled into a sneer. His yellowed teeth snarled. "Old books, new books, I have no dealings in either." He stood up. He couldn't have been more than five feet tall, at least a foot shorter than the rest of the men in the pub.

Aiden stood up quickly and interposed himself between Yarborough and the door.

"I'd not stand in my way, lad. I may separate your head from your body."

Lauren believed him. "Yarborough," she said.

He turned, "How do you know my name, lass?" His hand gripped the hammer in his belt tighter.

Quietly, she said, "Because I made you."

Yarborough's eyebrows fell. "What trickery is this?"

Oliver stood. "We both made you."

He eyed them crossways, hand still on the head of his hammer. "You speak blasphemies. Harland is Adonai's."

At Lauren's smile, Yarborough's muscles slackened as if it diffused his anxiety. He believed them but didn't want to. He needed more proof. Through the din of the off-key singing and the stomping of feet, Lauren moved close to Yarborough and whispered in his ear. Pointing to Oliver, she said, "He is the Agent of Creation, and we are the Hand of Adonai. This is how we know you, and how we know the things to come."

Yarborough let loose of his hammer. "How can this be?"

Oliver moved closer as well. "We know you are the Nameless Heir. We know you will return your people to their love of Adonai."

Yarborough's eyes slicked with inebriation and sorrow. His frown insisted a hesitancy and intense desire to believe. He mustn't believe himself the nameless heir, but it made sense. "My people are dead."

"Not all of them," Aiden said.

Yarborough pulled his white beard to a point. "Your words are convincing, but Shedoah is the deceiver of old."

Lauren touched his hand. She let her palm warm the back of his hand. "Search your heart, Yarborough. You know we oppose Shedoah. You may know our loyalties by our actions. You've read *The Book of Things to Come*. You know our coming has been foretold. The time has come for you to join us."

With his free hand, Yarborough wiped the golden droplets of honeyed beer from his beard and quietly spluttered, "Never in all my years did I dream this day would come."

CHAPTER SEVEN

Though His people forsook Adonai, the Nameless Heir will return their hearts to their creator. He will return to his people, though they banished him. He will return his people to their place in Alrujah. Though they will call him Nameless, all will know his name.
— The Book of Things to Come

ERICA WOKE, FLEXED HER fingers, curled and uncurled her toes. No pain. She opened her eyes. No piercing pain from the light. But when she swung her legs over the side of the bed, her pain rushed back. She lay back down, took a deep breath. The cold stung her skin. But unlike the gentle numbing effect the chilling touch of the angel brought her, this cold made her ache. Pulling stitched animal skins over herself, she shivered herself to sleep.

When she woke up again, a lantern next to her bed glowed red. The night wind slipped in through the window and circled over the top of the fluted glass. The flame moved intermittently. Outside, crickets chirped and owls hooted.

Her body still ached with cold and bruises, but she breathed without much pain. She closed her eyes again and let the sounds of Alrujah lull her back to sleep.

The next morning, she woke again. The greater sun ascended over the Alrujahn Sea, revealing its full spherical splendor. Orange and red light illuminated her room. The lantern had long been extinguished, leaving only a blackened wick as evidence it had ever burned. Hunger overcame her. She hadn't felt hungry in so long, the sensation seemed foreign, new. Her mind conjured images of three-egg omelets and pans of bacon. And orange juice. She might even go toe-to-toe with the sasquatch again if it meant a plate of pancakes.

Without thinking, she stood up, but dizziness forced her to sit again. Most of her pain had vanished, but weakness replaced it. She must have been out for a month to have healed to this degree—so why didn't it feel like that long?

The rock floor chilled her bare feet. She took her time standing up, gathering the animal skins—wolf and bear, mainly—from the bed. She wrapped a wolf skin around her arm and lay the others end to end on the floor, stepping on each, gathering those behind her, so as to make a moving skin-carpet. Wooden walls joined with wooden rafters to support a thatch roof. She'd never been to a place like this—not the castle, not the monastery, not the caves.

For a minute, fear tickled her mind. But hadn't Ullwen said something? If he was here, if he was okay, she would be, too.

She steadied herself on the threshold. A dying fireplace glowed in the small adjoining room, illuminating a tiny table with three chairs. Another door stood closed on the far wall. Whoever lived here must be sleeping.

She smelled something pungent, something terribly salty and starchy. Potatoes, and meat. Stew. An iron rod and hook suspended a black pot over the fire. The coals glowed red and orange. A small portion of stew still simmered.

Four wood bowls rested on a splintery wooden mantle over the fireplace. She reached up to grab one, but dizziness knocked her back. Whatever pain she'd had was replaced by fatigue to the point of exhaustion. She sat in a chair and pushed her toes into the furry side of a wolf's skin.

Sparky. Where was he? If she called for him, she might wake someone. And while that possibility frightened her—she had no interest in meeting anyone new—the alternative scared her more.

"Sparky!" she called in a terrified whisper. No answer. "Sparky!" She called, louder this time, with every ounce of force within her.

The closed door rattled.

Her heart leapt. Slowly, she steadied herself on the table and walked toward the door.

It swung open, and there stood Ullwen, his face unshaven, his eyes rimmed red. "Lakia," he whispered harshly. "Why are you up? You should be resting." He shut the door quickly behind himself and reached out to her elbows.

Dizzy again, she faltered, and he caught her.

He set her back in the chair. "It's early," he said. Examining her carefully, he said, "By the breath of Adonai."

"Where's Sparky?"

"Your bruises, your wounds …" He reached a hand to her face. She caught it with her own hand and twisted it down to the table.

Ullwen pulled his hand free and rubbed his wrist. "Sparky is resting, as you should be. But what a glorious wonder has transpired on you! Your wounds are healed!"

"Hooray for me. Is Sparky okay?"

Ullwen's face moved from wonder to sadness. "Relina is working on him. He will not be well for many days. But you …"

"I get it," she said. She didn't mean to be so short-tempered, but her stomach knotted from hunger and fear. She thought of telling Ullwen about the angel, a memory floating somewhere between the foggy recollection of a dream and a repressed memory.

"Do you feel well enough to eat?"

She did. The smell of the stew—the potatoes and celery, the carrots and herbs, and the meat—likely rabbit—bent her stomach until she thought of little else. "I want to see Sparky," she said.

"Very well." Ullwen walked back into the room and closed the door. The door muffled the sound of three voices—Ullwen's, a woman's, and another man's. She listened carefully, sitting as still and silent as possible, but the weathered wood door stifled the mumbles.

Shortly after he disappeared, Ullwen came back out, this time dressed in shabby Renaissance faire clothes. He took her elbow in one hand, her hand in the other, and helped her stand. "Sparky is in Relina's room. She's been watching him closely. Are you sure you wish to see him?"

Her legs shook, but not from pain. Past the door, Relina knelt over Sparky. The plump woman blocked Erica's view, but her mind conjured up the worst picture imaginable: Sparky broken and bruised, swollen like an oversaturated sponge. Her stomach boiled.

A man, tall as Ullwen but broader in the belly, stood in the corner of the room. He averted his eyes and blushed. "Mornin'," he mumbled.

His embarrassment made Erica realize how little she had on. Instead of her green dress, she wore bandages wound tightly around her chest and abdomen. Bandages encircled her left arm, wrapped from wrist to elbow. An animal skin hung snugly around her hips like a hairy skirt. And her legs—ugh. Every bit as hairy as the skin above them. Man, did she need to shave.

Relina stood up. The portly woman had a gentle voice, and her eyes widened at the sight of Erica.

"Lakia," she whispered. "Ullwen said healed, but I had no idea.

There's not a mark on you."

Erica swallowed and marveled at the lack of pain. "Is Sparky okay?"

Relina's wonder melted to melancholy. "He should survive, but it will take some doing. I'm not sure he's fit to do much but sleep for now." She stepped to the side.

Sparky lay on a skin mat on the floor. His side rose and fell with his shallow breaths. Blood matted his fur. Someone had splinted his front leg with a staff and bandages. Eyes closed, he didn't move.

"He may fair better than he appears," Ullwen said. He put a hand on Erica's shoulder, and she didn't pull away. "Much of the blood is from the sasquatch. Relina feeds him crushed mushroom caps from the vira trees to keep his strength up and clove and wintergreen to ease the pain."

Staring at Sparky, Erica said in a low voice, "Please tell me the sasquatch is dead."

"Aye, lady. I put six arrows in him, and he breathed no more." He sounded so old, not like the college-aged kids she knew from North Chester. *But then, I guess war grew a man up.*

Erica knelt next to Sparky. She put her hand on him tentatively.

Sparky whimpered.

Erica's eyes grew hot. She stood quickly, ignoring the lightheadedness that dizzied her. She moved outside into the cold morning. She squawked, and the call echoed over the thatched roofs of Varuth. A razorbeak alighted in a nearby tree and returned her call. "Tell Oliver I need him. Tell him Sparky needs him."

The purple bird lifted into the air with a flap of its long wings. She turned back inside. "Ullwen. Take me to Alrujah."

"M'lady. I must protest. You need more rest."

"I'm fine."

Ullwen nodded. "Very well. We'll leave soon. But first, you must eat, and we must find you clothes to disguise you. The dress you packed is far too befitting a woman of your stature. You're well known in Alrujah, and your presence may make Ribillius suspect betrayal. If we're not careful, we both may end up with your parents."

She sat at the table, trying to let Ullwen's reason pierce her fear and her anger over Sparky's injuries. A phantom heat scalded her hands, and she wished she still had her gloves on.

An idea hit her. "Relina, do you know anyone who is good with hair?"

"Aye, love. You fancy a new hairstyle?" She pulled a bowl from above the hearth and ladled some leftover stew into it. She set it on the table and gestured for Erica to sit and eat.

The smell of it made her stomach angry. How long had it been since she'd eaten? She brought the wooden spoon to her lips and sipped the thick brown broth. Her mouth watered so much it hurt. She took a bite of potato and chewed it slowly. Her jaw ached. "Thank you," she said. "And yes, I do."

"You'll be wanting Gabby. She does wonders."

"Can she turn my hair black?"

"I suppose."

"Ullwen, I need some money."

* * *

Shortly after they left the pub, Yarborough led Oliver, Lauren, and Aiden to a manor on the outskirts of Harland. They followed a winding path up the hill on the north side of town in the dark. Leafless trees lined the path, and the wind hopscotched through the branches. While nowhere near the size of the boxy castle looming in the west, the home qualified as a mansion in any of Alrujah's major cities. The two-story Victorian style home contrasted with the plain architecture of the surrounding residential area. Oliver recognized it immediately despite the nagging, distracting pain in his back. "Langley's house?"

"Aye," Yarborough said.

Oliver slowed his pace. Not only did he need a break from walking—his back was killing him—he wanted more time to talk to Lauren. "About Langley," he said. "I programmed the identity of the Mage Lord to randomly select from a group of about one hundred different NPCs. But in several of my tests, it turned out to be Langley."

"I know," she said. "You told me back in North Chester."

"You think this time will be any different?"

She shrugged—something that made his back and neck hurt just watching. "If he is, he'll know where *The Book of Sealed Magic* is, and we can take it from him."

"If he lets us."

Aiden slowed his pace to match theirs. "So we don't take no for an answer."

Yarborough paused, turned back to the meandering group. "You are coming, yes?"

Oliver had an idea. "You know Langley well. Has he been acting strangely of late?"

Yarborough said, "He is an elf. He is always strange. But his demeanor hasn't altered if that is what you mean to imply."

"No talk of strange books? Random trips to places abroad for reasons other than politics?" Lauren asked.

Yarborough shook his head. "What is it you suspect?"

"Don't know," Lauren said. "Just curious."

"Your suspicions, whatever they may be, are unfounded. He is the same contentious, arrogant elf as he's always been."

Behind Yarborough, Langley's immense home loomed.

"Just because he's not the Mage Lord now," Lauren whispered, "doesn't mean he won't be eventually."

Aiden followed her lead and lowered his voice. "I say keep your enemies close."

Oliver didn't like the idea, but Aiden had a point. He nodded. "Thank you, Yarborough, for your honesty. The days are strange, and we must be cautious in such a politically charged climate." He began moving again, slowly, step by agonizing step.

Before long, they'd reached the top of the hill. Yarborough smacked the golden knocker against the door. An elf, taller than Aiden by a head, opened the door and surveyed the peculiar group suspiciously. "Who are your friends, Yarborough?" he asked in a pompous tone.

"Evening, Cleejal. We need to speak with Langley. Business of Harland," he said.

The elf scowled down at them, no doubt disdaining the tattered clothing they wore to better blend in with the crowd. "I believe you know the way to the dining area, Master Yarborough. Be good enough to show your acquaintances along. I'll have Master Langley meet you promptly. He retired some time ago, so I must rouse him. I'll urge him to be expedient."

"Thank you," Yarborough said. He led them through the massive house. An upstairs balcony hovered overhead with straight staircases jutting down on either side. The elf took the one on the left, and Yarborough walked past the stairs to the next downstairs room. The room housed trophies for archery and fencing. Most had been fashioned from gold, but several silver and bronze medallions hung on the wall as well. In the center of the room, a glass case housed a golden gauntlet. More for show than practicality. A golden glove would be too heavy and too soft to be of much use in actual combat. It was an old family heirloom from a time long before the War of the Suns. Alone, the gauntlet was worth more than the house. A strong, but familiar, enchantment guarded it. Nothing so strong as to make Oliver suspect Langley for being the Mage Lord, though.

The next room had a lengthy harspus-wood table and bench-style seats. Yarborough seated himself near a bowl of fruit, took an apple, and bit into it. The crunch made Oliver's teeth hurt, which made his back hurt.

"So who is this guy we're meeting?" Aiden asked Lauren quietly.

"A half-elf named Langley. He's the Elvish ambassador to Harland. Since he has political connections, he should be able to help us find *The Book of Sealed Magic.*"

"Got it." He sat next to Yarborough, took a banana, peeled it, and handed it to Lauren. "Potassium," he said. "Keep up your strength."

* * *

Bailey Renee opened her eyes expecting to be half-on and half-off Lauren's bed. Instead, she lay flat on her back. Her hand stung. She blinked, let her eyes adjust to the lights above her. In the corner of the white room, a television hung. On it, some guy shelled shrimps and threw them onto an indoor barbecue. An IV needle poked the back of her hand and a tube connected it to a bag of clear fluid.

Why would she be in a hospital? Had she been in an accident? Maybe she hit her head and got a concussion?

She sat up slowly, dizzy, checked for a call button, and found one on the rail of her bed. She rang it twice, and a nurse's voice came across a speaker behind her head. "Nurse."

Her mind moved slowly and searched for the right question to ask. Eventually, she settled on, "Where am I?"

"Hang on, I'll be right in."

"Why am I here?" she asked.

The line clicked dead.

Bailey sighed and searched for the remote to turn the station. She tried to clear the fog from her head, to remember what had happened. Maybe carbon monoxide poisoning? Would explain the sluggish brain. But then, her mother would be sick, too, wouldn't she?

A nurse came in dressed in pink scrubs and white tennis shoes.

Her eyes sparkled gold, and she smiled warmly. "Nice to see you awake. You've been asleep for quite some time."

"What happened?"

The nurse checked the machines and made some notes on a clipboard hanging on the wall. "I'll let your doctor explain. Your mother is on her way. I paged her. She just stepped out for some breakfast. I told her I'd keep an eye on you."

Bailey groaned. She hadn't had a headache like this in some time. "Who are you?"

"I'm Nicole."

"Nice to meet you." Bailey turned the television down. She had no interest in watching anything now.

A moment later, her mother came in, coffee in hand. "Oh thank God you're up! How do you feel?" She set her coffee down and felt Bailey's forehead. "You're so cold, honey."

Bailey blinked. "Maybe because your hand is hot from holding the coffee."

Her mom smiled. "Sorry. I'm a little frantic."

Nurse Nicole smiled. "She's doing well, Ms. Knowles. Vitals are still strong."

"My head is killing me."

"On a scale of one to ten?" Nurse Nicole asked.

Bailey frowned. She didn't want to think. Thinking hurt. Finally, she chose the number she felt was safest—five—though her head hurt more like an eight.

"I'll let your doctor know."

"Why am I here?"

Her mom sat in a chair next to her and took Bailey's hand. "You don't remember?"

"I remember going to sleep."

"Going to sleep?" her mom asked, her voice sharp. "Sweetie, you staggered around like you were drunk or high or something. Had me scared to death. Then you passed out on Lauren's bed. I tried to wake you up, but you wouldn't move, wouldn't respond." She paused here, each word coming out slowly. "I thought you were …"

"I'm fine," Bailey said, but she didn't feel fine. In the window, dark clouds hid the sun and made it difficult to gauge the time. She wanted to see the sun. Even better, two suns.

"Well, I don't think a sixteen-hour coma qualifies as being 'fine.'"

She sipped her coffee and wiped her eyes with the sleeve of her coat.

"What time is it?"

"Almost eight."

"I slept the whole night?"

"Didn't you hear me, sweetie? You've been in a coma for sixteen hours."

Bailey closed her eyes. Sixteen hours? No way. "I'm missing school. Can't you tell them to let me out of here? I'm fine."

A short man with a tangle of black hair and a white lab coat walked into the room. "Morning, Ms. Knowles. Bailey, it's good to see you awake. I'm Doctor Walsh. Can you tell me how you feel?"

"Tired, but fine."

"She has a headache," her mother said.

"Yes, Nurse Nicole told me. I'll get her something for it right away. Good news, though. So far, most tests came back normal, but we did find some electrical abnormalities in your brain, like dreaming, but not exactly. My guess is that you had some sort of sleep-seizure. I'd like to monitor you a little longer. If we can find something soon, great. If not, we send you home with a fancy cap to monitor your brain activity throughout the day."

"I've never had seizures before."

The doctor smiled, folded his arms with the tablet PC close to his chest. "First time for everything, right?"

"I don't believe this," she muttered. "Can I go? You said most of the tests were normal. I don't want to get behind." She had no real interest in returning to school, not for her grades. But she couldn't shake the feeling that she might stumble across a clue there.

Ms. Knowles put a hand on Bailey's arm. "Your teachers will understand. I've already called the school to let them know."

Bailey sat up, stared out the window, thought about making a break for it. Already, the thrumming pulse of pain in her head eased. "I've got a game tomorrow night. The season's wrapping up, and they need me."

Doctor Walsh clucked his tongue. "No basketball for you, young lady. Not until we get some more answers, yes?"

Her head was wrapped in gauze, and something pulled her skin along her hairline. Wires? Behind her head, a tangle of wires was wrapped up like a ponytail. They fed into a machine beside the bed. She lay back down, took a deep breath. "Are you going into work, Mom?"

"I have the next few days off."

"Can you run to the school and turn in my work from last night? And pick up whatever I'm going to miss. And bring me my backpack and iPad. Please?"

Ms. Knowles glanced at Doctor Walsh.

He shrugged. "We can let her work. See how her brain does under stress. If it's too much, we'll cut her off."

Ms. Knowles nodded and picked up her oversized black purse. "I'll be back soon, sweetie, okay?" She handed Bailey her cell phone. "Call me if you need anything."

Bailey told her she would. Before Ms. Knowles got completely out the door, Bailey called her back in. "One more thing, Mom. Can you call Detective Parker for me?"

CHAPTER EIGHT

The elves raised for themselves idols. They cast in gold and silver the images of their forebears. They offered fruit and grain sacrifices and honored the memory of their tyranny. So Adonai passed judgment on their king. He cursed the sword that subjected human-kind to slavery. And the wicked elves revered it as the Blood Sword.
—The Book of the Ancients

L AUREN RECOGNIZED LANGLEY'S GAIT instantly. He carried himself with a confidence bordering on arrogance. Compared to Yarborough's stout frame, the half-elf was comically tall. Dwarves boasted round, robust features—bodies, faces, noses. Elves prided themselves on their long, linear, angular features. Dwarves were all ovals and circles; elves were all triangles and rectangles. If an elf and a dwarf ever had a child, the result would be very human. But what an amazing fighter such a child would make.

The tea Langley poured into their cups smelled of berries and spices. "I regret I have no substantial food to offer at this late hour," he said in a voice thin as his limbs. The lantern lit his face from beneath, casting sharp shadows over his lithe nose and eyes.

Lauren swallowed her fear, told herself to trust Langley, though it went against everything in her. "Thank you for the tea," she said, more a gesture to put herself at ease than to honor him.

Oliver seemed equally distrustful of Langley. Neither drank their tea immediately. After Yarborough and Aiden drank, they did too, but slowly. And as the hot liquid snaked down her throat, she waited for a wrenching sickness to overtake her. Before his ambassadorship, Langley had been rumored an assassin with a taste for poison.

Rumors only, she told herself. She had no reason to believe Langley played any part other than stubborn ambassador. She could feel the magic in him, and while he was powerful, he was nowhere near what the Mage Lord was. But she worried his quarrels with Harland's viceroy, and with Ribillius by extension, had some merit, as much as it pained her to think so. Certainly, her Alrujahn father had made some questionable decisions. But Ribillius was no Hitler, no Mussolini.

She pushed the tea away. "I'm not thirsty."

Staring into his tea, Langley said, "You distrust me, Indigo."

How had he learned her name? She wore the same tattered green and white dress as Harland's other citizens. Must be her wispy blonde hair. He must recognize her from his previous visits to Alrujah on political business. Knowing her identity may give him a slight advantage. She sighed. "Your quarrels with my father are well documented."

"How did you know?" Aiden asked.

Langley smiled. "One does not become an ambassador because they are unobservant. The tips of her ears are round enough for most people, but elves can always sense the presence of other elves."

"She's a human," Aiden said.

"Only half-human," Lauren said quietly. She ran her fingers over her ears, felt the nub at the top of each.

Aiden stared at her with new eyes, with a sense of wonder or fear.

Yarborough harrumphed. "They become an ambassador because they're a lousy halfling, and neither race wants to claim them. Because they're hated by both races, they put them in the only place imaginable—politics. Everyone hates politicians."

Langley glared at him. "Not every halfling is elected to a position of influence."

Yarborough folded his arms. "You insufferable elf. They tried to elect me, but I wouldn't let them. Some of us still have standards."

Langley grinned and slapped Yarborough's shoulder hard enough to make an echo. "You're a funny old man. Tell me how you fell into a dirty Alrujahn lot like this."

"Dirty?" Aiden asked, his voice gravelly with irritation.

Yarborough pulled his hammer from his belt and set it on the table. The bowl of fruit bounced, and bananas and apples leapt under the shock. He checked the room to ensure no servants still lurked in the shadowy corners. "This may be hard for you to believe, but they are the Hand of Adonai."

Langley put the kettle of tea in the center of the table. The sleeves of his green tunic hung loosely over his thin wrists. He put a foot up on a chair and crossed his arms on his knee. "It is difficult to believe. If so, why are there not five of them?"

Lauren spoke up. The way Langley treated Yarborough encouraged her. "Two of us have split off to accomplish a secondary mission. Put your mind at ease. We are the Hand."

"How can we be sure?" Langley asked.

Oliver said, "I am a monk, of the Cerulean Order. Our coming has been foretold in *The Book of Things to Come*. We have secured the last copy of this book and are using it to root out the Mage Lord, for the good of Alrujah, the good of the humans and the dwarves and the elves." Strange to ask for his help finding the Mage Lord after his earlier suspicions.

Langley buried his hands in his sleeves, something Oliver had done countless times. "The dwarves have long been extinct, Monk. Were you as well versed in ancient texts as you propose, you would know that."

"Bro, we've been to Margwar. We've seen the tunneling. The dwarves aren't exactly popping out of the mountains, but we're pretty sure they're on the other side. We don't need books to tell us that."

Langley shook his head. "And now we have your story as a lie, by your own mouth. Margwar is the home of countless nar'esh and an ancient evil. Had you traveled there, you would have been killed as surely as the dwarves."

Aiden stood up. "Not sure I like your tone, Stick Man. Ambassador or not, you'll speak to us with respect, or I'll use you to clean the apple skin from my teeth. Understand?"

Without moving, Langley glowered at Aiden. "You must be Jaurru."

"You know us," Aiden continued, despite Lauren's hand on his elbow. "So you must know what we can do to you if you don't help us."

"Threatening an ambassador is a capital offense in Harland," Langley said coldly.

Oliver stood up and winced. "Easy, Aiden. Please. We can handle this."

"This dude's a chump," he whispered.

"He's an ambassador," Oliver whispered back. "I apologize, Ambassador. Jaurru is very devoted to cause and country."

Langley had only brittle patience. "You are guests in my home and friends of my friend. I will allow him this one oversight. But I'll thank him to guard his tongue as fiercely as he guards the honor of Alrujah. Speak, Monk. Tell me why you're here."

"We seek *The Book of Sealed Magic* in order to keep it from the Mage Lord. We have reason to believe its current secret location is no longer secure."

Langley peeled a banana. He took a small bite. "Men have unsuccessfully sought the book for centuries. Why do you say its safety is now compromised?"

"The Mage Lord," Lauren offered. She also stood. "*The Book of Things to Come* is clear. If we do not find the book soon, the Mage Lord will. And if he does, all Alrujah will be bent to his will. Even Harael."

Langley put the banana down. "The Mage Lord seeks to overthrow Ribillius. We have no cause to believe he intends harm to the city of the elves."

"Bro, if he gets the book, everyone hurts."

"This man speaks like an Otherlander," Langley said.

"I'm aware," Yarborough muttered.

Lauren said, "The Mage Lord has no allegiance. His victory means defeat for all races."

Langley sipped his tea, checked Lauren's and Oliver's full cups. "You believe I can help you?"

"*The Book of Things to Come* does," Oliver said.

"Judging by your full teacups, I'd say we have some trust issues. If I'm to help you, we will need to trust each other completely."

Yarborough slipped his hammer back in his belt. "This again?"

"What?" Aiden asked.

Langley said, "There's an item of certain value to my people. If you help me retrieve it, I will accompany you on your journey to secure *The Book of Sealed Magic*."

Oliver glanced at Lauren. He must be thinking the same thing as her. "The Blood Sword."

* * *

The smell of yeast and wheat, of bread baking in the hearth, woke Erica. She ran her fingers through her shorter, black hair, as if she didn't believe she'd actually had it cut and dyed last night. Embroidered silver flowers and leaves adorned the torso of her new dress, sewn from a fabric two shades the blue side of black, also purchased last night. But the sleeves didn't last long. Erica ripped those off before she even got back to Relina's.

When she came into the kitchen, Ullwen sat at the table while Relina waddled around like the librarian in North Chester High. Erica spent a lot of time in the library, studying vampire books and the like. Relina's waddling made Erica more comfortable with her, but Erica had been hurt enough not to trust right away.

Relina stoked the glowing coals under the hearth. "You've gone daft, do you hear? Positively daft," she said. "I've heard enough of your lunatic ideas in my day to know you're still crazy."

Ullwen ignored her harsh words. "I'm asking you to make the potion, not to swim. Lakia and I can handle the rest."

"Swimming into Alrujah. Whoever heard of such a thing?" She settled herself onto the bench on the opposite side of the table. "The channel is colder than Vesper's Mountain. And you know it feeds the moat. Demons swim beneath the surface and make eagles think twice before swooping down for their meals. Parial-barbed vi-fish, water dragons. Death swims those waters."

"But your potions will guard us from the cold and allow us to breathe water."

"And what about those finned fiends? I can't make a potion to make them vanish."

"So, what are we talking about?" Erica asked.

Relina continued as if Erica hadn't spoken at all. "And once you're inside Alrujah? Where will you go from there? Guards line the docks."

Ullwen growled, "Aye, and well they should. From us."

"Right. Anyone want to fill me in?" Erica said.

"And to make her swim, too? She's been out of bed a few hours and you want her to pretend to be a fish?"

"It's the only way," Ullwen said.

By now, Erica had put the pieces together. "Why swim? Why not a boat?"

Ullwen put his hand on hers, a gesture of gentle reassurance. "Alrujah's ceased all trade with outlying cities. No boats run between Varuth and Alrujah. Swimming is our only option."

"I'm kind of with Relina on this one. I suck at swimming."

Ullwen nodded. "I will be with you. All you need do is hold on."

Didn't sound like too bad of an idea.

Relina sighed. "Ullwen. I'm an alchemist, not a miracle worker."

"Your husband says otherwise."

Relina's face brightened. Her innocent smile infected Erica, and she smiled too.

Ullwen leaned in close to Relina's ear and whispered. "Wouldn't you like to get one over on old Ribillius?"

"That's dangerous talk," she said, hoisting her corpulent frame and waddling back to the hearth. She checked the bread, and Erica's stomach growled again. She'd kill for a pizza right about now.

"Aye, dangerous. But tempting."

She pulled the bread from the hearth and set the oval loaf on a breadboard. She cut it into pieces with a large serrated knife and handed them to Ullwen and Erica. "It would take some time."

"We will wait."

"If I make them for you," she said, "I'll be sending you to your death."

"Let me worry about what happens inside Alrujah. We'll be back pestering you again before you can scrub our stench from your sheets."

* * *

Bailey Renee finished her work quickly and went back to reading Lauren's journal. She'd been reading for over an hour when Detective Parker, complete with snow-crusted black hair and overcoat, walked in. He hung his overcoat on the door. He held an unmarked manila file folder in one hand and used the other to slip his unlit cigarette behind his ear. He smiled at Bailey, a completely unnatural expression for him. Sitting down and crossing his legs, he nodded toward the machines. "You take a spill?"

She made another note in her iPad. "I'm a deep sleeper. Freaked my mom out, I guess. All precautionary."

"No pain?"

Her headache had subsided shortly after she took the two ibuprofen the nurse brought her. "No pain."

"Good," he said. Behind him, snow swirled outside the window, collecting on the corners in cottony mounds. "Your mom called."

Bailey sat up and crossed her legs Indian style. "I asked her to. That Lauren's file?"

"Nah. A get well gift." He handed it to her.

Perplexed, Bailey took it. Several sketches of Lauren and of Bailey spilled out. More than sketches, the charcoal lines, shadowed and illuminated with blank spaces, made art. She recognized each as a rendering of several photos they'd given Detective Parker when he showed up at their house the first night Lauren went missing. "Where'd you get these?"

"Drew them."

"You?" she asked.

"Started as a police artist. You know, projecting what people would look like when they were older. Using victims' descriptions of perpetrators to put something together. That kind of thing. Still like the feel of charcoal on paper. Helps me think. I do this a lot on tough cases."

Bailey filed through the pictures, stunned Parker produced anything this beautiful. "They're amazing," she said.

"Glad you like them. Here." He took the pictures and taped them to the wall beside the bed. "Little something to brighten this place up."

"Just when you think you know a guy," Bailey whispered.

Standing over the bed, Parker frowned down at her. "You didn't call me here to chat."

"Swear you won't send me to a shrink?"

He stuck his hands in the pockets of his black slacks. "No promises. But you've got me interested."

"Guess a shrink's office is no worse than this place." She handed him the journal. "This is Lauren's journal. It may be the only way to prove I'm not super crazy."

"How so?"

"Here's the thing." Bailey leaned back in the bed, pulled the covers up to her neck. The thin blue gown they had her in did very little to keep her warm, even in a heated room. "I think Lauren and the rest of the kids are in some sort of parallel universe."

"I'm going to need to sit down for this, aren't I?"

Bailey continued. "Read it tonight. Twice."

Parker shut the door, turned off the television, and sat down next to the bed again. Crossing his arms, he said, "I'll bite. Why twice?"

"It will change. When you read it twice, you'll know I'm not crazy."

"What if it doesn't?"

"I give you full permission to put me in the crazy hatch. I'll need it."

He flipped through the pages of the journal. "This is what you didn't want to talk to me about at the basketball game?"

"And the dreams."

"Dreams, too?" Parker inspected the sketches of Lauren and Bailey. He grimaced. "Could have done better on that one. Eyes are too dark."

Bailey closed her eyes. Sleep pressed in on her temples. She yawned and stretched while the fog of unconsciousness rolled in. It'd only been a few hours since she woke up this morning. She shouldn't be this tired, especially after sleeping for sixteen hours the night before. She pressed on, hoping to tell Parker everything clearly. "In my dreams, I'm an angel. I fly over the land Lauren created, the one she sketched out in her journals and diaries."

"Sounds like fun." Parker sounded as if he stood outside the window. She wanted to open her eyes to check, but fatigue weighed her eyelids down.

"I saw Erica there. She was hurt."

Parker's voice came stronger now, "You okay? Something's beeping over there."

On the outskirts of her perception, a door opened. Indistinct voices swirled like food coloring in water. She tried to count them, to see the colors of their different tones. Three? Four? They ran together, voices mixing from red and yellow to orange, blue and yellow to green, green and orange to black. Moments after they began, they vanished.

CHAPTER NINE

Moloch took unto himself a body of death. He became a living death, a desecration of the holiness of life. To him, wicked men made offerings. For him, they slew their friends. They murdered each other, sacrificed the willing and the unwilling. And Moloch's power grew stronger. They worshiped him as the Lord of the Flies.
—The Book of the Ancients

ERICA SAT ON THE bed next to Sparky. She rested her hand on his side as it rose and dropped with his shallow breaths. Blood matted his hair. The cracks in his ribs raised his thick skin and fur in a row of jagged mountains. His injuries made her sick, made her want to throw up. But she stayed with him. She spoke to him while Relina and Ullwen pored over maps of Alrujah.

"If Oliver had known me any better, I'm sure he wouldn't have made me a caller," she whispered. "I hated animals. Really hated them."

She moved her hand from Sparky's chest to his head. "But I'm glad he didn't know me better. I can't imagine going through all this without you, Sparky."

A knot formed in her throat. She didn't want to cry. She'd cried enough already in her life. But the sight of Sparky broken ripped her spirit. "Without getting too mushy, you taught me what love can be. And for what it's worth, I love you." The last words came as little more than whispers.

Someone knocked, and Ullwen glanced in the door. "How is he?"

Erica wiped her tears quickly. "Not good."

"Do you think Oliver can help?"

She traced the thin skin on Sparky's ear. "I'm guessing he had something to do with me being healed, but I'm not exactly sure how. If he did, he could probably do something for Sparky, if my razorbeak can ever find them. There's no telling how far they've gone or where they even are."

Ullwen nodded. "It is in the hands of Adonai, now."

"Whatever good that will do."

"You are not a believer, are you?" Ullwen said. He sat on the edge of the bed.

"What? In Adonai? No. Not really." Sparky's chest compressed slightly as he exhaled. "Kind of hard to believe in a made-up god."

Ullwen moved from the bed to kneel beside her. "Vicmorn insists Adonai is real, that He is the creator of Alrujah and of your world."

When she touched Sparky, his matted coat, his shallow breathing, she wanted to believe. What made something real? If Oliver created Alrujah, someone else might have created the world they lived in. "Before this. Before Alrujah and Sparky and you, I never believed in a creator. We have science classes where I live. Our books tell us our world was created by chance, a chain of events culminating in a cosmic explosion to form our universe."

"Your world must be chaos," he said. He put his hand on her shoulder.

Erica remembered the fire on the backs of her hands. "That's an understatement."

"When you look at Alrujah, the trees of the Cerulean Woods, the expansive Dragon's Back Mountains dividing the suns and the earth, the Alrujahn Sea and all the fish within it—it's hard to think there's no creator. How could random chance produce such fearfully balanced wonders? Alrujah bears the signatures of its designer."

Erica smiled. "Good thing Oliver's not here. His head would get too big to fit through the door."

"His head still grows?"

"Never mind. A designer, you say?"

"Aye, Lakia."

She put her hand on his. "Call me Erica."

* * *

Somewhere near the edge of the cliff of Vesper's Mountain, Oliver stood next to Aiden, who had his arm around Lauren. How long had it been since Oliver found Lauren in her pajamas on the edge of the cliff in North Chester? Weeks? Months? Years?

Shortly before sunrise, Aiden visited the merchant and retrieved their old garb, their weapons and armor. Oliver in his blue monastic robe, Lauren in her enchanted white dress, and Aiden in his silver

Alrujahn armor—they followed Langley's lead out of Harland and up to the Callbred Mountains south of the city. An hour later, they climbed the stairs up Vesper's Mountain to the Ruins of Norgren.

The Ruins of Norgren lay like a slaughtered city. The once strong elvish fort fell into disrepair nearly a century ago, and the decades of neglect had worked slowly to reclaim the mountaintop it once had. Thick, thorny bushes pressed through the cracked white flooring, now covered in snow. White rock columns stood as a reminder: they had once supported a roof. Trees cracked walls and floor. Vines hugged the stone columns like constrictors suffocating their prey.

Turning back to the cliff, Oliver said, "Brings back memories, doesn't it? You wanted to be in Alrujah, on Vesper's Mountain, and now, here we are."

"It's not exactly what I imagined," she said.

"Bro, wicked cold up here." With his free hand, he swung his sword in short arcs.

Yarborough ascended the final step up the winding path. He leaned on his hammer like a walking staff, hunched and panting. "Aye, Jaurru. The air here is thin."

Oliver didn't mind the cold. It numbed his back, not to mention his fingers and face.

Langley glided up the last few steps two at a time. He'd donned a heavy cloak of fine green linen. "We must hurry if we're to return before sunset."

The thin crust of snow ran halfway down the mountain. The sand-colored plains moved in the wind like a horse twitching its skin.

"Kinda makes you feel small, doesn't it?" Lauren said.

It did. He stomped his feet in the snow, hoping to regain the feeling in his toes.

The sound of rock grinding on rock broke the still morning air. Langley pressed his weight against a stone door fashioned in the rock wall. The white stone shrieked across those beneath it.

"Leverage," Oliver said, remembering how the simple principle had worked so effectively against Belphegor, the ancient Minotaur-like abomination. He handed Aiden his rognak staff.

Aiden took it, moved from the precipice toward the abandoned fort. He wedged the staff into the small opening between the wall and the false door, used the corner of the wall as a fulcrum. He pressed on it, leaned on it, but the rock wouldn't move. Oliver thought of helping, but with his wrenched back, he wouldn't be of much use.

Yarborough came beside Aiden to help. When he touched the staff, he said, "By Adonai's beard. Is this rognak?"

"It is," Oliver said.

"Where did you find such a staff?" Yarborough asked. His mustache spilled over his top lip, and the hairs quivered with his punctuated speech.

Langley stood next to Yarborough, and the three pushed with all their might. The squeal and scrape of rock on rock hurt Oliver's ears, but at least it opened.

"In a cave near the edge of the Cerulean Woods," Oliver said. The false door finally opened. Dust and dark spilled into the early morning.

Aiden leaned against the wall and caught his breath. "Bro, that thing may have been heavier than the beast of a door in Margwar."

"Margwar," Yarborough breathed. "I still find it hard to fathom. Some day, I hope you will show me the way."

"You'll return to Margwar, Yarborough," Lauren said. She came to him, put her hand on his shoulder. "Remember, you are the Nameless Heir."

"It doesn't seem possible."

Oliver said, "With Adonai, all things are possible." He handed the staff to Yarborough.

Yarborough held it in one hand, balancing it on his palm. With his other hand, he twisted his mustache. "Light, but strong as iron." He spun the staff over his head, brought it down so it extended in front of and behind him, tucked firmly under his arm.

As a halfling, Yarborough had the speed of a human and the strength of a dwarf. And though dwarves seldom used staffs in combat, Yarborough's skill demonstrated Oliver's programming prowess. He'd coded the halfling to be resourceful, capable with nearly every weapon imaginable.

Yarborough ran his fat fingers over the staff. Voice thick with memory, he said, "We grew the trees that made this staff. Long before they died. Long before we died. Our hands cultivated the greatest wood in Alrujah."

Tenebrous clouds marched overhead. The light from the suns cast strange double-shadows. The distant shrilling caw of a razorbeak stopped Oliver from following Yarborough and Langley further into the unlit passage.

"What is it?" Lauren asked.

"Not sure." He walked outside and scanned the early morning sky for any disturbance.

Aiden stood next to him. "Should I be worried?"

"Probably not." But Oliver worried. Razorbeaks naturally flew in murders unless they carried messages. Erica, he thought.

The bird pulled its wings behind its back and dove beak-first toward Oliver.

"Is it going to hit you?" Aiden asked as he drew his sword.

"No," Oliver said. He put his arm out and the purple-feathered bird alighted on his forearm.

"Okay. Weird," Lauren said.

Oliver stared at the bird. The tips of its claws poked through his heavy monk's robe.

The bird lifted off his arm and perched on the top of his staff. It cawed again. Someone had tied a paper to its left leg. Oliver read it.

"What's it say?" Lauren asked.

"It's from my father," he said. "They got a message from the bird. One of the yearlings is a speaker."

"Slow up," Aiden said. "What's a yearling?"

Oliver sighed. "A young monk, an orphan raised by our order. I was a yearling once. Anyhow, one is a speaker, like a caller. The yearling says Erica sent this bird. Sparky's hurt."

Lauren's face fell. "Is he okay?"

"Dillard is on his way to Varuth."

"Varuth? I thought Erica was going to Alrujah," Aiden said.

"They must be planning on crossing the bay by boat," Oliver said.

"So what do we do?" Lauren asked.

Oliver frowned. "What can we do?"

"Dillard will take care of him," Lauren said. She touched his arm.

Oliver wanted to compose a note to send back to his father but lacked the parchment and quill. "I don't suppose anyone speaks razorbeak?" No one did. So he raised his arm quickly.

The bird disappeared with a flap of its wings.

Oliver closed his eyes for a moment, prayed silently for Sparky, for Erica. He would kneel, but his back hurt so much, he didn't think he'd be able to get back up. When he opened his eyes, purple feathers floated down from the sky. Oliver caught one and slipped it in the pocket of the pants he wore under his blue monastic robe. This feather was the only piece of Erica he had left.

He turned and followed the strangely silent Langley into the dark chamber atop Vesper's Mountain.

* * *

Bailey awoke again in Alrujah, this time perched on a massive tree reaching over some sort of ruins. White columns shot up out of cobbled white stone flooring but supported nothing more than air. Whatever ceiling may have existed had long since crumbled, and the remains blended into the cracked, decimated flooring on the exposed mountaintop. Weeds pushed through crevices, forcing the cracks to further rupture. In some places, entire evergreens pushed through larger fissures. Only a few buildings stood, and only one had any sort of visible entrance.

Bailey spread her wings and alighted on the ground. Her boots crunched on the thin crust of snow covering the weathered ground. She wrapped her wings around herself and proceeded forward on foot, toward the opening to the dark, dank chamber. A tomb? Had to be. Little bigger than a shack, the white stone walls leaned as if they might fall soon, too. But something drew her to it, toward the opening and the darkness, the stale air and dusty motes.

Voices. Like the ones outside the cave a few dreams ago. One voice, more than the others, called her siren-like.

Lauren's.

She followed the hollow echoing voices into the thick darkness, but the moment she stepped into the chamber, the voices ceased. At least, Lauren's did. Another voice chilled her, crawled through her head like worms through an apple.

"You are not welcome here, servant of Adonai."

Bailey opened her wings, reached for the jeweled hilt of her sword. She needed light. She pulled the blade from its sheath, and the sterling metal glowed a hot white. The dark pulled back, an undertow of blackness receding from the gleam of the sword. The chamber was empty.

"What would you have of me, messenger?"

Alone in the chamber, Bailey shivered. No way the voice spoke to her, but if not her, then who? Bailey cleared her throat, wondered for a moment what the doctors saw inside her brain right now. Would they see her fear? Would they see how the voice terrified her? Would the chill in her neck and spine register as tiny digital spikes on some overly-complex medical monitor?

Sword in hand, she drew in a breath, held it in her lungs, prayed for confidence, for assurance, for peace. She concentrated on giving each word an outline of courage. "I have no message."

"Then you have no business with me. If you are here without Adonai's blessing, you are vulnerable."

Immediately, black-boned skeletons clattered up from the floor. Bones circled her, flew as if on invisible wires, assembled themselves into human skeletons, bear skeletons, boar skeletons; skeletons of goats and of children. What kind of tomb was this? What darkness had Lauren imagined?

Bailey tightened her grip on her gleaming sword. "Let me pass. I will leave you and fly away from this place."

The voice spoke again, like the hiss from a punctured steam pipe. "Bring me her flesh. Bring me her bones."

The skeletons quickly lunged at her. Weren't zombies and skeletons supposed to be slow? These had no muscles, no tendons. Movements shouldn't be possible for them, but still they moved, claws and fangs flashing in shadows.

Instinct seized her, and she struck out with her sword while twisting her body away from the attacking skeletons. Bony hands grabbed at her shoulders; brittle, broken teeth cracked together. She spun away, swung the sword in a broad arc. Bone separated from bone, and reassembled just as quickly. She smashed a skull, and the bones beneath it fell.

That must be the key. Rather than the edge, she shifted her fighting style to incorporate the flat of the blade. Something bit her shoulder. She kicked away, backed toward a wall. In quarters this close, her wings seemed more a hindrance than a help. But if she used them to help knock the bones back, she might buy herself some time.

She put a foot on the wall behind her, leapt, planted the second foot on the wall, and launched off like an Olympic swimmer. She stretched her wings, glided low over the crowd of grabbing skeletons. Her wings clipped the heads off several skeletons. Each impact shivered her wing, sent vibrations through her back, through her neck.

Bony hands clawed at her, grabbed at her light armor, but did not hold her long. She beat her wings, up, down, and clipped more heads. She had to find the exit. If she stayed too long, they'd overwhelm her.

She angled her sword up, flew as close to the walls as possible until the exit fell under the illumination of her blade.

Something grabbed her ankle. She kicked hard, twisted sideways, and folded her wings around herself. Barrel rolling out of the entrance, she hit the cobbled floor hard. Her wing snapped. The feathers split wide and blood oozed from the top. She took a deep breath, stood, and backed away. The skeletons didn't venture outside. They huddled near the entrance, crawled over each other like cockroaches, slunk back into the darkness.

Bailey slowed her breathing, checked her left wing.

Broken and freezing, she sat down, leaned back against the column, and closed her eyes.

CHAPTER TEN

*The Hand of Adonai will reach out and seize the Blood Sword, the
ancient cursed blade. But the curse of Adonai will not touch His Hand.
The holiness of Adonai broke the curse of the blade, and the Hand
wielded it with power and with courage and with strength. And none
shall be able to wrest it from His Hand.*
—The Book of Things to Come

ERICA'S GOLDEN MA'ATT'TAL BRACELETS clanked on her wrist
as she bent over and kissed Sparky. She tightened his old collar
around her other wrist. In his wild spending spree the night
before, Ullwen purchased a white-gold tiara stylized in the shape of
dragon wings. In the middle, where the wings met, rested an opal the
size of a quarter. Ridiculous, but Ullwen insisted.

"After the last few weeks, you deserve a bit of beauty," he'd said.

Cute of him. Endearing, really.

She wore it on her new hair. What used to be lifeless and brown,
Relina's hairdresser friend turned short and vibrant. Most importantly,
she'd been able to dye it black.

Erica didn't put much faith in this Adonai everyone kept going on
about, but she prayed anyway. If Oliver healed her, he might be able to
heal Sparky. She prayed her razorbeak would find him, prayed it'd be
able to deliver the message in a way Oliver understood.

Sparky's ragged, gasping breaths pained her in a way she'd never
experienced. She had to move, had to get away for a while.

"I'll be back soon. You hang on, okay? Hang on for me."

She left the room, hoping Relina and Ullwen wouldn't see her tears.
Boldly, she took Ullwen by his hand and said, "Come on."

"Where are we going?" he asked.

"Anywhere but here."

Ullwen quickened his steps to keep her pace. "Relina has not
completed our potions. It's too early to journey to Alrujah."

"I don't care where we go, but I have to go." She tried to push the image of Sparky out of her mind.

Ullwen yanked her hand and pulled her between two houses. Erica nearly turned her ankle on the cobbled street. The suns warmed the fog-lined air. Villagers swept up and down the road, mumbling as they went. "Erica," he whispered urgently.

She took a deep breath and smelled the salt of the Alrujah Bay. "I couldn't breathe in there anymore."

Ullwen took her other hand so he held both. "I understand your heart breaks for Sparky. But you must remember Chameleon Soldiers likely walk the streets unseen. We must be careful. Strolling through Varuth without the cover of night could be disastrous."

"They won't recognize us," she said and shivered.

"Never underestimate an enemy. Need I remind you we once believed them our allies?" He lowered his voice further. "Besides, I am a criminal here, the worst kind, a deserter. If the Varuthian Elite find me, I'll be hanged. I cannot let that happen."

Erica put her head against the wall. The shadows chilled her. She wanted to move, to do something. She was tired of hiding in the dark, tired of waiting for something to happen. "I can't stay there," she said.

Something caught her attention—a blue monastic robe fluttered past them. "Oliver?" She jumped from between the houses, followed the blue robe, grabbed its shoulder, and spun it around.

The tall man grinned. Beneath his hood, even under the heavy shadows, his face shone white. His eyes burned red. No hair grew from his face or his head. Albino. Dillard. "Good morrow, Lakia. I was looking for you."

Behind Erica, Ullwen said, "Brother Dillard. It is good to see you."

"As it is you, Ullwen of Varuth, and Lakia of Alrujah. Perhaps you can assist me. I came at the behest of a razorbeak. It seems you have a dog in need of healing."

* * *

Darkness filled the chamber they'd opened. From outside, the early morning light crept in and illuminated several torches along the wall, all of which had burned out centuries ago. The wood had rotted and the fabric had pulled into thin, useless strips. Long dead, the torches passed from uselessness to decay decades ago—no way to relight them now.

Lauren put her hand on Oliver's shoulder. "How are we supposed to see? I can make a light, but it'd take more magic than I want to use."

"Yeah. We'll need all the magic we can get."

Aiden scanned the depths of the darkness beyond them. "Going to be tough to fight blind."

Langley said, "Magic is only as effective as it is efficient. Here."

One by one, he put his thumbs on the eyes of his companions.

Lauren closed her eyes as his cold thumbs pressed lightly on her eyelids. For a minute, she imagined he might try to scoop her eyes out, or press them through the back of her head, but she ignored the fear. She would have to trust him if they wanted to make it through the Ruins of Norgren.

When she opened her eyes again, the dark ruins appeared green and dim. The little light in the chamber flashed in deep emerald. Shadows took the color of Spanish olives. She'd like it to be a bit brighter, but whatever spell Langley used at least allowed her to see through the swirling darkness.

"That should last us the trip," Langley said. "And it took very little magic to accomplish. I took the liberty of having Yarborough pack extra Fellian mushrooms in case we exhaust our magic."

Lauren designed the spell years ago and quickly forgot about it. Now, relief washed over her. If she hadn't designed the spell, this trip would be near impossible. Of course, Langley would know every obscure spell she'd told Oliver to put in the game. Next to the Mage Lord, she doubted anyone had more magic ability than he.

"Follow me," Langley said. "Yarborough, take the back. The rest of you fill in however you see fit. Make sure we don't get caught by surprise."

"Aye aye, captain," Lauren muttered. He still made her uneasy. Sure, he'd allied himself with them for now, but what might he do after he had the Blood Sword? More importantly, should they even help him get it? It might be the only way to get *The Book of Sealed Magic*, but she still didn't like the idea. Nerves, she told herself.

Aiden wrinkled his nose. "Does it always smell like this?"

"It gets worse further on, closer to the altar," Yarborough said.

"What altar?" Aiden asked.

Oliver said, "Long story."

"Do we have time?"

Oliver shrugged, winced. He stepped slowly, aided by his rognak staff. "About a hundred years ago, some of Captain Norgren's elves turned to strange gods. They'd been isolated on this mountain for years, spying on Harland before King Theramin conquered it and added it to his empire. The elves never worshiped Adonai ..."

"And why should we?" Langley said.

Oliver ignored him. "Anyhow, they turned from their gods to a demon called Moloch."

"You sound like *The Book of the Ancients*," Langley said.

"He should. He wrote it," Lauren said.

"Enough," Yarborough said. He stamped the butt end of his axe on the rough floor. "The undead will trouble us enough without us turning on each other."

"Undead? What do you mean undead?" Aiden said. He gripped his sword a little tighter. "What, like zombies or something?"

"Not nearly so comical," Lauren said. She took up the story where Oliver left off. "The elvish soldiers, two in particular, started experimenting with sacrifices and necromancy. They called on ancient devils imprisoned by Adonai centuries ago. At one time, they sought to break the barrier that sealed the evil away. They thought, in their twisted minds, they would serve as the masters of the devils and control them."

"They were wrong, of course," Yarborough said. He kept the line moving, scanning the dark from side to side. He held his double crescent axe with one hand. "None but Adonai can control such evil."

Through the veil of Langley's spell, everyone appeared green and sickly. What little light had been in the front room vanished as they forged down a spiral staircase. Lauren said, "Eventually, the soldiers they sacrificed were raised again, but faster and stronger. The undead of Alrujah are powered by the ancient evil, by the demon who eventually consumed the two necromancers. The stories say the necromancers still guard a sword of great power."

"A cursed sword," Yarborough said. "All who wield it are corrupted by its power."

"Not all," Langley said. "I can break the spell and have the power without the corruption."

"You should hope you can," Aiden said. "You get any crazy ideas, Langley, and I'll cut you down myself."

"Brave, Knight, but foolish. The Blood Sword has centuries' worth of power in its blade. What chance would a child like you have against one who wields it?"

"You sound ambitious," Oliver said. "Adonai does not bless those who wield power irresponsibly."

Langley said, "The Blood Sword belongs to my people. Adonai's blessing is the least of my concerns."

"Which is exactly why humans rule Alrujah," Yarborough said. "If our peoples would but turn their hearts to their creator, Adonai would again restore the elves and the dwarves to their prominent positions throughout Alrujah."

Langley moved a greenish hand along a dark wall. "Spare me your proselytizing. I've heard enough of it over the years. Respect my religion as I respect yours."

A cold, watery breeze, only ankle high, raced up the steps leading toward the upper chamber. The chill and dampness of the trickling air made Lauren wonder if the lower chambers had mysteriously flooded. But the inconsistent pressure, like a pack of rats racing under her dress, couldn't be water.

"Quiet," Lauren seethed. She grabbed Oliver's shoulder. A quiet, mournful squeal fell from his lips. He steadied himself with his staff, leaned back against the wall.

"What?" Aiden whispered.

"Something's down there," she said.

"Of course there is," Langley whispered harshly. "The bones of my people. The heritage of Norgren. I've been here before."

"Evil lurks in these chambers," Yarborough said.

Her stomach roiled. In the distance, a low, disembodied moan filled the chamber.

A throaty, dusty whisper said, "Who enters my domain?"

Yarborough grabbed his axe with both hands. "Here is where things get dangerous."

* * *

Blurry, amoebic shapes slouched across her mind. The column she'd leaned against had vanished. Must be back in the hospital. She would open her eyes, but she feared she wouldn't see anything.

A voice, far away and soft. "Nurse? Come look at this."

"Almost normal," another muffled voice said. A nurse?

Bailey opened her eyes. It took a moment for the soft edges of the amorphous shapes in front of her to sharpen. When they did, they took the shape of her mother and Nicole, the golden-eyed nurse. She blinked again.

"You back with us?" Nicole asked, her voice clearer now, but cottony.

"I fall asleep again?" she asked.

Her mother shook her head.

The nurse said, "Can't really call it a nap. I've paged Doctor Walsh. He's home now, but should be here in about ten minutes."

"How long was I sleeping?"

"A few hours. It's nearly midnight," her mother said, rubbing her cheek with her fingers.

Bailey closed her eyes. "I'm still tired."

"Don't go back to sleep," Nicole said sharply.

Her mother took Bailey's hand. "Hey," she said. "The nurse said not to go back to sleep."

Eyes still closed, her hand heavy in her mother's grasp, Bailey said, "A few more minutes."

Nurse Nicole tapped her cheek with her soft hand, and her hospital bed started to sit her up.

She opened her eyes. "Come on, guys, really. Just a few minutes."

"Not until Doctor Walsh gets here," Nicole said. She handed Bailey a plastic cup of apple juice. "Drink this."

Detective Parker came in with two cups of coffee. "Sleeping Beauty join the world of the living?" He handed a cup to Bailey's mom.

"What are you doing here?" Bailey asked. Her head swam with fatigue and drowsiness.

"Checking on you."

Her mother asked, "What's going on with you, honey?"

Bailey drank the apple juice. Her head cleared a little. "I don't know, Mom."

* * *

Erica sat on the bed while Dillard leaned over Sparky's swollen body. He ran a hand over Sparky's chest. His knotted red knuckles flexed slightly. For a minute, Erica thought about pulling him back, afraid he might do more harm than good, but she kept her spot and fought to keep her eyes dry. "Be careful," she snapped.

Dillard did not open his eyes. He bent over Sparky, his shoulders slumped toward the broken wolf. His lips moved soundlessly.

"Did you hear me?"

"I am always careful." Without getting up, he asked her, "And what of your wounds? How have those come to be healed?"

Erica didn't want to talk about her injuries. She wanted Sparky to jump up and put his paws on her shoulders again. "An angel," she said softly.

Ullwen put his hand on hers. "You never told me this."

She let him hold her hand in his warm grasp. It comforted her. She felt safe with Ullwen, a strange connection strengthening each moment she shared with him. "She came in one night, I think. Hard to remember exactly. She kinda moved her hands over me, my arms and legs, back. My neck and face." She remembered something else. "Does Lauren have a sister?"

"Indigo has no sister," Ullwen said. "Why?"

Dillard stood. "Not Indigo. Lauren. And I don't know."

Erica bit her lip. "I think I remember her saying she was Lauren's sister. She told me her name. It was like two names. B something. Barbara Rachel or Betsy Rebecca or something."

"Bailey Renee," Dillard said. He put his hands in his sleeves, something Oliver used to do often.

Erica missed Oliver, missed his confidence, missed his affections. But, sitting next to Ullwen, she felt the same confidence, the same assurance, the same affection. She squeezed his hand. What did it mean to hold hands in this world? "Yeah, I think that was it."

Relina stood in the corner of the room and leaned heavily on a harspus wood broom. "It was the Hand of Adonai, to be sure. She was torn up something fierce, and then she wakes up all healed and saucy."

"I agree," Ullwen said. "Brother Dillard, you are well aware of the mercies of Adonai and his angels. This angel must be a part of the Hand."

Sleeves covering his hands, Dillard glanced at Sparky before turning back to Erica. "It is hard to say if the angel is part of the Hand. But her name is mentioned in *The Book of Things to Come*. She is mentioned as an angel of light and destruction." He pulled his hood back over his head and smiled. Erica found it hard not to stare at his bald head, his nearly translucent skin. "The power of Adonai is mighty. There is no power under heaven greater. Do you believe it?"

She felt as if she should, but it didn't make sense. Why would Adonai, or God or whatever, allow her father to burn her hands? Why would he let her suffer in foster family after foster family? "I'd like to," she said.

Dillard nodded. "I understand." Kneeling over the bloodied wolf again, he put his hand on Sparky's chest. "Already, Adonai heals."

Sparky's chest moved deeply, regularly. The swelling receded, and his puffy face almost looked normal again. "Is he …"

"His healing will take a few more days. For now, he must rest. And we must speak."

"I thought we already were."

Dillard turned to Relina, who leaned on the broom in the threshold between Erica's room and the kitchen. "Good lady, be kind enough to close your front door for us, please."

"Sounds serious," she said.

CHAPTER ELEVEN

Though she was broken, she became whole again. As surely as she bled,
Adonai healed her wounds. Her body was made whole, and she again
lifted up with wings like eagles. Those who saw her called her the Broken
Angel. Adonai called her Bailey Renee.
—The Book of Things to Come

DETECTIVE PARKER DEALT ANOTHER hand of draw poker to Bailey Renee and Ms. Knowles when Doctor Walsh walked in the room, hair hastily combed and white lab coat wrinkled. "Who's winning?" he asked.

Ms. Knowles and Detective Parker both pointed to Bailey.

"Lucky, or good?" he asked.

"She's a shark," Parker said. He took an unlit cigarette from behind his ear and slipped it between his lips.

"Detective, we don't allow ..."

"Not lit, Doc. Nicole's keeping an eye on me."

"A very close eye," Nicole the nurse called from the hallway.

Doctor Walsh smiled. He took the chart and glanced over some of the readings, checked them against the numerous peaks and valleys the machine next to her head spit out.

Bailey scratched at the wires running down her head and across her face. She checked her cards. Two pair. She discarded one, hoping for a full house.

"You'll never fill an inside straight," Parker said, the cigarette dancing between his lips.

"Probably right," she said.

Ms. Knowles smiled at Bailey. She knew. She discarded three cards and asked Doctor Walsh what he thought.

"I think I'm going to have to refer her to a specialist. I've never seen anything like this. I even spent a few hours researching it tonight after work. Called a few friends. I've got a colleague here in the hospital. I'll make sure she takes a look at this. She should get to you tomorrow." He pulled a pen from his breast pocket and signed a few pages in her file. He peeked at Bailey's cards. "When you're done here, you can get some more rest if you'd like."

"The nurse told me not to sleep. Put me on some pretty terrible coffee."

"Well, you have my okay now." He put his hand on her shoulder. "Good luck. I'll be checking in on you from time to time."

"Sounds good." To Parker and her mother, Bailey said, "How about I sleep, and you two get some sleep, too. I'll still be here tomorrow morning, I guess."

Detective Parker put his cards on the small eating tray between him and Ms. Knowles. "I got two pair, aces over sevens." He stood up, moved out the door.

Ms. Knowles put her cards down; she had a pair of eights. She kissed Bailey on the head, squeezed her hand tightly. "I'm coming tomorrow. Be safe, okay? I'm really scared."

"I know, Mom." She kissed her mother's cheek.

Before Ms. Knowles left the room, Bailey called after her. "Can you bring me some food tomorrow? The stuff here sucks."

"Sure," she said.

Once the room emptied, Bailey closed her eyes. How long had it been since she'd had a natural sleep? But, though she was tired, her body refused to sleep. Sighing, she opened her eyes and flipped on the television. She'd rather read Lauren's journal, but Parker still had it, and she'd long ago finished the schoolwork her mother brought.

If this strange narcolepsy didn't kill her, the boredom would.

* * *

Green funnels of dust, like tiny broccoli-colored tornados, swirled from the stone flooring. Lauren moved a solitary bone with the heel of her boot.

The dusty voice continued, "Why have you come?"

A dark olive green mist crawled over the walls until it took the vague shape of a man.

"We come in service of Adonai," Oliver said. He stood tall, held his staff like a weapon instead of a crutch. Either his back felt better, or he faked it convincingly.

Langley shouted down the dank corridor. "We've come for the

Blood Sword."

Dust scurried like bugs under Lauren's feet. She thought of beetles, of engorged ticks. It rushed under her, like the tide taking the sand from under her feet at a beach. The dusty bones of the corpses assembled themselves into walking dead. She held the gold-wire wrapped hilt of her dagger and moved closer to Aiden.

The voice of the spirit in front of them continued. "Adonai's followers are not welcome here. And we have grown tired of you, Langley half-elf. We will not allow you to leave alive again. You will join us, as will your friends."

The tiny chamber filled with the noises of bones scraping floor, of half-petrified skeletons reassembling, bone on bone. Tenuous muscles sprouted from joints, grew larger and stronger, formed tendons that swallowed the ends of the bones.

The corpses' breaths came in slow, deep, rattling inhales with exhales just as chilling.

An animalistic roar echoed from down the black corridor. In an emerald smear, Langley rushed it. With one quick slash, the arm of the undead, which held a heavy mace, fell from the body and dropped to the ground. Another quick slash and the head joined the arm.

It had never occurred to Lauren, when she'd drawn these monsters, how they would see without eyes, hear without ears, but they did. She remembered her tenth-grade year, the human anatomy textbook she'd used to design these featureless masses of muscle and tendon and bone. No skin, no noses, no hair. Without lips and tongues, their teeth snapped together in loud clacks.

"Those skeletons remind you of Sarah?" Oliver asked Lauren.

"Yup. Let's kill them." Her breath grew hot. A fever-like burning replaced the chill in the air. The warmth radiated from her skin, from the burning within her chest, the volcanic pit in her belly.

Langley shouted, "Separate them from their heads. Otherwise, they join back up again."

"Sounds like he's done this before," Aiden said. With a resounding war cry, he delved into the sage green shadows along the wall. With his left hand, he lifted his golden dwarvish shield a second before a screeching corpse brought a star-shaped iron mace down on him. The force dropped Aiden to his knees. With a grimace and another shout, Aiden stood up with surprising speed and ran his sword through the corpse's neck. Its face contorted in surprise, as much as a corpse could show shock, and staggered back. Aiden matched its steps and wrenched the blade from its throat. With his left hand, he rammed the head with his shield. The little threads of sinew holding head to body tore, and the thinly muscled skull fell to the floor like a bowling ball bouncing down an alley.

Lauren's stomach tightened. Sweat stung her eyes. The heat inside her needed out, needed release. Wind rushed over her skin, and she leaned back instinctively. An iron claymore whooshed past her, inches from her face. She fell on her back, closed her eyes, and stretched out her hand. A ball of fire leapt from her palms and engulfed the walking corpse. It staggered back, but then reared toward her, its massive two-handed sword poised above her, ready to cleave her head.

Something crunched.

Oliver's staff pushed the corpse back to a safe distance. In one fluid motion, he brought the staff down and swept it under the legs of the carcass. It fell on its back. Dust floated up in a sage mist. A heavy axe chopped the head off the body.

Yarborough said, "Your fire may stun them, but it does little to stop them."

Langley and Aiden seemed to be in a competition. Each had felled nearly ten corpses. Yarborough trailed by little. His axe separated limb from body, head from torso, in equally swift and savage motions.

Lauren's dagger had no chance to decapitate any of the corpses, all of which towered over her by a foot or more. Thick with muscle and heavy with bone, their feet slapped the stone floor like fish smacking on river rocks.

She had to do something, but what?

She ticked off the spells she knew—fire, useless; ice, took too long; lightning, too dangerous with her friends in close quarters; quake, same as lightning; sleep and plague, corpses were immune.

Langley lifted a mace from the limp arm of a body and used it as a shield. He moved with grace and savagery.

Yarborough grunted. "Something is wrong," he said. "There are too many of them. There were not this many last time."

"Of course not," Oliver muttered. "The more in the party, the more enemies spawn."

Lauren had to help. She took a deep breath and exhaled slowly. Her breath came out in a thin mist. It mixed with the sage dust. Cold chilled her veins. She remembered the nar'esh, the ice thorns sprouting from her body. Could she do it again? No, she had no sense of it. She'd have to do something else, find another way. Corpses clambered and crawled through a narrow doorway to the left, a doorway that led to the burial grounds outside. If she cut the entry off, it should stem the tide of the undead.

"Watch my back," she called to Aiden. "I've got a plan."

Aiden shouted, "Langley! Little help!"

Langley and Aiden stood on either side of Lauren, felling corpses quickly. Groaning with exertion, they tired quickly. They wouldn't be able to keep their pace for long.

Lauren knelt at the base of the door, barely dodging a kick from a tall corpse. Oliver stood over her, barring the door with his staff. The corpse brought its mace down on the staff, but it bounced back.

"Nice, bro." Aiden stabbed the corpse with his dwarvish sword. The corpse reeled back.

Lauren worked her hands over the floor, bringing thick ice up, almost like a door. "This may take a bit."

"So long as it allows us to access the next floor," Langley said. "It's not far beyond that."

As her fear grew, the ice came faster. She worked her hands over it like a puppeteer controlling a marionette—fingers pulling invisible strings. The heat that consumed her moments earlier vanished instantly.

"Little faster, please," Oliver said. He poked at the bodies as they piled near the doorway.

"Going as fast as I can," she sang.

The corpses moaned and kicked at the ice. They swung their maces and swords, but the others blocked their attacks.

The energy left her quickly, but she had sealed off half the doorway. The ice shimmered in green, a deep emerald refracting what little light filtered in from the burial ground beyond. She finished three-quarters of the door, up to the corpse's necks. They stopped attacking the people and aimed their maces at the ice. They crashed the ice with terrifying force. Quickly, she thickened the ice.

"How are you feeling?" Aiden asked.

"Tired," she said.

"Can you continue?" Langley asked.

"I'll finish the door, but I'll need to rest after."

Aiden steadied her. "Don't overdo it."

Twisted carcasses smashed and slashed at her through the green ice.

Yarborough said, "Enough. That should hold them." He reached into a small leather sack tied to his belt. From it, he pulled a mushroom cap wrapped in a leaf. Handing it to Lauren, he said, "It's not much, but it should strengthen you long enough to reach the sword."

The bitter, dry leaf-wrapped mushroom irritated her mouth, her throat. But, after swallowing awkwardly, a new energy crawled through her limbs. Her core warmed with a vitality she'd not remembered feeling since she came to Alrujah, one she rarely experienced in North Chester. Eager anticipation, a longing desire, eased the soreness in her limbs. "Thank you," she said.

"Listen, bro," Aiden said to Langley. "Since you want this stupid sword so bad, why don't you go grab it? We'll wait here for you."

Oliver set his jaw tight and shifted gracelessly from one leg to the other. His protection had come at a steep price, a price clear in his grimace. "Never make it alone." Oliver moved toward a set of stairs in the far corner of the entryway. "Follow me."

Aiden asked Lauren, "Sure you're good?"

Better than Oliver, she thought. She didn't want to wait for the corpses to burst through the wall. "Let's go," she said.

* * *

After Relina closed her front door, Dillard sat on a chair in the corner of the room. He rested a prayer staff, one much like Oliver's, against the wall. "Alrujah is no longer safe."

"Oh, perfect beginning," Relina sighed from the doorway between the kitchen and Erica's room.

Ullwen sat beside Erica, her hand still in his. "I told her as much already. The Chameleon Soldiers. Should we even be speaking of this here?"

"There are no Chameleon Soldiers here now," Dillard said. "I would have sensed them already. Our conversation will not be heard by any outside this house, but we must act quickly after this conversation."

Erica took her hand from Ullwen's and knelt next to Sparky. She pet his head gently. "What about Sparky?"

"I'll watch over him," Relina said.

"I'm afraid your home is no longer safe, fair Relina," Dillard said. "Hear me out, please. And I promise to answer all your questions." Leaning forward, he continued, "I believe the Shedoahn Order monitors our movements."

Relina's face drained of color.

"Heard of them, but still not quite clear on what they do," Erica said.

"Those who worship Shedoah. They seek to unbind him," Ullwen said.

"Okay, maybe I missed this in Alrujah 101, but who in the world is Shedoah?"

"Can we please stop using that word in this house?" Relina whispered.

Dillard nodded. "It is best if we do." To Erica, he said, "He is the Deceiver of Old, the demon who opposes Adonai, who sought to overthrow Him shortly after the creation of Alrujah."

Sparky's breath seemed stronger, which strengthened Erica in turn. "So he's the Devil. Got it. He's got some crazy whack-jobs doing his bidding, I take it. Probably want to kill us. Worst case scenario and all that?"

Ullwen gaped at her, astonishment lining his eyes. "Sweet Erica, how can you be so unconcerned?"

She liked being called "sweet," so she smiled at him. "After getting beat to a pulp by a sasquatch, creepy cultists don't sound so scary."

"If you knew of their atrocities," Relina said coldly, one hand over her mouth. "Oh, my dear Adonai, they'll know I've helped you." Her voice cracked.

Ullwen stood and took Relina's shoulders in his firm grasp. "Be strong. Adonai will protect you. You are in His service. Their order cannot touch you."

Dillard stood as well, his head hovering near the rafters. "Take courage. It is as Ullwen says. Already, we are rebuilding the monastery, but we are being watched. Each day, their number grows. We must move quickly."

"Wait, how do they even know to look for us? How do they know who we are?"

"A book with very sensitive information went missing from our temporary home in the nar'esh cave."

"What book?" Ullwen asked.

Dillard said, "A leather-bound journal penned by the finger of Adonai. One of the famed Books of Power. It contained a list of every prominent name in Alrujah."

"Chameleon Soldiers?" Ullwen asked.

"We would have noticed them. The Monks of the Cerulean Order are not blinded by their invisible armor. We sense with our spirits. Someone snuck past our guard. Worse, they may operate from within our Order."

"Impossible," Ullwen snapped. He turned to Dillard. "How could a follower of Shedoah infiltrate the Monks? Your discernment is infallible."

"Only Adonai is infallible," Dillard said. "I wish I could say the same for us, but I worry we may have been, in some way, blinded to his influence."

Sparky whined. His chest skipped a breath. For a moment, Erica's heart seized in her chest. But as his breath returned, so her heart beat again.

"This book carries the names Lauren Knowles, Oliver Shaw, Erica Hall, and Aiden Price."

Erica took her hand back from Sparky. "Shut. Up."

"Trust no one outside the Hand, save for Relina, myself, and Eljah."

Erica had almost forgotten about Eljah, Vicmorn's adoptive father. "How do you know he's safe to trust?"

"His name was in the book as well, and was listed as an ally."

"Did it name enemies?" Ullwen asked.

"Several, but none we are familiar with."

"What about the Mage Lord?" Relina asked quietly.

"No identity was linked to the Mage Lord. We checked that first."

Ullwen knelt next to Erica. With a hand on her shoulder, he whispered in her ear, "If ever there was a time for you to seek Adonai's favor, now would be it."

His hot breath tickled her ear, and she stood up, a little weak-kneed, both from the news and from the closeness of Ullwen. "So what do we do?"

Dillard pushed his fingers into his temples. "Most in your position would hide. They would run to the Dragon's Back Mountains and live in the crevices until they breathed their last."

"I'm not most people."

"There's more," he said. "The book has the possible locations of *The Book of Sealed Magic*. It's only a matter of time before the Mage Lord seizes it and uses it to rend the world."

What had Lauren said in the nar'esh cave? *If we die here, we are absolutely dead.*

"You've known where the book is and you haven't told us?" Erica asked.

"We know of the possible locations only. And Vicmorn is well versed in the book. He knows what we know."

"So we move faster. Keep the book away from the Mage Lord. We put our little history lesson on hold, and we get my parents. And once we have them, we'll worry about the Sherpa Order or whatever they're called." Erica should be scared, but she'd had enough fear in her life. Sparky's wounds seemed to be mending quickly. Her injuries all but vanished. Soon, she'd free her parents and meet them for the first time.

"Take this," Dillard said. From his sleeve, he extracted a silver necklace with a shining opal, much like the one on her tiara. "As long as you wear it, no water beasts will see you."

The thin gold chain, light and soft and cold, felt like silk. The opal weighed no more than an ounce, more like a crumb than a jewel. "If you say so, but what about Ullwen?"

"Small as the opal may be, it is imbued with strong magic. It will cover Ullwen in invisibility as well. With the potions Relina is concocting for you, this should be enough for you to successfully carry out your plan."

"And what about you?" she asked. "What will you do now?"

"What I am sworn to do: Protect *The Book of Sealed Magic*."

CHAPTER TWELVE

The elves abandoned their first love. They came to worship the creation rather than the creator. They made for themselves idols, imbued a portion of their spirit on those artifacts, then worshiped them as gods, as holy objects for the use of profane gods."
—The Book of the Ancients

TWO HOURS AFTER PARKER and Ms. Knowles left, Bailey turned the television off and closed her eyes. She should be tired, but try as she might, sleep wouldn't come. She slowed her breathing, concentrated on relaxing the muscles in her neck, in her back. Her muscles ached from lying down all day. The stupid wires on her head tangled every time she tried to walk around. At some point, the hospital became a prison. Might as well throw some bars on the windows.

Rolling to her left side, she pushed the wires away from her face and pulled her knees up. Would she be able to finish the basketball season? Would she ever sleep normally again?

And as if on cue, the familiar dizziness of sleep spun her consciousness. More than sleepiness, though, this spinning constricted around her like octopus tentacles. She recognized the feeling, knew when she opened her eyes, she'd have wings again.

But, for the first time since she'd had the angel dreams, she opened her eyes to find herself sitting down. One wing hung limp at her side, the other wrapped around her front. A large, battered wolf sat at the foot of the bed on which she sat. She'd been here before when she came to heal Erica. Now, Bailey wished someone would heal her. Pain arced up her wing to her spine. Must still be broken from her fight with the creepy skeletons. She'd hoped it'd be healed when she next returned to Alrujah.

The door to the tiny room opened, and Bailey leapt up. Her left wing, still limp with broken bones, cried against the effort. Immediately, she drew her sword from her belt and held it outstretched, chest-level, ready for more bones, for city archers, for the king's guard, ready for anything.

Instead, the angel who told her to heal Erica moved into the room and closed the door behind him. He held something, some sort of white metal adorned with green jewels. Emeralds maybe? "Adonai has need of you again."

She nodded to the device the other angel held. "What's that for?"

"Your wing." He walked toward her. Taller by at least a head, he gazed down at her as he gently lifted her broken wing.

Bailey winced at the stabbing pain. Her knees weakened, and she wanted to push him away. But, as he touched it, the pain eased a bit, and her mind cleared. "It will heal my wing?"

"It will protect your wing and ease your pain. Healing will take time." He slipped it over the top of her wing. Immediately the cold metal warmed. It drew the pain up toward the surface of her feathered skin and held it within the metal cast.

"It's still broken?" Bailey asked.

The angel said, "You are not sick as some count sickness." He stepped toward the wolf, knelt beside the beast, touched its head and its chest.

Bailey tested her wing, stretching it wide, then wrapping it around herself. The metal sheath moved seamlessly with it as if it had a million invisible hinges. But what the angel said disturbed her. "What do you mean, sick?"

The angel, still focused on the wolf, said, "There are those who believe you ill. They've bound you to machines to read the inner workings of your body. But you are not sick. They cannot understand."

North Chester, she reasoned. "I know."

"You must leave the place they've put you."

"The hospital?"

"They seek to stop your transit from your world to ours. They call it a cure. If they stop it, there will be dire consequences in Alrujah."

Bailey sheathed her sword and wrapped her wings around herself for warmth. "What kind of consequences?"

The angel stood and spoke gravely. "Without your help, Oliver will die."

* * *

The circular stairwell terminated abruptly in a stone chamber. Jade shadows spread across the stone walls like moss. Dust and decay choked

Oliver. Death made his home here.

Mold and condensation from the cold mountain air slicked the steps beneath Oliver's feet. Stepping carefully and quickly, he leaned a shoulder against the wall. His back ached from the exertion of protecting Lauren from the masses of the undead while she walled up the entrance to the outer burial grounds.

"Where are we?" Aiden asked.

"Originally, this was a common room, where the soldiers would eat or be briefed on coming missions," Langley said.

"Now it is the Chamber of Death," Yarborough said.

"I bet I can guess how it got its name," Aiden said.

Lauren pointed to the rooms branching off from the main chamber. Four on either side made a total of eight. "These rooms were intended to be barracks, but the soldiers turned them into mini-temples. Each built to a different deity. They still used them for sleeping, all except for that one." She gestured to the far left door.

The moldy air nearly asphyxiated Oliver. Each breath seemed harder to take. Even the dark green shadows grew blacker. He'd not experienced anything like this since he walked into the throne room of Margwar, where he faced the nine-foot tall Minotaur Belphegor. Evil crawled along the walls, oppressed him with silent pressure.

Oliver spoke quietly. "Anyone else having trouble breathing in here?"

"Very much," Yarborough wheezed, and the others nodded agreement.

Oliver offered up a prayer to Adonai. *Breath*, he thought. Immediately, the darkness filling his nose and mouth receded. His vision brightened to its previous green hue. He touched the others' chests, one at a time, and repeated the one-word prayer in the Ancient Language.

All thanked him, save for Langley. He eyed Oliver, an irritated wrinkle at the top of his nose. "We each take a door. This way, we can retrieve the artifacts efficiently. After they've been recovered, we enter Moloch's chamber together."

"Two problems, bro. There's only five of us, and seven doors. And you never said anything about artifacts."

"The Blood Sword is an artifact, you witless buffoon," Langley snapped.

Yarborough grabbed Langley's arm and pulled him back from Aiden. "Guard your tongue, elf. This one might match your prowess with a blade. Speak to him with civility."

"No, it's cool," Aiden said, drawing his sword. "He wants to name call, that's all good. He and I can settle this real quick. Because right now, I'm thinking we walk away. He wants this sword so bad, let him face down big bad Moloch himself."

Oliver stood between the two quickly. "Enough. We've made it this far. Let's grab the sword and go. The other relics aren't worth risking our lives, which is exactly what we'd be doing if we entered any of these chambers alone."

"The relics belong to my people and must be returned. Help me retrieve them, and you'll have a friend in Harael," Langley said.

Aiden dropped his sword, but his gaze never left Langley's eyes.

Lauren stood next to him. "Like it or not, we still need him. Without him, Moloch would surely kill us."

"If he even appears," Oliver said. "We don't know for sure that he's awake."

"What is this Moloch thing anyway?" Aiden asked.

Oliver coldly described the demonic beast as if he read the description from Lauren's journal. "An enemy composed of the remains of corpses—fourteen eyes arranged in an arch and the horns of a bull, six rows of teeth and the strength of a hundred men."

Lauren continued, "The necromancers thought they could control it. But with each human sacrifice, it got stronger. When they ran out of bodies for Moloch to feed on, he turned on them."

The disembodied whisper echoed in the chamber. "We are pleased you've made it so far. It has been long since our master has eaten living flesh."

The necromancers.

Aiden's dwarvish blade glowed red as he said, "Then let him come and take the flesh he craves."

The door to Moloch's chamber opened slowly. Oliver gripped his staff, steadied his heart. Moloch was too big to fit through the door.

Instead, a tall man in a white robe stepped from the shadows. Black arcane symbols adorned the robe, ran along the sleeves and hood, down the sides. In his left hand, the man held *The Book of Sealed Magic*; in his right, he held an obsidian-tipped partisan. Both relics showed the same arcane lettering as the robe, but these had been inscribed in gold. The mage's eyes glowed gold from beneath his black mask.

The Mage Lord again.

Oliver tucked his staff under his arm and raised a hand. He wouldn't let the Mage Lord vanish again, not without a fight. Offering a prayer to Adonai, he imagined bonds around the mage's wrists and ankles.

The Mage Lord considered the blue-glowing bonds, and stepped out of them.

Lauren crafted fire, directed a searing blaze toward the Mage Lord. The mage dissipated the flame with his staff.

"Who are you?" Langley sneered.

"He's the Mage Lord," Aiden said, his voice firm, his shield raised.

"I do not come to fight," the Mage Lord said.

"Then why are you here?" Yarborough asked.

"I come to help," he said.

"Last time we saw you, you pulled Belphegor into Alrujah to crush our bones," Aiden said. "That your idea of help?"

The Mage Lord lowered his head. "Our time is limited," he said, his voice like a choir of men. The tip of his partisan flashed gold, and behind him, a menacing roar echoed. "I must prepare your way," he said, and then he vanished.

* * *

"The docks are this way," Ullwen said. He pointed down a narrow path cutting through the rickety homes with thatched roofs. It bent to the right a bit and disappeared in the light fog rolling in from the finger of Alrujah Bay.

The blue water undulated. The salty ocean air reminded Erica of being three. In the memory, she sat on the beach somewhere along the Pacific Ocean, miles and years from North Chester, with a boy about her age. She didn't remember the boy, or who else she came to the beach with then. Not her parents, she knew that. She and the blond boy buried their feet in the sand and stared over the ocean as the sun dropped beneath the horizon. Seagulls flocked overhead. They squawked, but it sounded like crying. The breeze, thick with salinity, cooled her sunburned skin.

Something in her memory prompted Erica to say, "I've never been on a boat."

"Never?" Ullwen asked. He'd shaved his beard and cut his hair. He'd abandoned his uniform at Relina's house in favor of a common villager's trousers and a plain white shirt.

"Never," she said.

In the waning light, children rushed through the streets, chasing each other and laughing. Adults busied themselves with chores—washing laundry in the bay, selling trinkets in shops and on the streets, sweeping spider webs from under their roofs.

Ullwen smiled. "It can be very relaxing. At some point, I will take you on a boat if you like. After we save your parents, stop the Mage Lord, and save Alrujah."

"Sounds nice." Erica sighed. Going back to Alrujah—nearly dying, and having Sparky so close to death—may have been a poor choice. But her parents had risked their lives for her. She would do the same for them. Though she'd never met these digital parents, she imagined them as the couple from the beach, the one with the blond boy sitting beside her.

Ullwen steered her toward an alleyway between two rows of houses. He pushed her back against the wall. Her mind replayed every movie she'd seen where the boy pushes the girl up against the wall and kisses her hard on the lips. She almost closed her eyes, expecting to find his lips on hers, but his head turned, gazed down the street.

She cleared her throat and smoothed her dress.

"The guards are changing shift." He handed her a small bottle of a glowing blue potion from his breast pocket. "Drink," he said, doing the same with an identical bottle.

When they'd drained the last drops, he took her hand and led her to a spot where the homes gave way, and the cobbled street ended in a steep edge that plunged deep into the glittering water. Its heaving surface reflected the light like a million tiny mirrors, each working separately. He pulled Erica by the elbow to the edge of the water. "Slide in. Be as quiet as you can."

"Good call." She spun around, dropped her feet over the edge. Water seeped into her boots. It should be cold, but Relina's potion kept the chill from her skin. She took a deep breath, held Ullwen's hand, and dropped the rest of the way under.

The dark murky water stung her eyes. Before long, her lungs burned. A heavy weightlessness possessed her. The drag on her boots and dress made swimming nearly impossible. She squeezed Ullwen's hand and pointed to the surface.

He shook his head, breathed out a stream of bubbles. The silver spheres of air raced to the surface. Her chest smoldered.

He inhaled, a deep swelling of his chest, water filling his lungs. He never broke eye contact.

She couldn't keep the air in her anymore. She exhaled, let the heated air rush from her.

Ullwen took her in his arms, held her so hard she thought he might break her ribs.

Air. Had to have air.

She pushed Ullwen, tried to wriggle out of his grasp and break for the surface. His unbreakable iron embrace trapped her mere feet from the surface. She punched him, but punching underwater proved useless.

Must breathe.

We are absolutely dead.

Her airless lungs screeched.

Ullwen held her head tight against his chest.

She tilted her head to the surface, to the silver moonlight diffusing and refracting through the water. So close, an arm's length from sweet oxygen. Ullwen's incredible strength held her immobile.

And then she inhaled.

Water rushed in her nose and mouth, filled her lungs, and she gasped, choked, convulsed. She shook in panic, grabbed onto Ullwen, pushed him, reached for the surface.

We are absolutely dead.

Was it moonlight, or heaven up there? The surface, or judgment? Salvation, or death?

Her short black hair floated around his face, caught in the stubble of his beard. She gave up resisting, sank into his embrace. She breathed.

In, out. Water moved in and out of her chest with each breath.

Ullwen stared at her, a self-satisfied smile stretching his face.

She'd never wanted to kiss anyone as badly as she wanted to kiss him there, in the Alrujah Bay, breathing water like a shark.

He nodded, a way of gauging her readiness. She reminded herself why she breathed water—for her parents, not for romance. Ignoring the romantic pull toward Ullwen, she nodded.

He turned toward Alrujah and swam deeper into the dark water. His legs and arms moved in large half-circles. Erica did her best to emulate his movements but felt as graceful as a sleep-deprived gorilla. She barely kept up with him. Ullwen held her with one hand, swam with his legs and his free arm. His guidance moved her through the water with more efficiency, but her wild movements, each awkward stroke, seemed to work against him. She wondered how much further Alrujah lay, and how long the potion would last. At what point, she wondered, would her body remember she wasn't supposed to be breathing water?

The deeper they swam, the darker the water became. Mud and silt swirled up from the bottom like a lazy tornado. The current pulled at her dress and her boots. Cold water froze her lungs. Why wasn't she dead?

Near the edge of her visibility, something dark shot by like a harpoon. It swam to the surface and split the silver water with its back. Long and eel-like, it moved with the fins of a sea turtle. Blood-red gills under pale blue scales rippled along either side of the giraffe-like neck. They swelled open and sealed shut in a rhythm consistent with the powerful thrusts of its flippers. Its long, pointed head terminated in a half-muzzle, half-beak. Jagged teeth ran along the sides of its mouth outside its lips.

Water dragon? Must be.

Ullwen slowed and allowed it to pass in front of them. He tread water with his legs, cutting them in alternating half-circles. She followed his lead, though her movements seemed jerky and imprecise, not nearly as efficient as his well-trained strokes.

They moved forward again, faster now. Her limbs ached, and she wished the cold of the water would soothe her burning muscles.

Several fish swam toward them, then cut beneath them, and Ullwen pressed on, but not before Erica got a good look at their sleek, agile bodies. Curved spikes—hooks, almost—lined their silver scales and twisted back toward their tails.

Parial-barbed vi-fish. Ullwen told her about those.

As one, the school turned up toward Ullwen and Erica. She grabbed Ullwen's ankle and yanked it in mute desperation.

Ullwen extracted two small knives from under his cloak, but the fish turned away from them. They accelerated toward the water dragon.

As if sensing them, the dragon slithered around in a circle and snapped one of the vi-fish in half. A vi-fish latched onto the dragon's tail while another snapped onto a flipper.

The dragon spiraled down into the darkness.

Erica lost sight of the battle. The other vi-fish did not follow. At first, Erica thought the vi-fish had killed the dragon, but dead fish floated, didn't they? They must still be fighting. Regardless, she didn't want to hang around to find out for sure.

They turned back toward Alrujah and swam with what strength they had left.

* * *

Bailey Renee missed the sound of Lauren's alarm waking her in the morning. Her head throbbed as it always did when she woke from Alrujah. How long had it been since she'd slept normally? Two days? Had to be longer.

She opened her eyes, stretched her arms through the tangle of cords running from her head to the machine beside her bed.

Home. Lauren's bed. Lauren. She had to get out of this hospital.

"You awake, beautiful?" Franky asked from a chair in the corner.

She smiled and sat up quickly, her head spinning with the sudden shift. "About time."

He walked to her bed, bent over her, and kissed her forehead. "I should have been here yesterday, for sure. Had some family drama. They said I'd just be in the way."

As he stood back up, she grabbed the front of his shirt, pulled him back to her, and kissed his lips hard. When she finally turned him loose, he staggered back. "You're never in the way. Now, you have to do me two favors."

"Wow."

She snapped her fingers. "Favors, I said. Pay attention."

He smiled. "Is one of them to marry you?"

"Please," she said, running her fingers over the thin white cords. They tugged at the skin of her forehead and scalp. "I'm fourteen. Talk to me in six years. Right now, what I need is a burger with extra pickles. And fries."

"Done. I'll grab some now."

"Not from the cafeteria," she said quickly. "Drive-thru. And there's one other thing."

"Anything, baby," he leaned in closer, touched his nose to her cheek.

"I want you to bust me out of here."

CHAPTER THIRTEEN

As the War of the Suns turned the swords of friends against one another, so shall the war that comes with Shedoah. City shall turn against city, elf shall again turn against human. The war will spread like a shadow of a demon across Alrujah.
—The Book of the Ancients

O LIVER DROPPED TO HIS knees and covered his head as the far wall exploded in a flash of greenish stones and dust. Remarkably, none of the rubble hit him. If it had, it surely would have flung him into the opposite wall. "Everyone okay?" he asked.

"We're good," Aiden said. He stood in front of Lauren, his shield outstretched.

"As are we," Yarborough growled. He pushed a large stone off his chest and sat up.

Langley had apparently dodged the debris as effectively as Oliver. "He's coming," he said.

A sickening growl crawled from the black hole in the far wall. Moloch's breath came as a cold wind and carried the stench of decay. The whispering of the necromancers swirled in the air. "Take these as our offering to you, Lord Moloch."

"Where is the Mage Lord?" Yarborough asked.

"He tucked tail and ran," Aiden said. "Dude's a coward."

Oliver stood up. The pain in his back eased, as it always did before battle. He tilted his head from one side to the other. Each joint cracked. He spun his staff around and tucked one end under his arm. Anticipation replaced his terror, and, for a moment, he understood Jaurru's blood-lust. The perversity before them stunk to Adonai. Oliver would take pleasure in destroying the abomination.

Moloch crawled through the hole. Filth swirled around him. His eyes blinked in alternating pairs. The severed arms of his victims, all in various stages of decay, linked together to form the limbs of the monster, formed decidedly human muscle groups. Little else humanized the beast.

The Ancient Language rolled off Oliver's tongue, and he lifted a prayer to heaven. "Adonai, protect us. Adonai, slay your foes."

* * *

The salty water in Erica's chest grew dangerously icy. Relina's cold potion must be wearing off, which meant the water-breathing potion wouldn't be far behind, and they had only made it to the southern gate. The heavy steel cross-bars spoke a simple message: "No Solicitors." A stonework bridge spanning the bay supported the gate. In times of peace and trade, Alrujah kept the gate raised. Boats sailed under the massive arch. Now, its bars ran well under the water.

Ullwen grabbed the bars and pulled himself down further. She followed close on his heels. She remembered the school of spooky fish attacking the water dragon. Down in the dark, bad things lurked.

Hand over hand, she clutched freezing bars. Each moment, the bars and water grew more frigid.

Must go faster.

Bar after bar, like climbing a ladder in reverse, she slowly descended until the silt completely obscured the pale silver moonlight. The loose sand stung her lungs, tickled her throat. She coughed, panicked with each sharp intake of seawater.

In the blackness, she reached for the next bar and found nothing. The pressure of the depths squeezed her. Each breath came with great effort. The immense, crushing cold of the bay pressed in on her. As she swam under the bars, her boots hit something solid. She jumped, spun in the water like an astronaut doing a double-take.

Nothing. Dirt. The bottom of the bay.

She stretched out her arm in the dark, measured the distance between the bottom of the gate and the bottom of the bay. Two feet, no more.

Ullwen latched on to the back of her dress the moment she cleared the gate. Water rushed around her in the wake of his powerful kicks as he swam upward. He pulled her faster than she swam. Where did he get his strength?

The silt cleared. The silvery moonlight illuminated the bay in cobalt ebullience. Erica wanted to dry off by a fire and collapse on the ground until the pins and needles of numbness left her limbs.

Up and up they swam, at a consistent forty-five-degree angle. Her chest blazed. How far to the surface? She kicked with the trickle of strength she had left. The surface of the water shimmered gently. So close.

Something long and skinny swam past the edge of her vision. Underwater trees? No. Posts. Hundreds of them. Wooden posts. They must be at the docks.

Ullwen's head splashed through the surface, and he pulled her up. She didn't have time to react. The water rushed out of her lungs; she coughed and spat, like throwing up, like the flu. Nauseated and chilled, she coughed and gasped and clutched at Ullwen.

"Help," he shouted in between spurts of water and gasps of air. "Help us!"

A shout came from the docks. "Be steady!" Feet from them, two men splashed into the water.

Erica blinked, hoping her eyes would clear enough to adjust to the sight of something other than the sea. Her legs kicked and she grasped at Ullwen's chest and arms.

Strong, gentle arms encircled her. Whatever panic seized her under the sea started to melt away. The soldiers pulled them from the water, and all went, for the most part, as planned.

Huddled together and shivering, Ullwen relayed the rehearsed story: they had walked too close to the edge and fallen in; Erica didn't know how to swim.

The guards brought them something hot to eat and something warm to drink, let them dry off next to the fire in the guard's quarters in the docks.

Soon after, they walked into Alrujah as if they'd lived there their entire lives.

So close now. By the next sunsdown, she'd be with her parents again. And after they'd rescued them, she'd repay Ullwen. Already, she formulated a few ideas of how to show her thanks—ways she'd enjoy as much as he would.

* * *

Moloch pounded his fists into the stone floor and set the ruins trembling. The rock beneath Lauren's feet rippled like windswept water. She collapsed and the cold floor smashed into the back of her head. The greenish tint illuminating her vision dimmed—emerald bled to sage, to olive, to a deep forest hue.

A hand touched her head. Her vision returned, and the pain shooting down her neck reversed its course dramatically and slipped away through the top of her head.

Oliver's hand. Had to be. "Thanks," she said.

The ground undulated like low tide beneath them. She'd never surfed before, but she imagined it would be much like this.

Moloch opened his mouth again and exhaled loudly. A fine mist issued from his gaping maw. "His breath is death!" Langley shouted.

Yarborough took up the cry. "Keep your air. Take as little of his stench as possible."

"Dude exhales poison?" Aiden whispered.

Lauren nodded but didn't speak.

Oliver knelt, his staff before him. So long as the poisonous gas clouded their vision and burned their lungs, victory remained improbable, possibly impossible. The chamber reeked of spoiled meat and sour milk.

The Ancient Language came from him again. "Adonai, give us breath. Give us sight."

Immediately, the gas filling the chamber rushed like a spinning tornado to the top of Oliver's staff.

Langley stared hard at him.

"By this you will know Adonai is God. This day, we will hand you the head of Moloch, and I will lift up the Blood Sword. It is by Adonai's hand you will be delivered."

Yarborough, still transfixed by the swirling gas, guffawed. "Impressive, eh, Langley?"

Oliver adopted a new pose. On one knee, he stretched his other leg in front of him, his staff held firmly in one hand and under his arm, the other hand stretching toward Moloch. He broke his consistent prayer in the Ancient Language long enough to tell Lauren to cover him. "It's not flammable," he said.

She grinned. "You got it." Her core temperature elevated to magma proportions, and she let free a stream of white-hot flames toward the demon.

* * *

Shortly after Franky embarked on a cheeseburger run, Detective Parker walked into Bailey's hospital room and closed the door behind him. He stripped off his outer coat and threw it on the chair in the corner. Tossing Lauren's journal on her bed, hands deep in his pockets, he said, "You're right."

Bailey picked it up. "You've read it twice?"

"Three times. Good stuff, too. Not even a fantasy fan. Girl's got talent." He pulled a hand free from his pocket long enough to stuff an unlit cigarette from behind his ear into his mouth. He pantomimed taking a drag and shook his head. "I gotta quit these things." He threw it in the trash.

Bailey held Lauren's leather bound journal, opened to the first page where she read the only words never to change. *The Book of Things to Come.* "Different each time?"

Parker scratched the back of his neck. "Some similarities, but for the most part, yeah. Trying to figure out how to tell the department. Or if I should tell them."

Someone knocked.

"She's fine," Parker said. "Napping."

"Doctor Fitzgerald will be here in an hour to check on her."

"Got it." He sat down and crossed his arms. "Ideas?"

The wires tickled her nose. "A couple." She sat up straighter and turned the television up. "You know I'm not crazy now, I can tell you this. I think the journal tells the story of whatever is happening in the game Oliver and Lauren created. I think they got pulled in somehow. And I think I'm getting pulled in, too."

Parker looked at her, then at the cigarette in the trash bin. "You sound bat-crap crazy right now." His voice didn't sound accusatory, more sympathetic.

"Listen," Bailey whispered, leaning forward so Parker could better hear her over the racket the television made. "Fitzgerald prescribed me some pills she wants me to take, but I can't take them. I can't explain exactly why, but I'm telling you, they could really mess things up. She's going to want to keep me here to see how the meds are working, and when she finds out I'm not taking them, she'll put them in the IV. I have to get out of here. I'm going to have Franky bust me out. Can you help?"

Parker narrowed his eyes. "What do you mean, bust you out?"

"I'm not sick," she snapped. "These episodes I'm having, they're what's pulling me into Alrujah. That's what's wrong with me. And they can't do anything for me here but screw it up. Here's what I know: if I don't get back to Alrujah, Oliver's going to die. Maybe even Lauren."

Pacha el Nai hadn't said anything about Lauren, but Bailey was sure that if Oliver died, the others wouldn't last long.

Parker's face paled. "Yeah. I read that in the journal, too."

"It never said that in the journal, not in the five times I read it. The game is changing. The only way to save them is for me to go in after them and bring them back."

Parker leaned back in his seat. "What makes you think you can pull that off?"

"For one thing, when I go to Alrujah, my body apparently stays here. I've seen Erica there. Parker, I've touched her. I'm telling you, I can get them back."

"You're crazier than me."

"We can be crazy together. Give me a chance to try something. I've got a copy of the instruction manual for the software Oliver created to make the game. Give me enough time with it, and maybe I can find something, some line of code, some file that somehow broke the barrier between our worlds."

"You keep yapping like this and I'm going to have to move you to the mental health wing."

"You read the journal. You know I'm not making this up."

Parker sighed. "The journal is changing, sure. And I saw mention of you in it, of you as an angel. But to say that the code created some rift between our worlds? Seems too sci-fi for me. There's got to be another explanation."

"You have to help, me. Please, Detective."

He stared at her, sorrow in the corners of his eyes. Almost as if he saw someone else when he looked at her, someone he loved, someone he missed. "I won't help bust you out. There's no need. Have your mom check you out. Even if it's AMA."

"I can't tell her what I've told you. And you can't tell her, either. It'll break her. She's fragile enough as is," Bailey said.

"She might surprise you."

"She hasn't yet."

"Give her a chance," Parker said. He stood up and opened the door. "If she won't take you out, then we can look into other options."

"So you believe me?"

"I believe you're out of your mind. But I also think you're smart.

Much as I hate to admit it, it's the best lead we've got."

* * *

Moloch roared and flailed his arms against Lauren's flames. Massive rocks plummeted from the stone ceiling. Aiden and Langley deftly rolled out of the way while Yarborough set his feet. He smashed the butt end of his axe into a falling boulder and sent it hurtling toward Moloch.

The beast plucked it from the air and smashed it into the wall. The green haze seeping from his mouth and nose twirled toward Oliver's staff.

Lauren took a deep breath. Electricity sizzled through her. She focused the energy in her core, heart beating with the static, chest rumbling. She called "Clear!" Energy crackled the air. In the green tint of her vision, the yellow sparks glowed blue.

Moloch jolted with the surge of electricity through the various disembodied limbs composing his musculature. He grunted and slammed his fists into the stone floor again.

Wise to the tactic, the group steadied themselves, keeping their footing and rolling out of the way of leaping debris. When the ripples slowed, they surged forward again.

Aiden rushed, his sword glowing red with heat. In a move defying the weight of his armor, he leapt, planted a foot on a nearby wall, and jumped even higher. He brought the heated blade across the face of Moloch, slicing his cheek open and falling back to the ground. He rolled under Moloch's swinging arm.

Yarborough hurled his axe toward the swinging arm. Blade met flesh and cleaved two decomposed arms from the larger whole.

"Gross," Lauren sneered.

Langley whispered something over his blade and extended it toward the left shoulder of Moloch. An intense beam of light shot from his sword.

The world went bright. Lauren's eyes burned. When the intense heat and light lessened, Lauren blinked. Moloch's left arm fell from his body. The composite arms separated and crawled along the floor toward Langley and Aiden. Yarborough raced around, crushing as many as possible under his heavy boots like cockroaches. The crunch of rotten bones echoed in the caverns. Lauren's stomach turned.

"Destroy them!" Langley shouted, "Before they join up again!"

Carefully, Lauren took aim. Her fingertips numbed, and she froze each crawling arm.

Moloch grabbed Aiden with his right arm and roared in his face. His gaseous breath enveloped Aiden's head.

Dear God, let him hold his breath.

Two corpses shuffled from behind the beast. Green and gold embroidery highlighted their black robes. Their skinless faces had peeled back, their lips rolled up, but their tongues seemed unscathed. Like Moloch, they opened their mouths and a green mist flowed from their stale lungs.

Corpses rolled down the stairs. They righted themselves, gathering their maces and their claymores.

Oliver did not move. The mist from Moloch and the necromancers' corpses flowed steadily into the tip of his staff. His hand grasped the amulet his father had given him. Lauren recognized a few words of Oliver's prayer in the Ancient Language. Something like "Breath of Adonai."

Aiden gasped for breath as the mist around his face cleared.

Lauren's hair circled her face. A wind blew down from the stairs and through the hole Moloch had punched in the wall. Dust spun up from the ground into a bottle green whirlwind, a verdant tornado. The cyclone traced the crags in the floor until it swirled around the hulking demon and the two necromancers. Their robes pulled around them, and they latched onto the grotesque leg of Moloch to keep from being blown into the night.

CHAPTER FOURTEEN

The Finger of Adonai shall breathe over the cursed blade. The evil forged within its steel will be vanquished. With a mighty cry of victory, the Hand shall bring a pointy reckoning on those who oppose Adonai.
—The Book of Things to Come

ERICA DID NOT SLEEP well. Had Sparky been with her, she would have huddled with him for warmth. Not knowing whether he would live or die made sleeping near impossible. But Dillard had worked whatever miracle he could, and Relina would care for Sparky while Erica sought to free her parents, so long as the Shedoahn Order left her alone long enough for her and Ullwen to get back.

When the suns filtered through the windows of the abandoned house she and Ullwen snuck into the night before, Erica had already been awake for an hour. The coals of the small fire Ullwen built next to the window glowed red. Ullwen, however, seemed to be in a coma. He snored, his mouth unhinged.

She rubbed her eyes and leaned back.

Sunlight slanted across Ullwen's eyes. He snapped his mouth shut and sat up quickly. "How long have you been awake?"

"Can't say."

He stood up, and Erica wondered why anyone would sleep shirtless in this cold, especially with his thick gold necklace. Must be like wearing ice. Still she wouldn't complain. He looked younger without the shirt, thickly muscled, the way she imagined college guys looking. Her eyes lingered momentarily before she wrapped her cloak over her shoulders.

The weight of the damp cloth comforted her.

Ullwen sheathed his sword and stepped on the coals. "One day, you must tell me all about your world."

Erica smiled. "You mean after we rescue my parents and stop the Mage Lord from getting *The Book of Sealed Magic* and restore peace to the land?"

His laugh startled her with its beauty. It rang with clarity and strength, forced her to relax. On a cold night, she could wrap her shoulders with that laugh, a laugh that felt like wings. "Perhaps when I take you on a boat for the first time. Just you and me."

Her face flushed with heat, and she searched for something to hide her embarrassment from Ullwen. Her eyes settled on the rickety, splintery door. It bore several scars, most inflicted, it seemed, with an axe. "You never told me why this house is abandoned."

"Not a pleasant story."

"Is it creepy? I like ghost stories."

Ullwen strapped his sword to his back beneath his cloak. It hung low so as to be completely hidden. "They say madness settled on this house, a madness of the kind of Norgren. It pushed a man to take an axe to his family. He spared none in the house. The violence spilled into the streets. Alrujah's soldiers were able to end the man's madness by taking his head."

"Right there in the street? Just cut the head right off?"

"They had little choice. They say he would not put down his axe, even after they took his head. Word of the story spread quickly with the merchants as they traveled between Alrujah and Varuth, as far up as Weileighn and Harland."

"Hard to sell a house with that kind of history, I guess."

"Aye." He strung a quiver of arrows and a short bow over his crowded shoulders.

"If you're trying to keep all that hidden, you may want to rearrange some of it. You look like Quasimodo."

"I've not met him. Is he a fair looking man?"

"He's a hunchback, sweetie."

Ullwen arched an eyebrow. "A fair looking hunchback, then?"

She smiled. "Gorgeous. Now let me take something."

"Are you better with sword or bow?"

She shrugged. "I'm better with a guitar if you must know."

"A guitar? Is that like an axe?"

She laughed. "You're cute when you're confused."

He nodded. "You'll excuse my embarrassment, but Alrujahn women don't often have your forthrightness."

She shrugged. "So I hear. I'll take the bow."

* * *

114

Chest heaving, Aiden circled behind Moloch. He leaned against the swirling wind still rampaging through the chamber, darted in and out of Moloch's legs, slipped past the flailing hands of the necromancers. He steadied himself with a foot on the back wall and one on the ground, hacked at the decomposing arms comprising the limbs of Moloch.

The demon grasped at the arch of his eyes and roared. His six rows of teeth gleamed.

Lauren shivered. Electricity crackled in her heart. Her hair snapped like millions of neurons.

She focused on the line of corpses falling over each other down the stairs. The wind knocked them over, kept them unfooted. A pile lay at the bottom of the steps, and those on top rolled off to secure weapons and attack. With them all lined up, a good blast of electricity should arc through them, and, ideally, cripple them all long enough for Langley to take their heads off. "The corpses." She had to shout over the gale.

Holding her hands high in the air, electricity sparked from Moloch and the necromancers into Lauren. She had never pulled electricity through anything before, and the surge of it added to the sizzling energy in her lungs.

Moloch and the necromancers howled. Lauren leveled her hands at the pile of corpses. Fat arcs leapt from her fingers to the mound. They convulsed and shook, their bones rattling in their loose musculature. The lines of blue energy leapt up the stairs, arcing from one corpse to the next.

Langley followed a split second behind the sparks. The minute the energy settled, he brought his blade through the necks of the corpses closest to him. The others still shook like nervous chickens.

The whirlwind waned.

Yarborough joined Langley, bringing the blade of his axe on the piles of undead.

The dust storm settled, and Moloch kicked Aiden. He slammed into the wall; the sound of steel on rock clapped through the cavern.

Yarborough's head snapped up from the heap of undead corpses. "Jaurru!" He leapt toward Moloch, narrowly escaping its wildly swinging arm.

Without the wind, a necromancer found his feet and smashed the halfling dwarf in the neck with his golden staff. Yarborough collapsed.

Already, Oliver called their names. He knelt in the middle of the chamber, remarkably out of the numerous dangers surrounding him.

His prayers provided the strength and protection they needed to win the battle. Otherwise, both Aiden and Yarborough would be dead.

Aiden struggled to his knees.

Moloch raised a foot over him.

With a speed that surprised even herself, Lauren pulled him out of the way. The stench of rotting flesh roiled in her mouth.

"Thanks," Aiden said.

"You okay?"

He spun around and sank his blade into the chest of the second necromancer. It screamed at him with its twisted tongue and broken teeth. He kicked it, extracted his sword, and sliced through its neck.

"I'll take that as a yes," she said.

"Let me have your dagger."

Moloch kicked at them, but they jumped to either side of the colossal foot.

Lauren pulled her dagger from its sheath and tossed it to Aiden, who caught it by the hilt.

"Hit him," he said.

"With what?"

"Anything. Everything. Just go!"

Lauren gathered her strength, and with one hand, sent electricity into the back of Moloch. With the other, she shot a line of concentrated flame toward his neck. Using two different spells simultaneously, something she'd never done before, came naturally to her. Must have leveled up again.

Moloch reeled around quickly, and Aiden leapt up. He sank the dagger hilt-deep in the small of Moloch's back. Moloch didn't flinch. Lauren's barrage of magic kept his attention on her instead of Aiden, who used his sword and the dagger to scale Moloch's massive back.

Too close. She had to move.

Moloch grabbed her. She wished she had her dagger, anything to stab him with, something to get her free.

The nar'esh cave. The ice spikes. How had she done it?

She conjured the same fear she had in the nar'esh cave, remembered dying, the pressing cold and blackness, the overwhelming despair. Something pushed from beneath her skin, near her elbows and knees, on the sides of her arm, her shoulders and ankles. It burned at each point of pain—a ripping. With a scream, ice spikes erupted from her skin.

Moloch dropped her quickly and spun around. Aiden crouched near the top of its back, holding fast to the dagger and sword.

"Be careful," she said.

Langley cried, "They're still coming!" He stretched out his hand and a piercing light shot from his palm toward the stairs.

The chamber lit up like day again. Corpses rained down from the stairwell, all with black holes burned in their chests and necks. Most had been cut in half.

Lauren made a mental note: learn that spell.

Yarborough righted himself in time to deflect another blow from the first necromancer. He blocked another attack, using his axe handle as a staff. The two traded blow after blow before Yarborough kicked the skeletal attacker in the knee. A sickening crunch, and Yarborough sunk the point of the axe under the chin of the necromancer. He pushed up hard. The head finally gave up its grip on the body. He pulled the head off his axe and spat at it. "Defiler of death! Traitor of Adonai!"

Langley called from the stairwell. "They've fallen!"

Yarborough turned his attention to Moloch, who spun from side to side. Aiden's grip slipped, but he held on by fingertips and a passionate determination.

Yarborough sank his axe into the calf of the monster. It screamed but did not stop twisting.

"Come on, Aiden."

Aiden climbed to Moloch's neck. He pulled his sword from the back of the beast, wrapped it under Moloch's chin, and pulled it back with his gauntleted hand.

The blade suffocated Moloch's screams. He reached over his shoulders and grabbed Aiden from behind.

Aiden gripped the sword firmly.

Moloch tore at him, finally pulling Aiden off his shoulders, and with him, the sword through its own neck.

The head fell a few feet from Lauren and smacked the rock floor with a wet thud. Lauren turned away and tried to keep her breakfast down.

The body of the demon fell backward, nearly crushing Yarborough.

Above its head, a black undulating cloud coalesced, like black blood coagulating into a scab.

"What is that?" Yarborough asked.

"May want to step back," Aiden said.

They did, as red sparks arced through the cloud.

"We don't know," Lauren said, her breath coming in heavy gasps. She tried not to look at the abomination.

The sparks united and leapt down toward the abomination, snatched it up and blistered it into oblivion in a massive red bolt of lightning.

"Just like Belphegor," Aiden said.

Pale and tired, Oliver stood up, a smile stretching his face. "Good job, guys," he said. Then, to Lauren, "Anything in *The Book of Things to Come* about red lightning?"

She shook her head, her heart still punching her chest. "Can't find anything."

"Let's get the sword and get out of here," Aiden said. He stared at the head of Moloch.

"It's in the next chamber," Oliver said. He stood over the head of Moloch and sneered. "So it is for those who challenge Adonai."

Langley sheathed his sword and bowed his head.

* * *

When Bailey's mom finally came back in, she sat in the chair beside the bed, clasping and unclasping her purse.

Bailey moved the wires from her forehead. She didn't have to ask, but she thought it better to get the bad news over with. "I take it your conversation didn't go well."

Her mother cleared her throat. "Doctor Fitzgerald says she wants you to stay here."

Bailey closed her eyes. The conversation would end in her getting a headache. "Not an option, Mom. I have to get out of here. I have to get home."

"I know, and I want to take you home. Believe me, there's nothing I want more. But leaving isn't an option," her mother said softly. The clasp on her purse clicked open and closed, open and closed.

Bailey made no effort to hide her irritation. Her sigh came out like an accusation, a skill she'd learned from her mother. "They're not going to find anything. They're going to put me on a bunch of medication, and the only effect it will have is to make me constipated. I've done the research, Mom. I know probably as much as the doctor does."

"Then you know how important it is that you stay."

"I'm not going to drive or operate heavy machinery. I'm going to go home and lay on the couch instead of this stupid bed."

"And what if you have another seizure? What if you take another twelve-hour nap? How am I supposed to feed you without an IV? I know you don't like the idea of staying here, but it's the best thing for you now."

But not what's best for Lauren or Oliver or Aiden or Erica. But she couldn't tell her mom that, not without making things worse. "So we take the IV bag home. We can do that, you know. There are places that will set it up for us."

"Be patient, sweetie. You'll be home soon enough. Please don't make this so hard."

"I'm not making it hard. Check me out AMA. People do it all the time. Detective Parker walked home after his first heart attack." Maybe she shouldn't have added Parker's personal information, but she thought it might help her case.

"That's just stupid."

"Mom, you have to."

"Do you know what Doctor Fitzgerald told me just now? She said if I checked you out AMA, that she could have me arrested for child endangerment. She threatened to have CPS take you away from me."

Bailey closed her eyes so her mother wouldn't see them roll. "She's bullying you, Mom. Don't let her bully you. It's a hollow threat."

Her mother closed the clasp hard. The snap reverberated through the room. She stood up, slung her purse over her shoulder, and said in a violent whisper, "I've lost one daughter already. I won't lose another."

"Said the woman who threatened to disown me if I left the house." Immediately, Bailey regretted saying it.

Her mother took a deep breath and looked down at her feet. "I may not be the perfect mother, but I'm not a complete failure. You're staying here because I love you."

Pacha el Nai's threat resonated in Bailey's ear. This was an argument she couldn't lose. "If you don't check me out, don't bother coming back here."

"Really? You're giving me an ultimatum?"

Bailey blinked back tears. "You did the same thing to me."

"You're right." She cleared her throat, then leaned over and kissed Bailey's forehead, wires and all. "And you left me." Clutching her purse, her mother walked out the door.

* * *

Lauren helped Oliver to his feet. His back seared with renewed pain. God had given him the strength he needed to survive the battle, but little more. His legs shook under him, from fatigue, from complete emotional exhaustion. The adrenaline crash left his knees loose, and he steadied himself with his staff, keeping one arm over Lauren's shoulder. "I never wanted any of this for us," he said.

"You guys okay?" Aiden asked. He put a hand on Oliver's shoulder.

For a moment, neither said anything. Soon, Oliver nodded.

"We must press on," Yarborough said quietly.

"Yeah," Lauren said.

Oliver leaned on his staff and began walking toward the far chamber that held the Blood Sword.

Lauren walked beside him, and Aiden beside her. They walked close, hand-in-hand. Langley took up the back, his sword at the ready, his fingers twitching like caught fish.

Several green pedestals stood in neat rows and columns, not unlike those in Langley's trophy room in Harland. But unlike Langley's display pedestals, each of which held some ancient artifact or family heirloom, these held nothing but dust. All but the center. There lay a brilliant sword glowing red with the power of its slain foes.

"That's it," Langley whispered with all the reverence of a church devotee.

The long black unbreakable onyx blade seemed to spring forth from the open mouth of a fangand wrought in gold. The fangand's teeth wrapped around the bottom of the blade tightly. The hilt, also fashioned from gold, had a large ruby at the bottom.

Langley stretched out his hand toward the sword, but Oliver grabbed his wrist before he even got close. "Don't touch it."

"It does not belong to humans," he sneered.

"We will return it to your people, but only after we've broken the curse," he said.

Langley leveled his sword at Oliver's chest. "It would be a political mistake to keep the sword from me."

"Easy, Langley," Yarborough said. He held his axe tightly, staring at the half-elf. "I cannot allow you to attack a monk of Adonai."

"This isn't religion, Dwarf. It's politics. If the humans want to show their goodwill toward the elves, they must give me the sword now."

Aiden slowly interposed himself between Langley and Oliver. "You want him, you come through me."

"And me," Yarborough said. "This is more than politics."

Oliver released Langley's hand and took a step back. "This sword drains the power of its victims, but whoever holds it must yield to the blade's madness. You pick this sword up, Langley, and it very well may be the end of us. None of us can touch it." Reaching into his robe, he extracted a folded cloth and threw it over the blade.

Lowering his sword, Langley turned his lip up. "You stole my linen?"

"A tablecloth I plan to return." He wrapped the sword in the soft fabric and tied it with the rope of his belt.

"How long do you plan to hold the sword?" Langley asked.

"Until I break the curse."

"When will that be?" Yarborough asked.

"Whenever Adonai wills it."

CHAPTER FIFTEEN

*The Lord Adonai opened his mouth and said, 'You mountains of
Alrujah, I shall stretch out my Hand toward you, and bring a sword
against you, and destroy your high places. Your altars will be demolished
and I will slay your people in front of your idols. I will lay the dead
bodies of the worshipers of Norgren in front of their idols, and will
scatter your bones around your altars, and you will know that I am the
Lord.*
—The Book of Things to Come

FRANKY MAY NOT HAVE been the brightest bulb in the box, but he
was at least punctual. He showed up exactly when Bailey told him
to, his backpack slung over his shoulder. "I can't believe I let you
talk me into this. Promise me I won't go to jail."

"Close the door," she said. When he did, she immediately pulled the
wires off her head. The electrodes stuck like glue, but she pulled and
pulled until they finally popped off, leaving red circles on her forehead.
She rubbed her temples and silenced the beeping machine. "Did you
bring my beanie?"

"Ask and you shall receive." Franky pulled a purple North Chester
High beanie from his backpack, and the rest of her clothes he'd had
Autumn get from her locker after school. "Won't that beeping alert the
nurses?"

"No. Patients get up and go for walks all the time. The nurse just
came in and checked on me. She won't be back for a while, so long as I
don't call her." She slipped into the bathroom and pulled her robe off. It
felt good to put on her own clothes, no matter how cold the jeans were,
or how tight the sweater was in her shoulders. Her skin itched where
the electrodes had been. She scratched her forehead and washed her
face. Lucky for her, she had the forethought to have Autumn grab her
spare make-up kit from the locker, too.

Outside the door, Franky sang softly. She didn't recognize the tune,
but the words were some embellishment of his nerves. "Hurry up," and

"Are you sure this is a good idea?"

She smiled, even though she felt little joy. Even if she never saw her mother again, at least she had Franky. "We'll be fine," she said, closing her kit. She'd put on enough blush and eye shadow, enough mascara to make her look presentable, and different enough from the girl who'd lain in the bed for the last couple days. "People walk out of the hospital all the time."

Shoes. Real shoes. And socks. Made her think of sneakers and gym floors, of basketballs on hardwood, the squealing of rubber, the swish of the net. Franky had earned himself a kiss, at least. Maybe two. She came out of the bathroom a new girl, ready to find her sister, ready to lay low. She grabbed Franky's hand, kissed his lips. "You're my hero," she said.

Franky beamed, kissed her back. "You get me arrested, and we're breaking up."

"You'd never break up with me."

"You're right. Ready?"

She grinned, feeling more like a complete person than she had in days. They walked out, hand in hand. Nurses swarmed the floor, but few looked their way. Those who did didn't look long. Bailey kept her eyes down until they made it to Franky's car.

No sooner had she sat down, than her lids got heavy. She groaned. "What? Cold?"

"Don't freak out," she said, her words coming out slowly. "I'm going to sleep again. I'll be up soon. But I swear to you, if you take me back, we are so over."

"I trust you," he said.

She'd never loved him more.

Franky's car vanished beneath her. The sprawling world of Alrujah lay before her. She stood on a cliff overlooking a city in the distance. She recognized the spires, fuzzy from this distance, as the spires she'd originally landed on when she first woke up in Alrujah. Her reception had been less than warm.

The brace on her left wing whirred and flexed while she stretched it. It still hurt, but the pain had lessened to a surprising degree. If she needed to fly, she could. But where? She had no way to tell where in Alrujah Lauren and the others might be.

Wind sang through dead pines. She covered herself with her wings, the mechanical brace tucking under her chin, and turned, gravel crunching under her boots. She recognized this cliff. She'd fought the mass of undead just ahead. She'd leaned against this pillar to rest her broken wing.

She walked toward the entrance of the ruins slowly, her hand on the hilt of her sword. The wind stilled. The chill in the air became imperceptible. Heat rose in her, a hot anger. She'd been so close to Lauren here before that stupid voice brought all those stupid zombies. She yanked her sword from its scabbard and proceeded into the chamber.

The blade glowed in her hands and illuminated the cavernous chamber. Bodies of the undead littered the floor, most missing limbs, all missing heads. The stench, like cat litter and blood, filled her nostrils, and her stomach soured. She heaved a moment before stilling herself and composing her stomach.

"You still here?" she called.

Who did she expect to respond? The disembodied voice? The animated corpses? Lauren?

Nothing answered. No corpses moved. No voices whispered or moaned. Lauren did not jump from behind a pillar and yell, "Surprise!"

Bailey pressed forward, kicking corpses from her path, stepping over others. Blade out, wings wrapped tightly around her, she proceeded down a flight of stairs.

In the lower chamber, illuminated only by the light from her blade, sharp shadows danced around the smashed pillars and altars. More corpses lined the stairwell and virtually every inch of the floor. But there, at the end of the light from her blade, something massive lurked. It didn't seem to be moving, but it had to be the size of a small house.

She approached it cautiously, as if she didn't trust it to be dead. A shiver ran up her spine and pain pricked her wing. Dark shadows played over it. Squat and bulky, it had lumpy, diseased arms and legs, and they seemed to be fashioned out of the limbs of dismembered corpses.

She fought back another wave of nausea.

A flash of light seared her shadow onto the far wall. Behind her, an angel stood. Tall, with radiant, glowing golden eyes and blond hair, she recognized him immediately—the angel who sent her to heal Erica. "You again," she said.

"Yes," he said. Light radiated from his skin. He stepped closer to her, made her feel small. If he stretched them out, his wings would reach from wall to wall. This close, his brilliant feathers shimmered pearly white. He wore a luminously silver breastplate, which covered his thick chest completely. His golden hair sparkled in the light of Bailey's sword.

"Who are you?"

"I am Pacha el Nai, servant of mighty Adonai. I come to you at His bidding."

Bailey took a moment to steady her heart. This angel could tear her in half if provoked. But some things warranted the risk. "Where's my sister? Where's Oliver?"

"On their way back to Harland. They are safe for now. They will not need you until later."

"Look, Pacha, what I really want to do is get my sister and her friends back home. As much as I love flying around and slicing up corpses, I'd like to go home and see my sister again. I got out of the hospital like you said. Now can I please see her?"

Pacha el Nai stretched out his hammer-hard hands. She put her sword away and took them. In his, hers looked like small spiders. Walking backward, he pulled her gently back up the stairs toward the entrance of the chamber. "The time for you to see your sister will come soon."

She followed after him, stepping over the bodies and glancing back at the hulking decayed beast near the wall. "What is that thing?"

"His name was Moloch, but he is no more. He was an abomination in Adonai's sight, and Adonai's Hand crushed his evil like a fist."

The chamber blackened with Bailey's sword in its sheath, but the radiance of Pacha el Nai provided the light she needed to navigate the narrow, corpse-strewn stairwell. "When you say Adonai's Hand, you mean Lauren, don't you? And Oliver?"

At the top of the stairs, still walking backward, still staring at her intently, he said, "Lauren and Oliver are two of Adonai's many fingers."

"So it was them, right?"

"They did not act alone, but by their efforts, they did slay Moloch." Pacha el Nai folded his wings tightly around himself and ducked as he passed through the doorway. Once outside, he spread his wings wide and lifted them both into the air.

Bailey opened her wings as well. They hovered in the air for a moment. "So, what do I have to do to see Lauren again?"

Pacha el Nai smiled. "You and I must speak with a king."

* * *

Erica smoothed her dress and pulled her cloak tighter around her. The early morning mist slicked the damp stones of the tower in front of her. And while the mist melted away, black clouds heavy with rain bulged overhead.

"Another minute or two. We need as many guards as possible to see it." Ullwen pulled the hood of his cloak up.

"You sure they won't be suspicious?"

"Of course they will. But by the time their suspicions are roused, we should have your parents safely out of the dungeon."

"And from there to Port Smalth, then to Eukara Island," she said.

"And then we find the others."

She fidgeted with her cloak. "Oliver couldn't think to put in cell phones. Sure would have made things a lot easier."

"What are cell phones?" Ullwen asked.

"Later. Looks like the guards are changing."

Twenty shiny soldiers filed out of the tower in front of them, all in steel plate armor. Each breastplate bore the stylized Razorbeak, wings outstretched to either sun, head tilted toward the greater sun. Their swords hung at their hips and stuck behind them like stiff tails.

Ullwen said, "Don't be afraid. The dungeon sentinels are not as well trained as Ribillius's guard. They may be well outfitted, but their skills do not compare with ours."

"Speak for yourself," she whispered. "Are we ready?"

A patrol of dungeon sentinels moved from the northern part of the city. They converged with each other outside the tower walls and began talking. One, with an ornate orange feather on his helmet, held parchment and a quill. He seemed to be taking a report and giving orders.

"Now," Ullwen whispered.

As discreetly as possible, Erica neighed like a horse. Seconds passed. In the distance, a rumbling, a shaking, moved through the earth like a bass beat.

Horses stampeded through the streets of the city. The soldiers' jaws dropped, and they flung themselves out of the way.

Erica and Ullwen moved closer to the tower at a slow pace.

The soldiers righted themselves as the sentinel with the feather in his helmet called out orders. "Those horses better be okay," Erica whispered as she slipped into the tower.

"They'll be fine." Ullwen closed the door behind them and drew his sword. He moved through the dark, dank dungeon with quick, quiet steps. Erica already sensed the presence of animals she could call to help—rats the size of cats, black snakes with big, diamond-shaped heads, bats clinging to the ceiling listening, lizards with inch-long teeth. Any of these would prove more useful than her bow and arrows, especially in a swarm.

They moved quickly toward the torch-lit staircase. Further in the dungeon, the walls lost their smooth texture, gave way to chiseled rock rather than careful masonry. Must be underground. The wet, spongy air chilled her skin. "There's a ton of animals down here," she said.

"How many is a ton?"

"A lot."

"Aye. No sentry wishes for dungeon patrol. Many soldiers have lost their lives from fatal snake bites. Often, the fact is not discovered until the body is removed from the dungeons, and the culprit slithers out of the armor as it is being removed for the next soldier."

"There's a happy thought. At least we won't have to worry about it. I can feel all the snakes in here. The lizards and rats and everything else, too."

"We will need that advantage."

Ullwen took a torch from the wall, handed it to Erica, and proceeded to extinguish the others by snuffing them in the corner of the flat black walls and slick floor.

"Must we travel in the darkest conditions possible?"

"It gives us another advantage." Each time he came to a torch, he extinguished it and left it on the darkened step beneath.

"Why not kill the torches toward the entrance?"

"They would know something was wrong immediately and pursue us swiftly. The sentry rarely passes down these stairs more than necessary. By the time they make their way this far down, we should be out. The dark will only delay them from learning we've made egress through the drainage pipes."

"And you leave it on the steps so they'll slip on it?"

"A broken leg makes pursuit difficult."

"Sometimes I'm really glad you're on our side."

* * *

Feet away from the walls of Harland, two shadows passed over

Lauren. She paused, let the rest of the group continue on, and checked the sky. The greater sun sank behind the tree-lined horizon. Two massive silhouettes soared under the lesser sun.

"Something wrong?" Aiden asked. He broke off from the group and took her hand.

"Griffins," she said, pointing up with her free hand.

He craned his neck up to where she stared. "You sure they're not birds?"

"Way too big."

Yarborough, his axe strapped to his back, followed their gaze. Hastily, he called back to them. "We must hurry. They are preparing to close the gates, and we must rest before our journey tomorrow."

Aiden pulled her forward, but Lauren didn't want to take her eyes off the strange shapes. She wanted to trace the flight of the griffins, to follow them until they settled back on the ground somewhere in Yeval Forest, near the Council of the Order of the Protectorate. Aiden's firm grip urged her on.

Langley walked briskly ahead of the group. Yarborough and Oliver hobbled along behind him. When they reached the guards, Langley simply nodded. The guards stepped aside and allowed the group to pass without the customary search—one of the advantages to traveling with a foreign dignitary.

The green mail and white shield identified the guards as two of Harland's Watch, a finely trained group of soldiers responsible for security. In times of war, they raced to the front lines to defend the multi-tiered walls. Still, they gave Langley a wide berth and inclined their heads in a begrudging, almost fearful sign of respect.

More of Harland's Watch walked up and down the streets, lighting the torches along the walls of the shops and homes. Though the lesser sun hadn't set completely, it moved closer and closer to the Dragon's Back Mountains looming in the distance. Because the city covered so much land, the lighting of the torches would take nearly an hour, even with a force of fifteen or more of Harland's Watch.

Shops closed. Merchants headed home while families scuttled off toward pubs. The streets filled with people. Getting through the masses felt a lot like fighting her way through the cafeteria in North Chester.

Langley moved purposely toward the hill on which his house stood. Once the group had put some distance between themselves and the denizens of Harland, Yarborough slowed his steps enough to walk beside Lauren. "Griffins, you said?"

"Sure looked like them. Had the wings and everything. Not dragon's wings, either. These were softer, more rounded. Why?"

"How much of *The Book of Things to Come* have you read?" he asked.

"A bit," Aiden said. He walked next to Lauren. The minute they'd cleared sight of the crowded streets of Harland, he'd taken her hand in his again.

"I saw two," Yarborough said, continuing. "How many did you see?"

"Two," she said.

"I still say they were too big for birds," Aiden said, "Pretty thick bodies. Like a tail or something."

Yarborough cracked his knuckles. Lowering his voice, he said, "They may well be griffins, but I don't believe they were. Only the Council rides griffins, and they are far too cautious to fly so low as to be spotted by the likes of men or dwarves or elves. But both *The Book of Things to Come* and *The Book of the Ancients* mention angels. Humans with birds' wings."

"We know what angels are," Aiden said.

Langley's house drew closer. Oliver kept pace with him, but barely. His staff dug into the gravelly path, then scratched through it as he drug it ahead of him. Plant, scratch, plant, scratch. The Blood Sword swung back and forth on his hip.

"Some say Adonai will send His messengers to aid in the final battles against the abominations."

"Sounds like you've done a bit of reading, Yarborough," Aiden said. The path crunched under the weight of his armor, and he left deep footprints.

"Aye. We had a copy, my father and I, before the Shedoahn Order had them all destroyed."

"So you think we're racing up on the final battles against the abominations? That might be a little scarier if we knew what the abominations were," Aiden said.

Langley plunged into his house, and Oliver followed. Yarborough stopped short of the threshold. "I don't wish to speak of this in front of Langley. It will only cause discord. But the abominations are demons. Once, they were angels, given dominion over parts of Alrujah by Adonai and King Solous. But the touch of Shedoah corrupted them. They established themselves as gods over their people."

"Moloch," Oliver said.

"Belphegor?" Aiden asked.

Lauren shuddered at the thought of the nine-foot tall Minotaur that nearly killed them all in the depths of the ancient dwarf city Margwar. "Has to be," Lauren said.

Yarborough closed the front door and continued in a hushed voice. "The dwarves worshiped Belphegor as a god. But my father refused to join in the worship of such a beast. He followed Adonai, as his human wife did, and so the dwarves put him out, only days before my naming day. He taught me the ways of Adonai."

Lauren shivered and stood closer to Aiden.

Yarborough continued quickly. "The elves of Norgren worshiped Moloch. The false gods are demons, according to *The Book of the Ancients,* which draw their power from the worship of the elves and dwarves and humans. There are six abominations, and one resides in Harael in two bodies."

"What's that supposed to mean?" Aiden asked.

"I am unsure," Yarborough continued. "That is how *The Book of the Ancients* tells it."

"The Seers," Lauren whispered. "Of course."

"No matter. We've killed two," Aiden said. "If it bleeds, it can be beat."

His arm around her shoulders offered little warmth. "Still."

"Let us pray the birds you saw were the angels prophesied about in *The Book of Things to Come.* And let us study the book to find what we may do to prepare ourselves."

"What should we tell Langley?" Lauren asked.

Yarborough said, "Nothing."

CHAPTER SIXTEEN

The Lord Adonai saw the wickedness of the elves, that they desired only evil, and each thought was vile and corrupt. Adonai was deeply troubled and grieved that He had created them. He vowed to wipe them from Alrujah, but Solous intervened for them. He bargained with Adonai and promised to return the hearts of the elves to Adonai.
—The Book of Things to Come

O LIVER SET THE BLOOD Sword on the table, pressed his hands against the fabric-wrapped obsidian blade. Intent on Oliver, Langley hadn't noticed the others hadn't come in. If they had something to talk about privately, it must have to do with Adonai, and the mention of Adonai always irritated Langley.

"Can you break the curse or not, Monk?"

Oliver, head bent over the blade, cut his eyes up to Langley's. "These things take time." He whispered in the Ancient Language, a murmur of a prayer. The words, though still foreign to him, came naturally, and with each, he became more aware of their meanings, the subtle differences in the pronunciations of harsh consonants and soft, flowing vowels. They created a rhythm, a bit of a punctuated staccato, each syllable, every intonation probing the magic contained within the stone blade. An inquisitive incantation, the words stemmed from the original language Adonai blessed the races with, and the power they summoned came from Adonai himself. They would better reveal what dark magic wove around the cursed blade.

Langley paced the antechamber of the house. He wiped blood from his face, tore off his blood-stained tunic. He undid the band in his black, silky hair and let it fall free. His pointed ears split his hair like jagged rocks split a waterfall.

Yarborough opened the door and walked in quietly. The others followed. "How's it going?" Aiden asked.

Oliver didn't break his prayer. The answer drew nearer. The magic of the curse began to reveal itself to him. Something dark, a blackness of sorts, wrapped itself around the blade. He saw it, inexplicably, through the fabric. The blackness shifted to a crimson hue, a diffused glow moving in and out of the blade like a sea serpent's spine splitting silver waters. He could break this curse, could unravel it, could snatch the serpent by the tail and pull it from the waters. But could he do it without being bitten?

But as he prayed, something told him it would be a bad idea. He must break the curse but must not do so now.

"How long will this take?" Langley asked.

Oliver didn't say anything.

"Can you break it?" Langley asked again.

What should he say? Withholding information had proven dangerous in the past, and monks did not lie, but telling Langley didn't seem like a good idea. He ceased his prayer and took his hands from the fabric-wrapped sword. "It seems Adonai doesn't wish me to break the curse right now."

In a dangerously thin voice, Langley asked Oliver, "When does he wish you to break it?"

"I don't know."

Langley balled his fists. "Are you saying I must wait on the whim of a broken god?"

Oliver straightened his back. "You must wait on the word of Almighty Adonai, creator of Alrujah and the heavens above, creator of the seas and the fish that swim in it."

Langley fumed. His anger reddened the sharp features of his blood-smudged face, and his eyes narrowed to dangerous proportions. His hand tightened around the hilt of his sword. Langley took a deep breath. "Cleejal. Prepare our guests' rooms. They will stay another night. We depart at first light for Harael."

* * *

Harael, the elvish water city, spread out beneath Bailey Renee in the center of the Harael Sea. The architecture mimicked ancient Rome. White stone buildings and sculptures rose up out of the water. Towers and spires, rounded domes and multi-columned entryways stood amid waterfalls on nearly every side. A calm section of water, much like a lake, probably the size of Laonis Lake back in North Chester—big enough to fish on, but not big enough to get lost on—rested in the center of the city. Pointy-eared people rowed kayak-like boats through the calm waters. Occasionally, they'd arrive at one side of the lake and ascend one of the various stairways leading to the upper levels, all the while pulling their boats up what looked like water slides.

Several of the pointy-eared people squinted up at her and Pacha el Nai.

Here, she had the eyes of an eagle. Even in the purpling sky, quickly darkening to black, her keen sight identified the facets in each stone, the cracks in each column, the slight discoloration of the stone near the rushing waters. Statues of lifelike fangands and beresus, of massive birds the size of mountain lions, and griffins.

Beyond the Romanesque architecture of community buildings lay a sprawling mass of squalid hovels. The elves stared at her with a strange mix of reverence and fear, of hope and dread.

Pacha el Nai pulled his left wing down, tilted his head toward the city below, and dove. Bailey followed him, the brace on her wing holding tight. The tip of her broken wing burned, but she managed the pain.

He set down among a mass of elves outside the capitol building. They stared at him, at her, in amazement and wonder. Many broke to their knees and inclined their heads. "The lips of the gods," they whispered.

She followed their gaze to the two towering white marble statues on either side of the tall building. Both represented massive, heavily-robed elves with flowing hair. Each crossed their arms over their chest, with each hand resting on the opposite shoulder. Each had one eye; the one on the left had only the right eye, the one on the right had only a left eye.

Pacha el Nai's face grew dark. Until now, Bailey Renee assumed he had no emotion, as if he'd never experienced pain or joy or anger or love. In hindsight, the thought became foolish, childish. But she wished she didn't have to witness his anger. He stretched his wings out as far as they'd go and stared at those who stared at him. "Get off your knees!"

They stood immediately, heads still bowed. Their knees knocked, and Bailey had to steady herself at the sound of his voice, once so beautiful, and now so terrifying. His wrath shook from him like an earthquake.

"We are not the lips of your gods. We are not the mouths of idols. We are the messengers of almighty Adonai, and we will speak with Neldohr, King of Elves."

By the reaction on the faces of the elves, they revered their king as a god. Shock and despair marred their sharp features, as if they wished to oppose Pacha el Nai but knew the results would be disastrous. Still, the crowd parted in front of him, slowly, afraid to make any sudden movements.

Pacha el Nai moved toward the expansive entryway. He enveloped himself in his wings and ducked through the doorway. Bailey did likewise. She kept pace with him while the crowd of elves, busy talking and writing with feathered quills on yellowed parchment, stared at them. Clearly, this building held the political leaders of the day. They conducted city business here, it seemed, as several people whispered "ordinance" and "protocol" and "restrictions" and "permit." Unlike the emaciated, poverty stricken elves behind the capitol building, these elves dressed as if they had money, and looked as if they'd never missed a meal.

All their talk ended when Pacha el Nai and Bailey entered.

He walked with purpose toward a flight of wide stairs leading down to the left. They worked their way down several flights of stairs, past several elves putting on traveling robes and staggering back at the sight of Pacha el Nai and Bailey Renee.

On the sixth floor down, Pacha el Nai led Bailey Renee to a room the size of a soccer field. Instead of walls, water flowed up and over the area as if glass held it back. She reached out and touched the water flowing beside her, drew her finger back soaking wet. Nothing held up the water surrounding them. Nothing visible at least.

"An enchantment," King Neldohr said in a baritone voice, much deeper than the other elves. He stood, tall and lanky, some bizarre mix of human features in giraffish proportions. A heavy golden crown sat on his head tucked under his pointy ears. His almond-shaped eyes latched on Pacha el Nai's unrelentingly.

Pacha spoke slowly. "King Neldohr. We come in the name of Adonai."

"Yes, of course. The Seers would never send winged humans to deliver a message." He descended from the white stone throne and stood inches from Pacha. Even with the king's impressive height, the angel towered over him. "The Seers would know better. They know we hate primitive humans." He grinned. "Still, I suppose winged humans are preferable to dwarves with gills."

Bailey swallowed her anger and stood next to Pacha. She had no desire to speak to this king. She'd rather slap him for his arrogance. But Pacha had told her exactly what to say if she wanted to save Oliver and

Lauren. With the voice of a crackling fire, Bailey said, "The Lord Adonai has seen your haughty heart. He will send to you a sign of His power. If you accept it and bless His name, He will bless you and bless your plans. But if you deny it, if you harden your heart, He will bring upon you a terrible reckoning."

Neldohr never acknowledged Bailey Renee. His neck bent back, face inclined toward Pacha's, he whispered, "Adonai sends a woman to speak? A sure sign of His weakness. Our Seers killed their mother for her devotion to the weak god Adonai. You must know this. She took an eye from each of her sons in the struggle. But that made them even more powerful. What weakness do you serve, winged one?"

"Wow. Rude," Bailey Renee said.

Pacha el Nai stared intently at Neldohr. "Your pride will destroy you unless you repent."

"You are wasting your time. I do not recognize Adonai's power over me. I serve the Seers."

Bailey Renee rested a hand on the hilt of her glowing sword. She wanted to pull it out, to teach this elf a few manners. But Pacha el Nai warned her not to. If she let her anger control her, it might inadvertently end with Lauren's and Oliver's deaths. Still, she had to say something. "You mean your one-eyed statues? Statues are blind, King Neldohr. They don't move or breathe or speak or think."

Neldohr finally turned his gaze to Bailey. "Guard your tongue, woman, or your fate will be the fate of the All-Mother. The Seers do not abide loose tongues, especially in the mouths of women."

Bailey stepped closer, spreading her wings to give the impression of size. The brace on her wing whirred with the extension. "I fear no hollow gods." She hadn't meant to say it. The words chose her, rather than the other way around. More words came the same way, surprising her as much as they did King Neldohr. "You've made your choice, and your arrogance has angered Adonai. Your Kingdom has been given into His Hand. Before the greater sun rises on the third day, the anger of Adonai will deliver your crown into the hands of another."

Neldohr sneered. He took a step back, pulled his hands toward his chest. The light dimmed near the edges of the room, and a white-hot sphere, small as a pea, gathered in his cupped hands. Whispering, the room darkened further, and the pea grew to the size of a head of lettuce, to a basketball. He extended his arms toward her, and a conical beam of light shot toward her.

Bailey flashed her sword from its sheath. The blade absorbed the beam, shimmered and vibrated for a moment before the illuminated blade dimmed. She replaced it in its sheath. "May Adonai spread His mercy over your people. May He not punish them for your arrogance."

Neldohr said nothing. His face contorted in wonder and fear.

"Their approach draws nearer, Neldohr. We have other matters to which we must attend." Pacha leapt up into the canopy of water stretching out like ceiling. Bailey followed, trading the warm, insulated throne room of Harael for the cold depths of the Harael Sea.

As much as she enjoyed swimming, she missed flying.

* * *

The rows of prisoners grew uneasy with each snuffed torch, but they remained silent. Their bare feet shuffled on cold stone flooring, bars rattled under pressing hands. What did they fear? What did they hope for? Had they been tortured in the dark? Soft sobs carried through the dungeon, bouncing off black stone walls.

Erica wanted to free them all, but many of them probably deserved to be in here. They may prove dangerous if freed. But even if they posed no threat, Ullwen had only brought enough solvent to dissolve the lock on two cells, and they had little enough time to free her parents.

Her parents. She had to focus on what mattered, had to shut out the simpering whimpers of passed prisoners, the dampness and chill of the dungeon, the nearness of Ullwen, the sound of his voice whispering her name, the memory of him saying, "Aye, my lady." So he was hot, who cared. This wasn't about him and that smoldering stare.

Parents who loved her. A selfless father. A courageous mother. Hard to wrap her mind around it, really.

"Hello?" a prisoner said. His voice tentative, the word came out as a tormented question.

Ullwen put his finger to his lips.

The dirty man quieted immediately. The half-light of Ullwen's torch made it impossible to distinguish the black splotches on his face as filth or shadows. How long had he been in there? His clothes, though too short for him, hung about his thread-thin limbs like flags hung on steel cable. An image flashed in her mind: a dog gnawing on his arm like a nylon bone. Voice hoarse, the man whispered something nearly inaudible. "Adonai bless your steps."

She shivered. What would her parents look like? Did they ever feed the prisoners here? Cell after cell, row by row, she followed Ullwen as he weaved through the snaking corridors. Her heart quickened. A hand grabbed her arm, and she yanked back instinctively. "Help me," a woman said. She must be eighty years old. Back hunched, nose broken, eyes wet, nails black with grease, grime, and old blood. Had she been digging at the stone walls?

"We must hurry," Ullwen said.

"Please," the woman said.

"We have to do something," Erica whispered to Ullwen. "We can't leave them here."

"There's no way to sort them out. Most of these are criminals. Thieves or assassins or worse."

"Worse than assassins?"

"Spies, mostly. Of the Mage Lord." He moved with practiced skill— quickly, but nearly silent. "Followers of Shedoah, even."

Erica's spine prickled. Torchlight shimmered in Ullwen's dark eyes.

She hissed, and two snakes crawled up her legs to her torso, to her arms. They rested their heads, mouths agape, in the palms of her hands. If someone tried to grab her now, someone unpleasant, they'd not forget their mistake. "How will you know which cell my parents are in?"

Ullwen shrugged. "Will you not recognize them?"

Probably not. She'd never met them before. But if she didn't, they should at least recognize her, right? If nothing else, she might be able to sense them the way she sensed the animals. The Alrujah in her might surface again and give rise to recognition.

They turned down a corridor lined with empty cells. "At least they're not all full."

"They look empty for a ways. Have we passed your parents?"

"Maybe they're not here. Are there no other dungeons in Alrujah?"

"None that would house your parents. Do you think," Ullwen began, but he never finished his thought.

He didn't have to. Erica understood what he meant. They may have died in captivity. But it didn't feel right.

She sighed. They'd worked too hard, risked too much, to come up empty-handed now. She straightened her back while the snakes squeezed her arms. She pushed forward. "I didn't breathe water for nothing. Let's go."

They walked for a half-mile before a gentle song, a lullaby, floated over the squeaking of rats and scurrying of lizards. Erica hummed along though she couldn't remember ever hearing the song. The snakes relaxed with her exhalation. "Follow that song, Ullwen."

He did. Around a slight bend to the right, six people, all dressed in brown burlap, sat in adjacent cells. "Easy," Ullwen said. "These are the traitors of the crown; those who are worse than assassins. They take money to start wars. Blood covers their hands. I've put many in here from Varuth myself."

"My parents are not traitors," she whispered harshly.

"Captain Korodeth would say otherwise. Anyone who hides a child who has shown aptitude in the arcane arts is labeled a traitor of the crown, and their fate is the same as instigators and guerilla soldiers. Your parents may be here because they hid you, but those in the cells around them may not be as noble as them."

"I'll remember that. But don't forget, I got about a hundred snakes and a thousand rats that might persuade them to leave us alone."

Ullwen nodded.

The torchlight spilled down the passage like gold mercury. The song, and Erica, stopped. "What happened?" she asked.

"They've seen the light. Perhaps they think we're guards and have ceased their singing out of fear."

"Keep singing," Erica said loudly.

"Who's there?" the soft voice asked.

"A friend," Erica said.

Tenderly, a man whispered, "Lakia?"

Little use in fighting the tears. Her chest tightened. "Daddy?"

"By Adonai," the singing voice said.

Erica brought the torch to the cell. The woman's filthy dress hung over her shoulders like a hanger. Her ice blue eyes shone from her soot-smudged face. The woman moved away from the bars of the cell. "This must be a trick," she said, eyeing the serpents encircling Erica's arms.

With a twitch of her palm, the snakes slithered down and away. "It's me, Mom," she said, nearly choking on the word.

"The snakes," the woman whispered. "You speak to them, don't you?"

A hand reached out from the other cell. "Sweet butterfly," a man said. He sounded hoarse. "We have missed you all these years. Let me look on you."

Erica moved to the next cell. The man shook his head, disbelief and grief and joy swirling in his damp eyes. "You are every bit as beautiful as the day they took us," he said.

"We'll have time for pleasantries later," Ullwen said. He extracted a vial of purple liquid from his cloak and sprinkled a few drops on each lock. He replaced the empty bottle in his cloak and said, "Step back, good people." He kicked each barred door and the locks smashed. He swung them open and pulled Erica's parents into the corridor. Her mother and father drew her into their arms immediately.

Erica's knees went slack. They smelled rank, cankerous, and her stomach flip-flopped. She wanted to throw up, but her arms would not let them go.

"Hey," a man said from another cell, his voice hushed and forceful. "The guards will be coming soon, no doubt. Hurry and turn us loose."

"We must go," Ullwen said.

"Turn us loose," the man said again. "Don't leave us here."

Erica said, "We can't take you. We have to go now. It's not safe to stay here."

"I'm not asking," the man said. Burly in the neck and shoulders, the hairy man must have been a recent arrest. "Turn us loose, or I'll call the guards."

Ullwen's severe gaze could have melted the lock.

"I don't think so," Erica said.

The two snakes that had encircled her arms returned, and two more slithered up the man's legs to his neck. He screamed and clutched at them, pulled them from his chest, but two more slithered over his legs.

"Settle down," Erica said, but the man went on screaming.

"Get them off me!"

"Hey!" Erica snapped. "Shut your mouth or they'll shut theirs, get it?"

"Too loud," Ullwen whispered.

"Help!" the man shouted, throwing the snakes and leaping to his bed. "Adonai, save me! Get them away!"

Erica rolled her eyes. "That didn't exactly go like I wanted."

Ullwen said, "They will have heard his shouts. We must go."

Erica grabbed her mother by her hand and thought she might never let go. "The snakes stay. They'll leave you to your bed, but you won't be going on this floor for a while, I think. And don't even think you'll be getting any of your food any time soon. My rat friends are quite hungry these days."

"Adonai, please," the man blubbered.

"Let's go," Ullwen said. He stepped behind Erica's father and urged him along with a gentle touch on his back. He took Erica's free hand.

Despite the dungeon, despite the dampness and filth and smell of decay, Erica had never been happier—one hand in Ullwen's, the other in her mother's.

CHAPTER SEVENTEEN

By his Hand, Adonai establishes the throne of kings. He places crowns
upon the heads of men, the heads of elves, the heads of dwarves.
—The Book of Things to Come

SURE, THE IDEA OF putting bath houses in the major cities seemed
superfluous at the time, but Oliver hadn't listened to Lauren, which,
for once, made her happy, especially since he'd put a bathing room
in Langley's house on the hills. After slicing through thousands of dead
bodies, charring corpses, and lighting Moloch like a bulb, she deserved
a bath—something she'd not had since she left North Chester.

She eased her weirdly thin body into the warm water. She'd lived
in the body for over a month now, but it still struck her as strange,
otherworldly. Whenever she felt convinced of the reality of Alrujah and
all around her, she'd catch a glimpse of herself in a burnished bronze
mirror and marvel at the dim reflection staring back at her.

She tipped her head backward until her hair lay completely
submerged in the bath. Oliver hadn't programmed much in the way of
shampoo, so she made use of what Langley had nearby—a bar of plain
white soap. She didn't care. It got the job done. The mud and blood
smeared on her skin lifted and dissipated in the now murky water. What
started as clear lake water turned to muddy silt. Gross. She hurried her
bath along and wished Oliver had gone the next step and left perfume
for her to wear. Nothing too powerful. Something flowery, enough to
get Aiden's attention.

The candles lining the bronze tub flickered. She finished washing
and put on the clean sleeping gown Langley had Cleejal pick up for her
in Harland. Unfortunately, he'd picked one too big for her—one that
might have fit her in North Chester. She wrapped it around herself,
appreciating the clean warmth of the heavy cotton fabric.

She pulled the drain for the tub. Though custom demanded several
people use the same bath water, as an ambassador, Langley had his
own supply of water. Oliver, true to character, found a way to convince

Langley to allow clean water for each of the party. Lauren had taken her turn last. After the bath, she'd head straight back to the room Cleejal prepared for her. The thought of sleeping on an actual mattress again made her already relaxed body sigh in relief.

But before she turned into her room, she made a quick stop at Aiden's. She knocked gently, and he answered. Dressed in a white gown, not unlike hers, he smiled. "Feels like a dress," he said.

She smiled. "Looks great on you."

"You look great," he said.

Blushing a bit, her mind raced for something to say. She had no idea why she'd come to his room, why she'd knocked. More than anything, she wanted to see him out of his armor, his face not smeared in nar'esh blood. "Listen," she said to buy some time. "I'm really glad you're here. I'm not happy you got pulled in, and I'll make sure you get home safe, but for now, I'm really glad you're here."

He stole a quick glance down the hall and kissed her lips. "I wouldn't want to be anywhere else."

She thought her face might burst into flames. Electricity crackled through her, but she pushed it down. "Glad we agree."

He touched her cheek and stared hard into her eyes. "Get some sleep, baby. I'll see you in the morning."

As he closed the door behind her, she moved down the hall, the feel of his lips still on hers, thankful for once she didn't have to worry about fangands or nar'esh or the Mage Lord or Shedoah. She would sleep tonight and, perhaps for the first time since coming to Alrujah, her sleep would be unmarred by nightmares.

* * *

Bailey's wings ached. She wanted to wake up in Franky's house so she could get some sleep, but Pacha El Nai insisted she make one more stop before returning to North Chester: Harland.

When she'd first woken up in Alrujah, she'd perched on a tower shooting up from the castle district of the city. Guards erupted from a spire and shot countless arrows at her.

But now she returned under the cover of night, flying high over the multi-tiered walls of the city. The guards below wouldn't be able to spot her, but her keen sight picked them out, even in the dark of the night.

Cold wind pressed her face. Her brace whirred with each extension, each flap of her left wing. Guards along the wall mumbled. Crickets chirped within the streets of the city. She turned toward the towers of the castle, but her destination lay just beyond, in the residential city behind the castle reserved for political officials and wealthy merchants.

The house she needed to visit sat alone atop a hill. The owner had money, and it showed. The architecture—clean lines, new paint, and windows—said as much. Must be the only building in the city with windows. The moon behind her, she folded her wings. Her brace whispered in the movement. Moments before crashing into the earth, she pulled up, flapped her wings twice, and landed at the door. Pacha had told her not to use the door. She leapt up to the window at the back of the house, opened it, and crawled in.

An elf slept in an ornate bed. Gold comprised the frame, and heavy blankets covered the mattress. While most people in Alrujah slept under animal skins, this elf slept in the closest thing to a four-star hotel Alrujah had.

The room glowed silver in the moonlight. Bailey shook her head, stood at the foot of the bed. Should she wake him? Nudge him? Call him?

She didn't have to. Langley sat up, eyes fixed on Bailey Renee. "Who are you?"

"A messenger," she said.

"No messenger wears wings and a sword of that caliber." He threw the covers from him and stood up. "You think to run your steel through my heart? What faction are you from? Are you from the Shedoahn Order?"

Bailey Renee took in the paintings adorning the walls: elves at sea aboard sprawling ships, engaged in bloody battles against humans, riding horses through densely wooded forests. "I speak on behalf of Adonai."

"I am no friend of Adonai," he said. "You come for my life, then?"

By now, Bailey Renee had grown accustomed to this part—words coming to her as clear as birdsong across a still morning, though she never clearly identified their origins. "I do not come for your life. I come to prove Adonai is God, and God alone; to prove the Seers are no gods, and their mother is no goddess. This is how you will know Adonai is Lord: By sundown on the third night, both Seers will lay in rubble, and King Neldohr will lay dead at your feet, and you will wear his crown, and you will hold in your hand the uncursed Blood Sword."

She thought he might be surprised, or perhaps excited. Instead, anger flooded his face. He squinted his almond-shaped eyes. His sharp nose wrinkled, and his pointed ears tilted back. "You speak of treason! I shall never defy King Neldohr!"

She hadn't expected this. No one had contradicted her messages before. Had to happen sometime, and she didn't have the energy to argue with him. More words pealed from across a deep chasm. "Then your fate will be the same as his, and the crown will pass from the elves to men."

The elf's ears returned to their normal position, and his eyebrows slipped down to his nose. His forehead wrinkled under his wispy black bangs. "You look familiar," he said.

It took less than a second for her to glimpse an image in the clear reflection of his green eyes. Lauren. She tried to say the name, but her eyes rolled back in her head, her knees buckled, and she woke up on her back, tucked into a bed, staring into the face of Nurse Nicole.

* * *

Erica struggled to keep up with Ullwen's pace. Her side hurt like it'd split open if she didn't slow down, but she pressed on. Had to. A torrent of guards poured down the stairs. Their armor clacked and clanked. One of them must have slipped on the torch Ullwen left on the top step. The others wouldn't be so unlucky.

Her mother and father trailed, faces anguished in the dim torchlight. Ullwen's brisk pace must be twice as hard for them to keep up. "Come on, Mom, Dad. We can make it."

She'd never called any of her foster parents by those words. But here, the words became an undeniable truth. Digital as they may be, Erica had never had more real parents.

The other prisoners' ululating screams followed behind them. "Free us! Don't leave us!"

Her parents' noodle legs barely supported them, struggled to propel them forward at the pace Ullwen demanded. They pulled her back, weighed her down, like walking a stubborn dog. "Lakia," her mother said, "I can't. I can't run that fast."

"You have to move, Mom. They're coming, and they won't ask you nicely to return to your cell."

Ullwen said, "The exit is still a ways off. It would be best if we didn't have to fight them."

Her father put both hands on his knees, bent heavy at the shoulder, and heaved with breath. "Your mother is right. We're too weak. Go on, Lakia, you and your friend. We didn't hide you for you to die trying to rescue us. We're not important."

"Don't you ever say that." Erica hadn't meant to whisper, but her voice lacked any strength. Her eyes burned hot, and her throat tightened, as if someone strangled her.

Ullwen took his sword from his sheath. "Take them, Erica. Follow this path. Do not turn right or left. The corridor will bend slightly to the right. The drainage hatch is not too far beyond."

"What did he call you?" her father asked.

"Later," Erica snapped. To Ullwen, she said, "You're not fighting them by yourself." She worked hard to hold back the tears of fear and elation.

"It's the only way. I will give you the time you need and meet you at the house. Remember, stay to the wall and move through the alleys where possible."

Erica hissed and squeaked. In seconds, the floors and walls crawled with snakes and rats and lizards, all moving toward the racket of the guards. "We keep going," she said. "I've enough friends who will gladly do our fighting for us."

A scream pealed down the hall, followed by another.

Ullwen sheathed his blade. "Very well. Quickly now."

Erica turned and led the way. Ullwen helped her father hobble through the dungeon.

More screams, and through them, another sound: footsteps, coming fast. Heavy, too, by the sound of them. Metal slapped on stone. Too close. Torchlight burned beyond the bend. She nocked an arrow on her string, pulled it to her ear, and let it fly.

The soldier came into view in front of the arrow, which lodged itself in the man's shoulder. By the time he'd realized the arrow hit him, another embedded itself in his abdomen, and another in his leg.

Her mother stared at her, shocked. "Lakia?"

Her father said, "You're either a very bad shot or a very good one."

Erica said, "He'll live." The clanging of guards died down, replaced instead by the horror-stricken shrieks of soldiers wrestling with the dungeon's unsavory inhabitants.

Erica wrapped her arm around her mother's waist and continued on. Her mother must weigh as much as a cocker spaniel. "The first thing you're going to do when we get out of this is eat."

Her mother laughed. "If we get out of this, you mean."

Ullwen said, "Bread and cheese. We'll cook a hearty soup for you both. Potatoes and vegetables and rabbit."

Erica said, "Nothing says lovin' like a pot full of rabbit."

* * *

Oliver didn't want to get out of bed. After a night on a decent mattress, he felt better than he had since wrenching his back in Margwar barring the door from the onslaught of nar'esh. When the first light of the greater sun illuminated the room Cleejal had prepared for him, he rose from the bed feeling nearly new, feeling strangely alone. He abandoned his sleeping gown for his newly laundered Monk's robe. Cleejal had done a great job cleaning the blood and sweat and dirt from the fabric. Before exiting the room, he took a moment in the quiet stillness of Langley's house to kneel at the foot of the bed. He put his hand over the amulet Dillard gave him the first day he'd awakened in Alrujah. The metal should be cold, but the gold warmed his chest. He pinched it between finger and thumb, bowed his head, closed his eyes, and touched the amulet to his forehead.

He thought of Erica, of how much he missed her. Before he woke, he'd dreamed of her. Because of the battle with the living corpses, with Moloch, because of the Blood Sword, he'd nearly forgotten about her. He didn't love her less, but the imminent danger seemed to eclipse what feelings he'd had for her when she traveled with them. His feelings for her had been forced to the back of his mind, but the dream brought it rushing back.

By now, she should be well on the road to recovery, and likely on her way to find her parents. He prayed for her, for her health and her safety, for Ullwen as well, even Erica's parents. The few moments free from mortal peril had given him an opportunity to remember these things. Perhaps God had simply called them to Oliver's mind so he'd cover them in prayer. The reason didn't matter nearly as much as the action.

"Let me be faithful," he mumbled. Rising, he smoothed the thick white covers of the bed and exited the room.

Aiden waited in the hallway. "Bro, had some crazy weird dreams last night. Think they were dreams, at least. Felt more like memories. I grew up in Harland? Not me, Jaurru. You know what I mean."

Oliver nodded, marveled how the action didn't send his back into agonizing spasms. "Yeah. At least until you were ten. Your father moved to Alrujah to help train the Watch. Captain Korodeth requested him personally." Aiden's memories of Alrujah didn't surprise Oliver. He'd had several himself, and Lauren had told him similar stories about her and Erica.

"Right," Aiden said, walking down the hall. He moved down the staircase toward the entry room. Paintings of well-dressed elves lined the walls. "And he taught me everything he knows. He's dead now, isn't he?"

Oliver took a deep breath, held the air in his chest. "Yes."

"I remember it," he said. "Some sort of rebellion, right?"

"A small band of elves."

Aiden's eyes shot up the stairs. "So you think I'm in love with Lauren because Jaurru is supposed to love Indigo?"

Oliver's eyebrows slouched toward his nose. So many things weren't the way they were supposed to be, who was to say Aiden would fall for Lauren simply because the script called for it? "You tell me."

"I liked her in North Chester. She was cute, smart, funny, you know."

Oliver moved toward the dining room, past the golden gauntlets and helmets and chalices on display in glass cases. "Well, she's the same here as in North Chester."

"I know, right? Same girl exactly." He paused. "You like Erica, don't you?"

Oliver sat at the oiled bench in front of the dining table. He took a banana from a bowl in the center of the table. "Pretty obvious?"

"In North Chester, too?"

"Yeah."

Aiden bit into an apple. "She's spicy. Gotta like that."

"Look, be careful with Lauren, okay? She really likes you."

Aiden grinned. "Almost as much as I like her."

* * *

Bailey Renee blinked twice, still weary from her trip to Alrujah. She must be imagining things. Nurse Nicole stood in front of her, her brownish eyes nearly gold, her long dark hair pulled back into a ponytail. Her lopsided grin hovered somewhere between disappointment and joy. Purple scrubs on olive skin, a warm hand on Bailey's wrist; no way Bailey imagined this.

Had Franky taken her back to the hospital when she fell asleep?

No. Light blue paint adorned the walls around her, and the window to her right had dark purple curtains covering them. Framed posters of Minnesota Vikings covered the wall. This was Franky's brother's room, practically untouched since he left for college a couple years earlier. But a machine stood next to her, beeped in slow spurts.

"Confused?" Nicole asked.

"Very."

Nicole's grin lost the edge of disappointment. "You and I have a mutual friend."

"Excuse me?"

Franky slipped in and closed the door softly behind him. "Thought I heard talking. Keep it down, okay? My mom's home now."

Bailey answered politely, though she didn't feel particularly polite. "Sorry." Then, "Where's your dad?"

"Out of town on business," Franky said. He sounded irritated.

Bailey's head swam in mist, a fog dense as stew. "You told your mom?" No—that wasn't right. If he had, he wouldn't be worried about them talking.

Nicole checked Bailey's pulse and temperature.

"She's good?" Franky asked.

"Healthy as a horse."

"I was seriously freaking out," Franky said, his voice unsteady.

"I told you not to," Bailey whispered.

"What was I supposed to do? You passed out, and I couldn't wake you up."

"How'd you get here?" Bailey asked Nicole.

"I followed you," she said. "My shift was done, and I saw you walking out with this gentleman here." She motioned to Franky as she checked Bailey's temperature. "Wasn't too tough to figure out what you two had in mind. And I figured he'd be in way over his head. So I brought a few spare machines from the hospital. They're old. Had to pull them out of storage, but they'll get the job done, and no one will miss them."

Bailey's head hurt. She wanted to go back to sleep, but her stomach growled angrily. How long had it been since she'd eaten? "I take it you called my mom?"

Franky knelt beside her and took her hand. "She promised she wouldn't. It was the only way I'd let her help."

Bailey lifted an eyebrow. Even that was exhausting, but the surprise at the level of Franky's dedication to her took her a little by surprise. She'd always assumed she loved him more than he loved her. A senior, after all, had no business dating a freshman, no matter how mature she may seem. But here he was, kneeling beside her, doing anything and everything she asked him to do without question. Plus, he was cute. "Thanks," she said to him. Then, to Nicole, she said, "Why are you helping me?"

She looked to Franky and frowned. "Shouldn't you check on your mom? Wouldn't want her coming up here, would you?"

"She won't. The television is on. She'll watch that until she goes to bed. That's all she really does."

"I think she wants you to leave," Bailey said. "Girl talk."

Franky frowned. "Yeah, sure. I'll come back and check on you when Mom goes to bed. Make sure you're comfortable and all that. You want me to sneak you some food up here?"

"Please."

"What do you want?"

"One of everything?"

"On it." He slipped out the door.

Once he'd left earshot, Nicole put her hand on Bailey's head. "You must be tired, too, I imagine. Flying through Alrujah isn't exactly relaxing, is it?"

Bailey closed her eyes. She must be dreaming. Her mind moved like a bike through thick mud. Had Parker said something to her? He must have. He was the only one she'd told about her dreams.

"You're not crazy, Bailey Renee. I've been sent to you in the same way you were sent to Erica."

"I'm not sure I understand what you're saying."

Nicole tilted her head back, moved it left and right. The lights dimmed. Nicole's olive skin glowed amber. Her eyes shone gold. "No wings here," she said. "Hard to hide under the scrubs."

Bailey's mouth dropped open. "No. Freaking. Way."

"Pacha sent me on Adonai's orders to watch over you and Parker. And your mother." Her voice sounded like Pacha el Nai's, as if two people spoke simultaneously, one soprano high, the other bass low.

Bailey sat forward again, covered her ears. "I am insane."

The light emanating from Nicole's skin softened. She sat next to

Bailey, put a reassuring hand on her shoulder. "I understand how hard it is to be in two worlds. But it's much easier when you understand why we're here."

When had life become so complicated, so convoluted? She longed for the days when she had only to worry about class work and which college she wanted to attend. "And why is that?"

"To do the will of Adonai. To do the will of God."

That should sound so much crazier than it did. But somehow, Bailey understood. "It's not a game, is it?"

CHAPTER EIGHTEEN

Thus says Adonai, "Behold, I have sheep that are not of this flock. They hear my voice and heed my call. Shall I not also bring them with me? Shall they not follow me as you follow me?"
—The Book of the Ancients

CLAD IN STEEL, SWORDS drawn, Alrujahn soldiers raced through the streets in their silver armor. Word of her parents' escape had clearly spread outside the dungeons. Korodeth did not take kindly to prison breaks, and he'd have the entire Watch on patrol, which meant Chameleon Soldiers.

Far deadlier than even the Palace Guard, Chameleon Soldiers moved soundlessly through shadows, skulked around corners, and struck with fatal speed.

Weeks before, they'd burned down the Cerulean Monastery on Korodeth's orders. They struck invisibly, moments after Erica and the others had departed for the nar'esh cave. According to Dillard, little survived their flames. Clearly, Korodeth had no respect for Adonai, and he had power. Why Ribillius trusted him, Erica would never know.

The greater sun rose over the Dragon's Back Mountains, but a deep purple hue still robed the sky. In the incipient light, Ullwen guided Erica and her parents through thickly shadowed alleys. He moved, Erica thought, much like a Chameleon Soldier. His time as a Varuthian Elite taught him the value of stealth and speed. Now, she hoped she didn't ruin his practiced skill with her clumsily huge feet.

Even when they arrived back at the abandoned house without confrontation, Erica did not trust their safety. "You sure we'll be safe here?"

Ullwen said, "We cannot have a fire. They will see the smoke. Last night, they did not know to search for us. We no longer have that advantage. The soldier you left alive will give an account of our appearance. Hiding will be harder, but we must rest here for a few hours, at least."

"You didn't answer my question," she said.

He pulled some extra blankets from the corner of the house and wrapped them around Erica's mother. "I am Ullwen," he said.

"Breniveer," she said weakly.

Her father extended his hand to Ullwen. "General Norby, though Ribillius stripped the title from me long ago."

Ullwen clasped the man's bony hand in his strong grip. "I've heard tales of your valor and cunning."

"Greatly exaggerated, I'm sure," Norby said meekly.

"I was unaware of your relation to the great General Norby," Ullwen said to Erica.

"So was I," she muttered. She should have introduced them earlier, but tragically, she didn't remember her parents' names until this moment.

"I can't believe this is truly happening," Breniveer said. She sat on the floor, pulled her knees up to her chest, and shivered.

Norby sat beside her and put a frail arm around her. "Adonai is good," he said.

Erica wanted to disagree, but she didn't. Why ruin the moment with a heated philosophical debate about the goodness of a God who allowed His worshipers to suffer as her parents had suffered, who allowed them to be captured and tortured for her sake?

Instead, she concentrated on quelling the onslaught of contradictory emotions: excitement, terror, confusion. For the first time, she had a set of parents who loved her, risked themselves for her, protected her despite the personal cost. She had no frame of reference to understand a love so strong. Hollywood made movies about it, authors wrote about it, but she'd never experienced anything like it, not even anything close. Now, prime, tangible examples of love sat feet away from her.

No wonder she risked her life for them, these skinny, weak creatures. For a moment, she felt like a mother looking at a frail child, rather than the other way around. She loved them, a feeling so foreign it baffled her. With no idea what to say, what to do, she paced the small room in the abandoned home, shoulders hunched and pointed to the floor.

Ullwen said, "Are you all right, Erica?"

When he said her name like that—his voice, the shivers. She looked to him, imagined him again smashing in the prison door to rescue her parents. She'd never seen anyone hotter.

"Erica?" Norby asked.

Breniveer put a hand on Norby's knee. "Changed her name, dear. You taught her well. She has to keep Korodeth off her trail."

Erica said, "Something like that. It's a long story, and I'm not sure I get it all."

Ullwen took bread from his pouch, broke it, and gave a half to each of Erica's parents. "Dip it," he said, pushing the pot of cold stew to them.

They did, happily. Erica thought they might cry. She might, too. "We have to get you someplace safe."

"We go where you go," Norby said. He reminded Erica of the children on commercials—the starving ones celebrities always hugged.

Ullwen said, "You're not strong enough to come with us."

"Where are you going?" Breniveer asked.

"Harland," Ullwen said. "We must meet some friends on urgent business."

"Don't worry, Mom and Dad." The words tasted wonderfully strange in her mouth. "We'll put you someplace safe."

"East Eukara Island remains uninhabited. You may hide there until we return for you."

"All respect, Ullwen, we've not seen our daughter in years. We'll not leave her again," Norby said.

"All respect, General, but we are not able to fight as efficiently if we're concerned about protecting you."

Norby stood and pulled the blanket tighter around his shoulders. "One does not attain the rank of General of the Alrujahn Army if he is unable to protect himself. Give me a sword, and you'll never need worry about me or my wife."

Breniveer also stood next to her husband. "And perhaps you wonder why the Chameleon Soldiers did not accost us on our way here, and why they do not spy on us now?"

Erica had wondered. "How do you know if we're being watched or not?"

"Because," Breniveer said, "I can sense their minds."

"A mind witch?" Ullwen breathed. "I thought they were children's stories."

"A what?" But Erica didn't have to ask. A vision formed clearly in her mind—her mother sending telepathic thoughts to the Chameleon Soldiers like some crazy Jedi mind-trick. "You plant thoughts in people's minds? But how could they hold you in a cell with a power like that?"

"The dungeon walls are thick with stone and enchantments," she said coldly. "But I'm a little beyond their reach now." She smiled.

Erica moved closer to Ullwen. "I guess we should be more worried about slowing them down," she said.

Ullwen didn't move. He didn't like the idea of them coming along. With a reluctant sigh, he said, "Very well. It is decided. We sleep here. Tomorrow, we begin our journey."

* * *

Lauren woke with the lesser sun. She had no desire to get out of the comfortable bed she'd slept in the previous night. If she stayed here in bed for the next three weeks, she'd not complain. But Aiden waited for her. Oliver waited for her. All of Alrujah waited for her. As part of the Hand of Adonai, she had a responsibility to end the Mage Lord's threat. He may not hold the throne of Alrujah yet, but his influence made itself clear in the world around them. And now he was waking the abominations, appearing just before Belphegor and Moloch reared their ugly heads.

She sat up and took *The Book of Things to Come* into her lap. She'd not had much time to read through its pages while she traipsed through abandoned elvish forts, or while hunting hostile ambassadors. She didn't have much time now, either, as Langley wanted to leave at sunup to cover as much ground as possible. Still, even with horses, they had little chance of making it to Harael in one day. They would have to camp. A few minutes of study shouldn't hurt.

She opened the dusty book, flipped toward the middle, where she'd left off last time, and read about the fall of the second abomination, Moloch. She read of their journey back to Harland, of their strained friendship with Langley, of their inevitable trip to Harael, which would take two days. "I knew it!" she said in a satisfied whisper.

The following pages detailed the events that would transpire after their arrival, but the text became vague, and discerning the exact future became incalculably difficult. The few passages she understood, however, terrified her.

A bloody battle.

Several deaths.

A slain king.

The fall and restoration of Harael.

For the Hand to have ultimate victory over the Mage Lord, they must fight. The crown of Harael must be removed and re-established. And the lives it would cost must be paid as restitution for the sins of an evil king.

None of those things terrified her as much as who would wear the crown, who would rule over Harael in two days.

Langley.

Must have read it wrong. She scanned through the text again, and, even racking her brain to interpret it another way, the text made the point clearly. Langley would wear the crown of Harael.

She closed the book quickly and put on the green dress Cleejal had purchased for her. Thicker than her white dress, this green one hung on her loosely but helped her stay warmer than the last. It would also help her avoid unneeded attention. Dressing like a princess had a way of drawing eyes. Not a good thing when the Shedoahn Order counted her as an enemy. It especially wasn't good when the Mage Lord still slinked around in the shadows of anonymity. No telling how long it'd take to root him out, or if they'd even be able to.

She raced out of the room and downstairs. Oliver and Aiden sat at the dining table eating fruit. Cleejal brought out scrambled eggs, and Lauren thought her stomach would leap through her skin and eat the entire plate on its own.

Langley and Yarborough were strangely absent. Must be heavy sleepers.

After Cleejal returned to the kitchen, Oliver continued whatever conversation he'd been having with Aiden. He spoke in a whisper, and looked toward the kitchen often, as if he didn't trust Cleejal to stay there. Whatever they discussed, Oliver didn't want Langley's servant knowing. Perfect. What she had to say shouldn't reach his ears either.

She sat next to Oliver mid-story.

"You can't really call them abominations. Their father was an elf like any other, but, their mother, Maewen, was an angel. They killed her and allowed the elves to worship them. As twins, they're kind of half-abominations."

"For real? Why would they kill their mom?" Aiden asked between bites of apple.

Oliver said, "Family quarrel, so to speak."

Aiden put the core on the table and smiled at Lauren. "You look great," he said. To Oliver, "So why are they called the Seers?"

Oliver sat straight up, a minor miracle for him. He ate a banana slowly. "During the fight with her sons, she tore an eye from each of them. Elves believe she inadvertently gave them some sort of supernatural perception."

"What, like seeing the future?"

"Exactly."

"Can they?" Aiden asked.

"Who knows?"

"You should. You made them, right?" Aiden asked him.

Oliver shook his head.

"I did," Lauren said. Sitting next to Aiden, she picked up the conversation in the same hushed voice. "The Seers are twins. Torap is the older, Uhesdey the younger. They work in tandem, though they often fought while they were alive."

Aiden asked. "So if they're dead, we don't have to worry about them, right?"

"I hope not. Uhesdey practiced some really dark magic. Real Fort of Norgren stuff. Probably taught the necromancers of Norgren everything they know. Torap only practiced good magic—alteration spells, divination spells, healing spells, restoration spells, those kinds of things. But even he had a mean streak. Some of his spells were far more destructive than even Uhesdey's. He's the one who struck the final blow to Maewen. He burned her with a light so intense, it incinerated her."

"Nice," Aiden said.

She hadn't really thought about it before, but mentioning it now made her remember the beam of light Langley shot at the corpses in Norgren. Must be the same spell, which meant his magic followed Torap's path of study. That should be helpful. If he'd studied Uhesdey's magic, he'd be much more frightening, much harder to trust. "Anyway, the point is, even though they're dead, they may still be a threat. The elves have studied their magic for centuries, and they're super dedicated to their gods."

Oliver stood up and stretched. "Yeah, but our God is way bigger. Way stronger."

"Listen," Lauren said, swinging her legs over the bench to face Oliver. Still whispering, and checking over her shoulder to ensure she wouldn't be overheard, she said, "We have to talk. I've been reading *The Book of Things to Come*. Best I can tell, when we get to Harael, we'll have a fight on our hands. Neldohr won't be happy to see us. We're going to have to kill him."

"Kill him?" Oliver asked.

"Who's Neldohr?" Aiden asked.

Oliver said, "King of the Elves."

"For now. Langley's going to replace him. He has to."

"Hold on a second," Aiden said, setting his third apple on the table. "That buggy little elf is going to be a king?"

Lauren frowned. "I know, right? But it's the only way we can defeat the Mage Lord."

Oliver put his hands behind his head and sighed. "Okay. We do what we have to."

"You'll have to give him the Blood Sword," Lauren said. "Where is it, anyway?"

Oliver said, "Locked in a trunk upstairs."

Footsteps on the stairwell halted the conversation. In moments, Langley entered the dining room dressed in a plain brown traveling cloak. "The suns are up," he said, but not in the confident voice Lauren had grown to expect from him. "Yarborough is preparing his things. We leave now."

His voice carried a tone of resignation, of someone going to work though they'd rather take the day off. Deeper still, a fearful tone rippled beneath his strained resignation.

* * *

Someone shook Bailey's shoulder and woke her from the first real sleep she'd had in days. Whoever it was was about to get a punch in the nose. But when she opened her eyes and saw the worry in Franky's face, she ignored her frustration and fatigue. "What?"

"I think you should call your mom."

"Why? What's going on?"

"Parker called me. The cops are on their way to pick her up for questioning. They think she has something to do with your disappearances—yours and Lauren's."

"But that's insane," Bailey said.

"Text her or something. Maybe that will get them off her back."

She fumbled with the phone, tried to slide it open to make the call. Still, her brain tried to take in the information, to process it, to put it into some sort of logical order. If they were taking her mother in, it wouldn't be long before they came knocking on Franky's door, especially if Nicole already knew. How much longer would it take the police to figure it out? "Maybe we should move first. What if they check here, too?"

"They already did," Franky said. "Well, Parker did."

"So he knows?"

"He's keeping your secret."

"Why?"

"I convinced him to," Nicole said from the corner. She sat in a chair reading the Bible. She smiled.

Bailey wished, for once, she'd wipe the stupid grin off her face. Must be nice not to have to worry about a family.

"I can be pretty persuasive when I need to be," Nicole said.

Bailey rolled her eyes and pressed her mother's number into her phone. She considered texting her so she wouldn't have to hear the anguish or disappointment in her mother's voice, but it'd be better for the police to have a voice record. It'd make her mother look less guilty.

Her mother answered. "Bailey Renee? Where are you, honey? I'm worried out of my mind! Are you okay?"

"I'm fine, Mom." She glanced at the IV needle in her hand.

"Where are you?"

Why hadn't she thought of an answer before she called?

"Are you there? Sweetie, you have to talk to me!"

"I'm here, Mom. I'm fine."

"Where are you? We've looked everywhere."

"I snuck out of the hospital," Bailey said. "I didn't really have a choice."

"Don't turn this around on me, Bailey. You should still be in the hospital. You're sick, and I'm worried out of my mind. What happens if you fall asleep again? There's no telling what strangers will do to you."

"I'm some place safe. I can't tell you where. Not yet. Not until I find Lauren."

"Don't do this," her mother said with a strange steel in her voice. "I've lost one daughter, I won't lose another because she's off playing cop. Let the police do their job. You have to get better."

"Mom, listen. The police can't help. I can't tell you where I am, but when I come home, I'll bring Lauren with me, okay? You have my word."

Nicole and Franky stared at her.

Ms. Knowles didn't say anything for a while. "I hear beeping. Are you in another hospital?"

"I gotta go." Hanging up, Bailey closed the phone and turned the ringer off. She put her head in her hands and cried.

Franky put a finger under her chin and lifted it until her wet eyes locked on his. "Hey," he said in a quiet voice. "I know. It's almost done. We'll get her back. We'll get you home."

We? What could Franky do? He had no idea what he was saying, but he said it with such assurance, such confidence. And his voice—smooth as a warm latte. She kissed him, her eyes slicked with tears.

"She's going to be fine. We'll get her back."

Bailey couldn't help but believe him.

CHAPTER NINETEEN

"Because of your pride," declares the Lord Adonai, "I will make of you an example of stubborn kings. I shall wrest the water crown from your brow, and sunder your power. I tell you the truth, you will lay at the feet of my servant, and he will stand above you in authority and power. He shall lead his people alongside my Hand and establish a unified kingdom. And your memory will pass from this land. Even your children shall forget your name."
—The Book of Things to Come

THE MOMENTARY RELIEF OF pain Oliver experienced from a good night's sleep on a decent mattress didn't last long. From the time he slung his leg over the white steed from Langley's stable, the familiar ache raced up from the small of his back to the base of his neck. It hurt so bad, Lauren had to ride beside him and keep her hand on his back, sending soothing cold up and down his spine. To make it to camp, he'd need her beside him each step of the way.

Uncharacteristically, Langley offered to ride ahead and make camp with Yarborough so it would be ready when Oliver arrived with Lauren and Aiden. And when their horses clopped to a stop, the tents had been erected, and Langley stoked the flames of a campfire beneath a cook pot. Yarborough, his axe on one side of his belt, his hammer on the other, held an armful of dry wood. "How is your back?" His gruff half-dwarf voice carried through the still night. He dropped the lumber next to a green and white tent.

"Been better," Oliver groaned while drill bits worked their way through his vertebrae.

Aiden slid off his horse, tied it to a tree, and came back to help Oliver off his horse. "I got you. Take it slow."

Yarborough raced over, as did Langley. Strange. Oliver leaned back gently and eased his leg over the oiled leather saddle. Yarborough put a hand under each of Oliver's feet. Langley and Aiden each took a hand. Working together, they pulled him from the horse and set him gently on the ground.

Oliver's legs shook from the long ride. He took a few steps toward the nearest tent and lay on the thickest bedroll. Lauren and Aiden followed him in, and Langley poked his head in after them. Yarborough knelt down and slid his head in under Langley's.

"He ails still?" Langley asked.

"He almost broke his back fighting Belphegor in Margwar," Aiden said. "Hasn't been the same since."

"He is unable to heal himself?" Yarborough asked.

Lauren shook her head. "Can't figure that one out. Seems like he can move when he needs to, when we're in battle. You saw him at Norgren. But if we're not in mortal danger," she motioned to Oliver, who cringed with pain, his head tilted back in agony.

"I have some herbs," Langley said, "and a salve." He disappeared into the other tent.

"You've prayed for him, of course," Yarborough said.

Aiden frowned. "Well, no. Not really."

Why hadn't it occurred to Oliver earlier? "Please," he said. "Please pray for me."

"I don't know how," Lauren said, sorrow lining her voice.

"Prayer's as easy as falling off a horse," Yarborough gruffed. He entered the tent and knelt next to Oliver. Putting his meaty hand on Oliver's back, he began with a simple prayer. "Almighty Adonai, You are the great healer. We pray for your healing touch upon Vicmorn, for your glory and honor."

The pain in his back lessened, but not much. Still, he thanked Yarborough.

Langley returned to the crowded tent with a leather pouch. From it, he pulled several dried leaves. "Open your mouth." Oliver did, and Langley pressed a small yellow leaf to his tongue. "Don't chew this. Suck on it for a few minutes before you bite into it."

Aiden said, "It's pretty crowded in here. I'll check on the fire."

"Be out in a minute," Lauren said. Then, quietly to Aiden, "I want to see what this mystery leaf does."

"You may bite it now. Chew it, but do not swallow. When you've chewed as much as you can, spit the rest of the leaf in this." Langley held a bowl next to Oliver's face. When Oliver did as told, Langley poured some mead from a pouch into Oliver's throat. "Rinse and spit."

Yarborough shook his head. "Such a waste of good dwarvish mead."

The mead tasted brilliant in his mouth, and Oliver wanted to swallow, but the leaf he'd sucked and chewed tasted miserable—bitter and dry. The sharp iron taste made him think he'd bit his tongue, but the lack of pain made him conclude the taste came from the flesh of the leaf. "I'm thirsty," he said.

"Later." Langley pressed a purplish leaf into Oliver's mouth. "This one you must swallow whole. Do not chew."

Oliver closed his eyes and swallowed. Like the other, this leaf had sharp edges. He wished he had water to wash it down. He thought of North Chester, of how he used to get carsick and take Dramamine before long drives. The leaf tasted like the tiny white pills. He wondered if it'd make him sleepy. Sleep would be amazing now.

"How do you feel? Do you ail still?" Yarborough asked.

Remarkably, Oliver shifted his weight, moved from his back to his side. "I still ail, but not as bad."

"The power of Adonai," Yarborough said.

Langley nodded. "Aye."

Oliver opened his eyes. "What?"

"I said aye," Langley repeated.

Lauren lifted a skeptical eyebrow.

Oliver turned his head to better see the half-elf. "You acknowledge Adonai has helped to heal me?"

"If Adonai created Alrujah, then He grew the trees and the leaves that have helped ease your suffering."

Oliver smiled, momentarily forgetting the stabbing pain in his back. Langley's answer gave Oliver the confidence he needed to trust the Blood Sword to the elf. But not now. The time would arrive quickly, but Oliver no longer dreaded the moment. To Langley, he said, "By sunsdown tomorrow night, you will wield the power of the Blood Sword."

Langley stood up. Before he left the tent, in a voice thick with worry, he said, "I know."

* * *

Erica woke up on Ullwen's shoulder. He stared at her, his eyes still blurry with sleep.

Creepy, but adorable.

She leaned forward and kissed his lips.

He pulled away in surprise, as if a snake had bit him.

"Stop it," she said. "You liked it, and there's nothing wrong with it." She leaned forward and kissed him again. This time, he did not pull away. Instead, he took her into his arms and held her tightly. When they stopped kissing, Erica said, "Finally."

Ullwen laughed, then quieted. "Your parents."

"I know." She sat up quickly, wiped the sleep from her eyes, ran her fingers through her short, black hair and, out of habit, checked her breath. She wished she hadn't. What she wouldn't give for a good toothbrush and cinnamon toothpaste.

"Good morrow," Ullwen said in a hushed voice.

"Back attcha," she whispered. She stood up, stretched, and paced the floor, hoping to get the blood back in her legs. Her parents' thin bodies made bumps beneath the animal skins Ullwen had brought the day before. "They're not strong enough to go with us."

"I know."

"I don't want to leave them."

"I know."

Her father stirred. He put an arm around his wife and stared at Erica. "I've waited too many years to wake up to your beautiful face, Lakia."

Erica smiled, something she might grow used to with practice.

Norby kissed Breniveer's neck, and she grinned like a love-struck teenager. Without opening her eyes, she said, "This may be the best day of my life." She stretched her arms far over her head and sat up. "I feel like making breakfast."

"I feel like eating it," Erica said.

"We've no time," Ullwen said. He checked the sword on his hip and gathered the scattered arrows into the quiver. "There is a man I know at the Northern gate. He'll let us pass for the right amount of gold."

"Korodeth will know of our escape. He'll have several guards posted at each exit," Norby said. The long years in jail hadn't dulled the general's cunning.

Erica rubbed her hands together, ran her fingers over the backs of her hands. Her smooth skin still scared her. She'd done this a lot since she found her parents, and, though she loved them, she found herself wanting to put her gloves back on.

Ullwen said, "It's possible. But their loyalties only extend to the depths of their pockets."

"I'm not thrilled with your plan, Ullwen. I mean, we swim the length of the bay to get in, but your plan is to pay off a guard to get out? If they're that easy to bribe, why didn't we walk in the front gates in the first place?"

"Timing. I know but one guard bold enough to look the other way. He is a man who knows how to convince others to hold their tongues. But our first step is disguise." He handed Norby and Breniveer a change of clothes he'd purchased the day before. "We walk in the crowds, and so are invisible."

Erica sighed. This wasn't what she'd planned, but she had little choice. "I still think this is a lame plan. We're saving the world, right? Seems stupid to have to slink around in shadows. We shouldn't be hiding."

"These are strange times," Ullwen said. "We do as we must."

She sighed and packed her things. "Might as well get this over with, then. Lead on, oh handsome warrior."

Ullwen grinned and opened the door. Outside, the sunslight split the morning air. Already, crowds bustled over the cobbled streets. Vendors called their wares from the marketplace near the center of the city. Droves of the populace strolled in and out of taverns, laughing and stumbling.

Norby and Brenniveer walked closely behind her, and she stayed immediately on Ullwen's heels. She wanted to get lost in the crowd but not separated from the others.

"Stay close," Ullwen said. His deep voice rang with determined compassion and a subtle undertone of fear, as if he worried he might lose her. Had he fallen for her? Had she fallen for him?

The thought shocked her—her falling for Ullwen, forgetting completely about Oliver—but she didn't care. Her crummy life had been transplanted by an amazingly cool adventure. She'd been given a gift, some strange reward, though she didn't deserve it. And no maniacal magician or power-crazed lackey would stand in her way of her newfound happiness.

Norby and Breniveer walked beside her now. She wanted to put her arms around them but thought it would look too conspicuous. She might be able to get away with it, though. Few people seemed to notice them. Instead, the guards watched the louder, rowdier bunch. Other guards pushed carts full of bodies toward the bay.

A corpse wagon? Pretty macabre. "What's with the stiffs?"

"The bodies?" Ullwen asked. "Droughtworm. More die each day."

"Gruesome." She took her father's hand in hers.

"It's worsened," Norby said. "I've not seen it claim so many so quickly."

"Best to keep our distance," Breniveer said.

The suns climbed up the blue sky. Wisps of clouds cast thin shadows on the cobbled streets. Breniveer took Erica's hand, and the three walked side-by-side, hand-in-hand, as if she were on her way into her first day of preschool, before her father lost his mind.

"There are Chameleon Soldiers all over the city," Breniveer said. "I'm encouraging them to look elsewhere. But I can only do so much. We may wish to hurry."

"Understood," Ullwen said. He quickened his pace through the market square toward the northern gates.

Overhead, a razorbeak cawed, its long wingspan silhouetted against the lesser sun. It swooped down and alighted on her shoulder, cawed three times. Erica said, "Tell them to meet us at the nar'esh cave whenever they're done."

Ullwen halted, turned to her. "What does it say?"

"The others are on their way to Harael to drop off a sword."

"Harael?" Breniveer said from the doorway.

"The Blood Sword?" Norby asked.

"It can't be," Ullwen said.

"If Neldohr still sits on the throne, your friends will never make it out of Harael alive."

Erica said, "Oh, they will. Count on it. Now, let's move. People are looking at me funny."

"Few can talk to animals," Norby said. "The guards will be stopping to ask us questions quickly."

"Really?" Erica said. "All this Cloak and Dagger spy stuff, and a bird gives us away? I swear this is the lamest thing ever."

In the distance, far on the hills, the castle loomed like a bad omen. Its spires stretched toward the dual suns, and the white stones fashioning the wall between the castle gardens and the city shone bright in the early morning.

She'd prefer to find another way to the gates, a way that didn't take them so close to the castle, but she trusted Ullwen to get her there safely. "How much farther?"

"Stop," Breniveer said, her voice a pinched whisper of fear.

Erica turned.

Her mother's chin was tilted up, and her arm twisted behind her back. Her eyes shone with fear and defiance.

"Show yourself," Ullwen demanded. He pulled his sword from its sheath and leveled it toward Breniveer's invisible assailant.

"Drop your sword, or I will kill the traitor."

Norby's muscles tensed.

Erica's heart seized. How had Breniveer not detected this Chameleon Soldier? She should have felt him a mile away. Unless this was a special Chameleon Soldier, one who had been warded against mind witches.

If it were, it meant he held high rank in the army of invisible soldiers, which meant he was deadly, and likely didn't make hollow threats. "Put it down," she said to Ullwen.

Ullwen clenched his jaw and dropped his sword.

* * *

In Bailey's dream, the skin of Oliver's face had been pulled away. His high cheekbones, crooked teeth, prominent chin poked through thin muscle. Red blood marbled over white bone. His eyes, brown as acorns, remained unscathed. His mouth fell open, closed with a clack of teeth. His tongue writhed like a fat, restless worm.

Bailey reached toward his skeletal grimace, touched his smooth black hair, followed it down to where his ears and sideburns should be. Her heart hammered her chest while her fingers moved in cautious exploration.

Behind him, the Harael Sea spilled out toward the horizon. The suns hung over him like disembodied candles. A stiff wind blew his cerulean robe back. His hood inflated like a plastic bag in the wind.

"Oliver," Bailey Renee said, her throat tight like a fist.

His eyes locked on her. His mouth unhinged again, his tongue flicking, doing silent sit-ups. Slowly, he reached toward her, put his hand on her shoulder.

No wings on her back. They'd have twitched at his touch.

She let out a breath, shivered as chills raced like trains down the rails of her spine.

No wings.

A dream?

Or a warning?

Oliver collapsed. Behind him, the stretch of greenish sea expanded toward Harael, toward the looming statues of the Seers, clearly visible, even from this distance. But something about them had changed. They no longer crossed their arms. Instead, they each raised a shielded arm and held a stone sword in the other. The empty eye sockets glowed red like ember light.

Bailey raced toward the sea, forgetting her lack of wings, forgetting her inability to fly. The Seers had done something to Oliver. Terror kept her feet on the ground, but a seething anger lifted her into the air.

She wouldn't allow anyone to touch Oliver, to hurt him. Not while she lived.

Seconds after she leapt into the air, her body dove headlong into the salty, frigid waters.

She awoke with Oliver's name on her lips. Nicole pressed her shoulders gently. "Easy, Bailey," she said.

Bailey steadied her ragged gasps for air. "Oliver's in trouble."

"I know," the nurse angel said.

Bailey threw her legs over the side of the bed and stood up. She dizzied with the quick change in elevation so soon after her dream or vision or whatever it was. She sat down again, waiting for the room to stop spinning. When her mind slowed and her breathing returned to normal, she looked at Nicole. "You're still here? Don't you ever go home?"

Nicole shrugged. "I live alone. I go out when you're in Alrujah, get some food, run errands, that kind of stuff. But I'm always here before you wake up again."

"So you know when I'm going to fall asleep and when I wake up?"

Nicole smiled. "I've got the inside track."

"Are you the one doing it? The one who makes me fall asleep and wake up in Alrujah?"

Nicole shook her head. "You're what we call a dreamer. There have been other dreamers—those are the ones who tell their stories of faraway lands and elves and dwarves and the like. But dreamers can't control when they slip between the worlds. There are only a few angels who can freely move between the realms. But humans? They can only move through the worlds by the power of Adonai."

"Then I need to talk to him. Can you get a message to him? Tell him to send me back, and let me stay there. I don't want to come back here until I've got Lauren and Oliver with me."

Nicole smiled. "Why don't you tell him yourself?"

* * *

Lauren paused on the dock stretching into the Harael Sea.

Yarborough nearly bumped into her while the others continued down toward Langley's ship. "What's wrong, Indigo?" the half-dwarf asked.

She touched her hand to her heart. "Something's really wrong. I've got a bad feeling about this whole thing."

Yarborough tugged at his white beard. "As do I. I've not seen Langley this quiet in some time. Something's worrying him. And if he's worried, we all should be."

The dock moved beneath her feet, rising with the gentle swells of the sea, and sinking with the ebb. The familiar rhythmic lull of the water reminded her of summers in North Chester. She and Oliver spent several days renting boats and going out on the lakes for her to sketch landscapes for Oliver to digitize for Alrujah. How long ago? Two years? More? Twenty?

In the distance, the tips of white marble buildings and the crown of two stone foreheads crested the horizon. The statues of the Seers. Had to be twenty feet tall, maybe more, given Oliver's penchant for making things bigger than she intended.

Her dress snapped in the stiff wind, and she sighed. "Too late to change plans now, isn't it?"

"Aye." He rammed the butt end of his war hammer into the docks and leaned his chin on it.

It still amazed her to stand next to Yarborough, a half-dwarf of her design. He fulfilled his role flawlessly, and, at times, she had difficulty remembering he'd sprung from her mind.

"If nothing else, we should drink ourselves silly before facing Neldohr. The elf-king is bad business."

She smiled despite the sense of foreboding. Oliver's cloak pulled tight around him. The wind caught his hood and billowed it in the breeze. He lowered himself into the boat, and Lauren's breath caught. Langley followed him in, but Aiden did not. He stood on the edge of the dock, waiting for Lauren and Yarborough to join them. Such a gentleman.

"Whatever happens over there," Lauren said to Yarborough, "I want you to know I'm proud of you."

Yarborough harrumphed. "An odd thing to say to a drunk half-dwarf."

"You're the Nameless Heir. You forfeited your right to the throne because of your father's dedication to Adonai, and you clung to his devotion though it cost you everything you could have."

He pulled himself up to his full height, which put him only to Lauren's shoulder. "If I am the Nameless Heir, as you say, I shall retrieve all I've lost."

She nodded. "I believe you will, with all my heart."

"But if I'm not, I can die as easily as a bug under boot. Harael is a good place for a dwarf to die."

Lauren bit her lip and walked toward Aiden and the boat. "I've already died once, and that's quite enough for me. If I have my way, no one else will die while I'm around, thank you very much."

Yarborough replaced his hammer in its shoulder loop. "If it comes to battle again, I can think of none I'd rather fight beside."

She said, "Same here."

CHAPTER TWENTY

"They call Me by a different name," declares the Lord Adonai, "but they are still My people. Their hearts search for Me, their voices cry out for Me. They are not of this world, but they are of My world. And I shall harvest them unto Myself just as I will harvest Alrujah when its time has come, and My promises have been fulfilled."
—The Book of Things to Come

OUTSIDE THE CASTLE WALLS, Korodeth stood with his arms folded across his chest. Oil slicked his short black hair. His gold tunic displayed the crest of Alrujah. He considered Erica. "I'm surprised it's taken you this long to mount an escape attempt. Truth be told, I planned for this eventuality the moment I threw your treasonous parents in the dungeon. Ribillius insisted you wouldn't mount a rescue attempt. He trusted his kindness in raising you would dissuade you from any foolish attempts to free your parents. Of course, I didn't share his optimism."

Erica wanted to scream at him, to punch him hard in his smug little face, but the invisible soldier had a knife to her mother's throat, and she didn't doubt that he'd use it at the slightest sign of trouble. She took a breath, cleared her mind. She wouldn't play games with him. She was tired of things happening to her in North Chester. Here, in Alrujah, she had a chance to make things happen. She was saving the world from an evil dictator, and this clown wanted to throw her parents in prison.

Not on her watch. "You know, maybe it's better you found us."

Korodeth lifted an eyebrow, as if he wanted to ask why. But he wasn't a man easily baited. He held his tongue, and by doing so, remained the one in control. Instead, he turned to Breniveer. "Your attempts to get into my mind will be as fruitless as your efforts to get into Argus's. I assure you, we are well warded against your dark magic. It would go better for you if you stopped your attempts. They're rather annoying."

"As is having a knife to my throat," she said, her Sylvonyan accent thick on her tongue.

Korodeth nodded, and Breniveer dropped her chin. "Be warned. I've six more soldiers at the ready, all similarly warded."

"You're bluffing," Norby said. His back straightened.

"It would be unwise to call his bluff," Ullwen said.

"Take them to the dungeon," Korodeth said. "I'll inform Ribillius of their treachery."

Erica stepped forward. "Actually, we'll talk to him ourselves. You forget, I'm on a mission to find and kill the Mage Lord in order to protect Ribillius's daughter. I doubt he'd be pleased to hear that you've thrown me in the dungeon."

Korodeth unfolded his arms and considered Erica. He was a man in thought, one weighing his options.

Of course, he had no reason to let them speak to Ribillius. He could throw them in the dungeon and make up whatever story he wanted, one that would likely convince Ribillius. Or he could simply refuse to tell him at all. "And, of course, if you refuse to let us speak with him, I'll send a razorbeak to do it. And who will he send for when he can't decipher the meaning of the message? The only caller in Alrujah. Let's save ourselves the time and talk to him now, what say? If he wants to throw us in the dungeon, let him say it himself."

"The king is unwell," Korodeth said. "I speak in his stead."

"How long has he been ill?" Norby asked, his eyes narrowing. His voice carried the threat of an Alrujahn general, one who itched to put on his armor and sword and settle the debate with steel.

"For some time now," Korodeth said. "But don't take my word for it. You're right. The king should speak with you. You may explain your treachery to him. Bring them." He turned and walked through the gates leading to the gardens outside the castle.

Four invisible hands grabbed Erica's arms, and the edge of an invisible knife pushed lightly into her back. She stiffened, stumbled forward, her heart thrumming in her chest. She walked slowly, defiantly, as did her father and mother and Ullwen, but the knives urged them forward.

＊ ＊ ＊

The boat ride proved much smoother than the horse ride to the boathouse, and the tension in Oliver's back eased. The stiff, salty sea breeze filled the white sails of Langley's dhow like a lung. The mast pointed back at a forty-five-degree angle, and the inflated sail, from the shore, resembled an elvish ear. Lauren worked her hands over his back, releasing a consistent numbing cold. Langley had given him another yellow leaf and another purple to ease his pain and nausea. Leaves from the tresica tree, Langley told him, from different seasons. The yellow leaf was poisonous to swallow, though when it reacted with saliva, it created a mild anesthesia. The purple, harvested weeks before winter, no longer remained poisonous, and aided quick-healing.

Langley stood at the front of the ship. Oliver sat on a crate near the center. They'd been on the sea for more than an hour when Harael came into view. The white-marble city had been built on a small cluster of islands in the middle of the sea. Each island, even the sea itself, seemed to be on a different elevation. The physics of a sea like this baffled him, though he had designed it. Seeing it in person swelled him with pride while simultaneously humbling him. Though he had coded it, he didn't have the power to give it life. Only Adonai, only God, had the power to make a miracle like Harael come to life.

"How long?" Aiden asked.

"Another hour. Maybe a bit more," Langley said.

The statues of the Seers, also crafted from white marble, stood twenty feet high. The likeness of the elvish half-abominations wore long, flowing robes and crossed their arms. Each had an eye missing. Oliver shivered. The cold in his back must be from Lauren's hands, but terror didn't make it any easier.

The statues felt ... alive. They seemed to glow, as the Chameleon Soldiers did. Their mirrored mail made them nearly invisible, but Vicmorn's father Eljah had taught him how to sense their life force, their spirits. The gift had served him well already, and it might again. But if those statues started moving, they'd all be in a world of trouble.

"Lauren," he whispered. "What do you make of those statues?"

"They're big," she said in an equally soft voice.

"You get a bad feeling about them?"

"You have no idea."

"Get the sense they're alive?"

"Please tell me you didn't make them into some crazy boss."

"No. Promise. But they're glowing. You don't see them glowing?"

"No."

Oliver frowned. "They could mean trouble for us."

Lauren's hands stopped on his back. She knelt beside him. "Harael won't fall without a fight."

"Did it say if we'd survive the fight?"

She shrugged. "Only that the hand would be divided, whatever that means. I figured it meant Erica and Ullwen were in Alrujah and we were here."

The sail rippled in the breeze. Oliver thought of clean sheets and freshly made beds. He thought of blank canvases, of a painter's palette, of the hand of Adonai painting the Harael Sea, the boat, and them in it.

"If they are alive, do you think we can beat them?"

Oliver wanted to say yes, but an unsettling doubt darkened his vision.

"I don't want to die again," Lauren said.

Oliver stood, back straight, his rognak staff firm in his hand. He wanted his voice to be firm, to sound of conviction and confidence. "We have Adonai. If our God is for us, who can be against us?"

* * *

Night fell on North Chester quick as a candle being blown out. Nicole removed Bailey's IV, and Bailey paced the room. *Tell Adonai herself?* Helplessness soured her stomach. She put her jacket on, considered jumping from the second story window into the foot-deep snow, considered running into the dark and the cold and screaming until she passed out, anything to get her back to Alrujah. But reason pressed against her anger, and though it didn't calm her, it kept her from following the rash desires of her adrenaline. "You mean prayer, right?"

"I assume you've done it before." Nicole's eyes glowed gold.

"Not really. But I've seen Oliver do it."

Oliver, her sister's dearest friend, might die if she didn't get back to Alrujah. The boy genius who helped her with her calculus, with her chemistry. She'd known him since first grade, and she wouldn't stand by while he raced headlong into some unforeseen danger.

The Seers. It had to be them. Somehow, prayer didn't seem like a very powerful weapon against the evil of the Seers. "So, what, I bow my head and close my eyes and talk to God?"

"That's the basic idea, yes."

"How are our worlds joined?"

Nicole unplugged the IV monitor from the wall. "I don't know. Pacha can explain it better than I. The way he said it, Alrujah is contained within earth, and earth within Alrujah."

"That makes no sense." Bailey took her jacket off. Too hot with it on. The air near the window felt ten degrees cooler. She moved to the center of the room, shoved her hands in her pockets. Pain twinged the back of her hand where the IV had been. "But Oliver and Lauren created the game, created the world. Even if it's real now, they still made it, right?"

Nicole shook her head. "Alrujah has existed as long as Earth. What Vicmorn and Indigo thought was creation was really revelation."

"What do you mean?"

"Adonai gave them the vision of Alrujah. They believed it came from their imaginations, but Adonai was the one who placed it within their minds, as He has done for centuries. Our worlds have crossed before, and they will cross again in the future."

Bailey stopped pacing. "Scoot over," she said. Nicole did, and Bailey sat down with a sigh next to her. "*The Book of Things to Come*," Bailey said.

"Exactly."

"But it keeps changing."

"As it must. Our decisions affect the future. Very few things are set in stone."

"So Oliver can die?"

Nicole nodded. "Everyone can die. Even angels."

She had to get back to Alrujah. "Sleeping pills," Bailey said.

Nicole's eyes narrowed, and, for a moment, Bailey thought she might start glowing again, might reveal her wings and speak with two voices.

"It's worth a shot. I have to do something."

Nicole stood up. "I'm not sure it will work, but you're welcome to try. After you pray."

Bailey had hoped it wouldn't come to that. She wasn't particularly religious and felt awkward talking to God. But if it meant saving Oliver, she'd try it.

* * *

Korodeth's office seemed simple enough. The stone walls and glassless window mimicked all the others in the castle. A black harspus-wood table sat near the center of the room, as did wood chairs on either side. Purple and gold Alrujahn banners adorned the walls. Korodeth had arranged several daggers of varying length along the table. Two unlit candles stood on opposite corners of the table in thick, silver holders.

Erica, her parents, and Ullwen refused to sit, so Korodeth stood as well. He rolled up a map of Alrujah and set it on a smaller table near the iron-banded wooden door. "When you departed with Indigo and the monk," he said, "I hadn't anticipated seeing you back here so soon. And I had not anticipated you arriving with such an odd group of traveling companions. A Varuthian traitor and two criminals."

"I am not a traitor," Ullwen said in a low, wolfish voice.

Norby adopted a similar growl. "Nor are we criminals. You arrested us to secure your position as Captain of the Watch. We committed no crime."

"Hiding a daughter with such a particular set of talents is a crime," Korodeth said. His arms strained against the mail under his uniform tunic. "The law clearly states all such talented individuals must be recorded by the Keeper of the Chronicles. You had several years to record her name and talents, yet you refused."

"Because you wanted to use her as a weapon," Breniveer said. Her thin arms crossed her chest, but her hands clenched into fists. Her fierce protectiveness made Erica's heart swell.

"Those were difficult times. King Ribillius saw the need for any and all assistance we could find. We are again in difficult times. You never submitted yourself for recording either, which is another fault, on the same lines as treason. You're nothing more than a wandering band of traitors."

"Watch it," Erica said. If she could, she'd scratch this man's face off, but if he was connected enough to have someone ward his mind, and his soldiers' minds, against mindwitching, she needed to be careful. Maybe he even knew a thing or two about magic himself. Plus, he was perhaps the best-trained soldier in all Alrujah. Somehow, she doubted she'd last long in a fight with him.

Korodeth removed the dagger in his hip sheath and replaced it with another, nearly identical blade. "By law, I can have you all executed."

Ullwen said, "Only Ribillius can demand life in payment for crimes. You wear no crown."

Korodeth's upper lip pulled back in a slight sneer before finding its place with the lower. He didn't speak for a moment. Smiling, he said, "You've put your trust in Ribillius. And so I find it fitting that, by his word, your fate will be sealed. Come, he is ill, but I will call for him.

Then you will see, his love for justice far outweighs his love for traitors."

Timing, Erica thought, is everything. She'd have her chance to smack this man, and when the opportunity presented itself, she'd make sure to enjoy it.

* * *

Yarborough steered Langley's dhow as well as any elf. In the distance, the sprawling water city grew larger and larger, its white marble structures tall and bright against the backdrop of the green sea. Each of the islands, clustered in the shape of a crescent moon, claimed a different elevation. The sea itself grew restless around Harael. Waterfalls flowed in, around, and through the islands, culminating in a deep crater of water like Niagara Falls.

The elves watched their coming. Several smaller boats, with thin, tall sails came out to meet them. The elves in the boats wore battle armor and scowls. The six smaller ships surrounded Langley's dhow quickly. Lauren took two steps back from the edge of the boat.

"State your business," an elf in a golden helm said.

Langley's eyebrows slanted toward his nose in anger or surprise. "I am Langley, ambassador to Harland, and I have urgent business to discuss with King Neldohr."

"The Seers have told us of your coming," the golden helmed elf said. "Follow us to Torap."

Aiden whispered to Lauren, "Isn't that one of the Seers' names?"

"Yes. The good one. It's also the name of the central island, where the throne room and capitol building are. It's the heart of Harael."

Yarborough adjusted the course of the boat to follow the elvish warships. The deck moved beneath Lauren's feet, and she steadied herself on Aiden's arm.

"I got a bad feeling about this," he said.

"That makes three of us."

Though Lauren had described the story of Harael in her journals, she had nearly forgotten the poverty and fear of the elvish populace. After spending so much time with Langley, a lithe warrior, she'd forgotten how frail the rest of the elves had become under the squandering reign of Neldohr.

Hunger emaciated the elves, all but the politicians, who ensured they had enough to eat, often to the detriment of the denizens. The impoverished elves ambled through the streets, picking berries from the thorny plants growing between the wooden homes of the residential area of Torap. Their chipped yellow teeth protruded from their lips at odd times, as if even their teeth searched for food.

Contrarily, the war elves all stood as tall as Langley and moved as swiftly. And just as Langley detected the magic within her, Lauren sensed the magic in the war elves. Each possessed a deep arcane arsenal. Their fingers twitched with the power undulating within them.

On either side of the capitol building, the twenty-foot statues of Torap and Uhesdey stood like sentries, their stone robes frozen in an invisible wind, arms crossed over their chests, hands draped on their shoulders in a position reminding her of the dead, of a corpse in an open casket.

"Something's very wrong here," Oliver said.

Neldohr stood in the entryway holding a spiked staff. "You have come without an invitation."

Langley stepped to the front of the group. "I was unaware I needed an invitation to visit the kingdom I serve."

"You have allied yourself with the enemy, and are thus a traitor of the crown."

"We come on a mission of peace, good King Neldohr," Yarborough gruffed. "We bring a gift for you." He nodded to the Blood Sword, still sheathed and attached to Oliver's golden rope belt.

Oliver touched the scabbard and closed his eyes. He mumbled something incoherent, likely breaking the curse on the obsidian sword. He'd waited this long, and no better time would present itself. Now or never.

"I'll have no gift from humans, nor from dwarves. The elves are beholden to no one."

Oliver lifted his chin. In a voice an octave lower than his normal tone, he said, "We come in service of Adonai."

"Adonai is no god of mine!" Neldohr shouted. His pale face took on a reddish hue in the waning sunlight. He rammed the butt of his pike into the marble steps in front of the capitol building. The war elves surrounding him unsheathed their swords. "I, Neldohr of Sumerya, King of Elves, declare Langley of Erul banished! He and his companions will leave my kingdom or they will perish!"

The golden armor of the war elves gleamed in the setting suns. Lauren sensed a surge of magic within them and braced herself for the coming battle. The crackle of electricity raced from her chest to her legs, to her feet. Blue sparks leapt from fingertip to fingertip. The ends of her hair crackled.

Aiden moved from her and bared his blade.

Langley and Yarborough steadied themselves, drew their weapons, and dug their heels into the soft soil beneath their feet.

"You have been warned." Oliver's voice sounded as if it belonged to someone else. He spoke in a guttural tone, one like Jaurru's war cries. He raised his staff, and the tip of it flashed blue and white. Lauren's eyes burned.

When she opened them again, all thirty-six war elves were gone.

Neldohr's eyebrows slouched in confusion. "Where?" he asked in a hushed whisper.

"Scattered across Alrujah," Oliver said in the voice of another.

Neldohr bent his ears back and bared his teeth. He inclined his staff in front of his mouth and shouted. The steel blade atop glowed red. The force of his shout, magically amplified by the blade, knocked her off her feet. She slid backward through the soft soil until her head lolled over the lip separating land and water. She sat up quickly, readied a burst of lightning. Langley, Yarborough, and Aiden lay on their backs as well. Only Oliver seemed unfazed.

No one hurt Aiden. She loosed a sizzling bolt of electricity at Neldohr.

But the arcing blue light never reached him.

The Mage Lord stood beside Neldohr. When had he shown up? He absorbed the electricity in the tip of his partisan, then stretched it out toward the two statues.

In his booming, magical voice, Neldohr shouted, "Seers! Heed the call of the king of your people! Smite the heretics!"

As Aiden and Yarborough and Langley righted themselves, the Mage Lord vanished, as if he'd never been there in the first place.

Then, the fingers of the giant stone statues twitched.

CHAPTER TWENTY-ONE

King Solous pulled the Blood Sword from the dead hand of Paramir,
King of Elves. He kept it in a locked room within the castle, away from
human and elvish eyes. But the elves would not be denied. They stole
into the castle, took the cursed blade, and returned to their post in Fort
Norgren, which is on Vesper's Mountain.
—The Book of Things to Come

ERICA THOUGHT OF SPARKY back in Varuth. She needed to get back to him, needed to see how well he recovered, needed to bury her gloved hands in his thick fur and feel the warmth of his body leaning against her leg. She wished he waited with her now, in her castle room with Ullwen and her parents, watched closely by ten Alrujahn guards.

Korodeth disappeared shortly after bringing them here. He posted the guards outside their room and several inside. It didn't leave much room for pacing.

Outside the window, gardens ran up toward the castle on softly sloping hills. Purple flowers grew in abundance, and, even in the cold, trees blossomed. The sweetly pungent smells reminded her of something, a ghost of a recollection, something strangely familiar and disconnected from anything familiar—like recalling someone else's memory.

She closed her eyes, drew in the sweetness carried by the chill air, and her mind conjured an image of herself as a child. Not in North Chester, not in the foster home, not on the beach with her friend. She remembered herself as Lakia, growing up in the castle of Alrujah.

Seven years old, she played with a little blonde girl in a flowing white dress. The blonde girl wore a silver band woven in her hair. Erica recognized her as Lauren, as Indigo. They hid in the trees, ran through the flowers, laughed.

Erica had never laughed so hard, been so happy, in North Chester or anywhere else. Guilt overtook her for a moment. If her parents had been thrown in a dungeon, the child Lakia should not have felt such joy. It made no sense. Opening her eyes, she turned to her parents. "How old was I when they took you away?"

Sitting on Erica's bed, Breniveer said, "Three."

"I remember," Erica said.

Ullwen sat near the window, arms crossed over his knee. His eyes traced the path of the silver-armored guards.

"Relax," Erica said. "Once we talk to Ribillius, we can get out of here."

"We shouldn't be speaking to him," her father said. "Korodeth is the archduke. He has the authority to imprison us without Ribillius's approval. He would not let us speak to the king if he didn't have something to gain."

"I agree," Ullwen said. "We are not among friends. Nor would we be wise to consider Ribillius an ally. He may prove as vengeful as Korodeth."

Erica whispered, "You think we should make a break for it? Maybe hop out the window and run for the hills?"

"We wouldn't make it far," Brenniveer said.

Her father put an arm around her. He stared at Ullwen, who nodded. Of course, they wouldn't say anything more, but Erica got the sense the two warriors were making plans. Wasn't that how generals and spies thought?

Another memory, somewhere around eight years old. A woman, tall and thin, in a green dress, opened the door to her room. Erica arranged flowers, sang to the bees. The woman had a voice of one who loved Erica—soft and patient.

The queen? Must be.

The woman in green cried; she fell on her knees and hugged Erica.

But the woman melted from the memory, replaced with a soldier in bloodstained armor. Erica, now eleven, stood on a hill overlooking a battle. The air rang brightly with the sound of metal on metal, men screaming and shrieking, armored horses trampling through the onslaught and chaos. Erica lifted up her arms and cawed. Soldiers raged around her—protected her from men who sought to kill her.

Razorbeaks purpled the sky. They dove down in droves. She grunted. Beresus marched from the neighboring forest and attacked the enemy soldiers. Pain seared her shoulder as someone grabbed her by the wrist and lifted her onto the back of his horse.

The woman in the green dress returned, knelt over Erica in her bed in the castle. Her hand worked Erica's shoulder. Warmth and relief spread through her shoulder, through the rest of her as well. A name came to her: Trinie.

The memory vanished, but the profound fear and love and relief still encircled her. Sadness washed over her. As much as Trinie cared for Erica, Breniveer had been denied the opportunity to raise her. Korodeth had no business letting an eleven-year-old stand in the midst of a war, caller or not. "Korodeth should be the one in prison," she muttered.

Her father took Erica into his thin arms. "Yes, he should, butterfly."

How long had it been since she'd heard him call her that? She put her head on his chest, wrapped him in her arms, and cried.

* * *

The words came out of his mouth, and whatever power scattered the war elves across Alrujah came through him, but Oliver didn't do any of it. Instead of scaring him, though, it comforted him. Adonai stood with them. Adonai was for them. And if their God was for them, who could stand against them?

No one. But the massive twenty-foot tall polished white marble Seers would try.

They moved slowly at first, stepping off the marble foundation stones and sinking inches deep in the soft soil of Torap Island. A faint, purplish glow radiated in their chests. Oliver shook his head. Adonai would get them out of this, but how? He steadied himself to move and move quickly. The others, Lauren, Aiden, Yarborough, Langley, would need him to be on constant vigil, healing whatever injuries they might sustain. But if they got crushed, Oliver doubted any of his prayers would bring them back from something so lethal.

Yarborough raised his war hammer, and with a throaty bellow called, "For Adonai, that Neldohr will see His mighty power! That Neldohr will bend his knees to the God of gods!" The half-dwarf raced toward the towering statues, hammer high over his head. Torap, discernable by the missing left eye, brought his leg up. The marble knee hovered two stories high before he brought it down again, directly over Yarborough. The spry halfling rolled out of the way, righted himself as the ground shook under the impact, and swung his hammer with enough force to put a horse into orbit. It hit Torap's ankle, and the marble cracked like an egg.

"They can be beat!" Aiden cried, his shield protecting his chest. "Steel your nerves, soldiers! Today, victory will be ours!"

Before he'd completed his war cry, new white marble melted into the cracks on Torap's ankle and healed it. The resulting sheen of new marble gleamed like the flesh of a scar.

Oliver unfastened the Blood Sword from his belt and tossed it to Langley. "Take Neldohr. It has to be you," Oliver said. Torap swung a hand the size of an SUV at him, and he leapt six feet in the air, barely clearing the attempted swat.

Langley caught the blade as Lauren worked spell after spell—lightning, ice, fire. Nothing worked.

"Try quake!" Oliver shouted.

Neldohr tucked one end of his bladed staff under his arm and rushed out to meet Langley. Deftly, he leapt, twisted, and brought the bladed portion of the staff spinning toward Langley's face. The half-elf ducked and extended the Blood Sword up, slicing the staff in two.

Neldohr didn't stop. He jabbed at Langley with the remaining stub. Langley parried it easily and leveled the obsidian blade at Neldohr's chest. "Command the Seers to retake their places, and I will allow you to live."

The elf-king sneered and brought his hands back. An intense, white light formed in the place his palms met. He extended his arms forward, and light burst from them.

Langley positioned the Blood Sword in front of him. The black sword absorbed the energy. "You cannot beat me. The Blood Sword holds the power of all its victims."

"You are a worthless traitor," Neldohr said.

Langley shook his head. "I'd hoped I'd not have to do this, my king." He closed the gap between the two. Neldohr stumbled backward to the steps of the capitol building, and Langley lanced him through the heart. Neldohr dropped to his knees, and Langley extracted the obsidian blade, now bathed entirely in the blood of the elf-king. Moments later, his blood vanished into the blade, absorbed as a sponge absorbs water.

For a moment, the Seers stopped their assault. Slowly, Uhesdey pulled a marble fist back, his elbow pointing toward the lesser sun, and brought it racing toward Oliver. Oliver dug his feet into the soil, extended his staff toward Uhesdey's rushing fist. The fist shattered on the staff. Stiff white fingers cracked and flew off in awkward angles, some landing knuckle deep in the soil, others impaling walls, some splashing into the

Harael Sea. The shattered remnants of the hand, all jagged marble up to the wrist, drew back to Uhesdey's chest like a frightened puppy.

Uhesdey groaned, a sound like an avalanche of granite. His marble lips parted, his milky eyelid blinked over his remaining eye. His tongue worked the top of his mouth, darted through his parted teeth, and words like boulders crashed from his mouth. The sky darkened with thick, black clouds. The suns vanished in inky fog.

Even through the gloom, the purplish radiance of life still glowed softly within the chest of the Seers. But, in the darkness, Oliver noticed something else—more purplish glows, brighter than the Seers, or anyone else's spirit luminosity. These radiated from beneath the ground, up the slight incline of the hill on which the capitol building had been built.

The pedestals. No—something in them.

"Smash the pedestals!" he shouted. "Something's in them!"

"Can't see them," Aiden shouted.

Yarborough's voice swam through the fog. "Vicmorn! We need your help! Clear the skies!"

Oliver knelt, but only for a second. Something massive and hard as stone hit him in the chest. He flew backward, hoping his breath would come back to him, hoping to be able to roll with the momentum and right himself.

But his breath never returned. And rather than landing on the island, he splashed into the water. He struggled to breathe, to move, but his limbs didn't respond to his commands. His mind darkened as the water of the Harael Sea closed over his shoulders, his face, the tip of his nose. He tried to scream, but the salty water rushed in the moment his jaws separated. He swallowed, choked, gasped. And still, his arms and legs would not move.

* * *

Erica remembered the throne room exactly as it appeared—expansive columns running the length of the hall, two purple upholstered golden high-back thrones, stairs running on either side behind the thrones, swords and shields hanging on the walls, glass cases displaying prominent weapons and documents near each column.

Ribillius waddled down the left flight of stairs and, with a flick of his left wrist, motioned the silver armored guards to exit the room. He'd changed since the last time she'd stood here, so many weeks ago. Or had it been months at this point? He'd lost an alarming amount of weight. His stately purple cape billowed around him, easily two sizes too big. His skin paled, and his hair whitened. He'd aged years, maybe even a decade.

"Lakia," he said, and coughed. He walked toward her, eyes wide, like a child seeing a spread of gifts under a Christmas tree. "You are well?"

She glared at Korodeth. "Well is a relative term."

"Your hair. What have you done to it?"

"Long story."

Ribillius took a step back. Ullwen, Norby, and Breniveer knelt, and Erica followed suit. Best not to upset the most powerful man in Alrujah.

"Enough with the kneeling." He pulled her up into his arms. His embrace felt cold, awkward and stiff. She hugged him back, only because she thought he wanted her to. He smelled sour, and she wondered when he'd last bathed.

How sick was he, exactly? What did he have? She wanted to shower in hand sanitizer.

"How are the others? I trust they're well. Captain Korodeth keeps me informed as he is able. They travel to Harael? I wonder what they may hope to accomplish there. The elves are no friends of humans."

She pushed away from him as politely as possible. "I'm not here because of them." She took Norby and Breniveer by their hands and raised them to their feet. "I'm here because of my parents."

Ribillius took his seat on the throne. "So you seek me as a king, and not as a father as you used to."

Memories soared in her mind like kites. He'd been a father to Lakia at times. "As much as I loved you, you were always king first and father second. To me, at least."

"Your Highness," Korodeth said, raising his hand like a child in school. "If I may."

Ribillius waved him off much as he had the guards. "You may speak when I ask, not before." He folded his hands and adopted his best kingly pose. "So be it, Lakia. If it is a king you seek, it is a king you will receive. But I am a just king and will hear you speak your case before I punish you for releasing two traitors from my dungeons."

"They're not traitors," she snapped. "The only thing they're guilty of is loving me. They knew Korodeth would put me on the battlefield long before I was ready. What child has business in the throes of war? They did not betray you, King. You betrayed them by allowing Korodeth to lock them up. All I've done is set right a wrong committed by the good Captain here." She pointed vehemently at Korodeth. All the hurt from North Chester joined with all her sorrow from Alrujah and welled up in her like a volcano.

"You want to talk about traitors," she continued, still pointing to Korodeth, who held his head high and did not break his gaze at Ribillius. "What about this guy? He took the best general you've ever had, the strongest mindwitch this side of the Fellian River, and locked them up in a dungeon where they were useless to you. And then he burns down the monastery in the Cerulean Woods. If that's not treachery, I don't know what is."

Ribillius straightened the crown on his head. The midnight sapphire glowed in the light of the torch-lit sconces adorning each column. "The monastery?"

Korodeth frowned. "The monks are not what they seem. They attacked and killed one of my Chameleon Soldiers."

"A lie, your highness," Breniveer said, her eyes still on the cobbled floor.

Ribillius stood, leaning a bit to his left, his crown slipping slightly on his scalp. His left hand held close to his stomach, he limped toward the steps leading from the elevated throne to the floor before him. The gold chains circling his neck swayed with his unsteady gait. Each finger glinted with a gold ring, which shone against his ashen pallor. Sweat collected under his white hair.

No way Erica had been gone this long. No way he'd been this old when she left. Did everyone age faster in Alrujah? No chance. Korodeth hadn't aged a day, nor had Ullwen. Something was seriously wrong.

Droughtworm? Is this what it did to you?

"Enough," Ribillius said. The word, elongated like a snake, slithered out of his mouth. To Korodeth, he said, "The monks are the very mouth of Adonai. You would cut off His blessing from Alrujah? From my throne?"

"They were the mouth of Adonai, my lord. Much has changed in Alrujah in the last few weeks. Your illness may be clouding your perception. This is why I never mentioned it to you. I did not want to upset you further, for fear of your health."

Ribillius coughed and made no attempt to keep his spittle from flying in Korodeth's face. He set his jaw and ran his tongue under his lips, pushing them out like he had something stuck in his teeth. "My health is fine. You forget your position, Captain. As long as there is breath in my lungs, I am king of Alrujah. You may not choose which information I need. Your duty is to tell me all you know."

Korodeth's lips pulled tight. "Yes, my lord."

Ullwen spoke softly. "Your honor, if I may."

Ribillius sat heavily in his throne and coughed again. "Who are you?"

Ullwen put a fist over his heart and bowed his head. "I am Ullwen of Varuth," he said. "Varuthian Elite, First Class, my liege."

Ribillius's face reddened. "You attacked my daughter," he whispered.

"No no no," Erica said. "Listen, my king or liege or whatever I'm supposed to call you." She put a hand on Ribillius's chest. She'd been here before, having to talk her way out of sticky situations. How many times had she and Indigo—Lauren, she reminded herself—gotten themselves into trouble? "He's on our side. He's saved our lives more times than I can count. He protected Indigo from the nar'esh when we made our way toward Margwar."

"Margwar?" Ribillius said. He glanced at Korodeth, an unspoken criticism of the poor job he'd done keeping Ribillius informed.

"You want Indigo safe? You let my parents stay free. They'll come with us to stand against the Mage Lord. Why wouldn't you let them free? They've done nothing wrong, and they give Indigo a better chance of survival."

Ribillius coughed harshly and cradled his ribs. He winced, rubbed his forehead with his thumb and forefinger.

"Highness, she speaks deceptively," Korodeth whispered.

Ribillius snapped. "Seal your lips, Korodeth, or I'll have them sealed for you."

Korodeth took three steps forward, his leather boots slapping the stone floor like bathmats on tile. "I want Indigo safe as much as you, sire, but your first duty is to your kingdom. These two have flown against your crown and denied your authority. Freeing them will invite riots in the streets, will elicit cries of deception and injustice."

Ribillius leaned his head back against the throne. Shoulders slumped, he said, "My daughter's safety is the safety of Alrujah. My duty to my kingdom is my duty to her. Without her, Alrujah has no hope against the Mage Lord."

"There are other ways," Korodeth said, moving forward again, each step slower than the last.

Erica moved between him and the king. "Wow. Talk about speaking deceptively. You sound like a lawyer."

"A what?" Ullwen asked.

"A lawyer. A slimy animal that crawls on its belly and hisses."

"Like a snake," Ullwen said.

"Exactly," Erica said. She turned back to Ribillius. "Let's face it. If Alrujah survives, it will be because of Indigo. Imagine what she could do with a mindwitch and an Alrujahn general."

Ribillius's voice wheezed. "Too many soldiers cannot a secret keep."

"Listen, the Mage Lord isn't exactly a secret, and neither is *The Book of Sealed Magic*."

Ribillius considered Norby and Breniveer. "You were a good general," he said.

"Thank you, sire."

"I will make your release conditional upon your consent to aid my daughter in her quest for *The Book of Sealed Magic*."

"We will, sire," Breniveer said, her face bright with her smile.

"Sire," Korodeth said.

"I've made my decision, Captain."

"It is a trap, sire."

Erica put her hand on Korodeth's shoulder. "It's over, sport. Deal with it."

Korodeth grabbed her wrist roughly. "It's never over."

CHAPTER TWENTY-TWO

*And I looked up, and behold, I saw another world, a new heaven and
a new Alrujah. Adonai moved among its people as He moves among
us. He speaks to them as He does to us. I walked among them, but they
could not see me. I spoke, but they did not hear.*
—The Book of the Ancients

S
OMETHING MUST BE WRONG. Oliver should have said something,
should have done something by now. But he never answered
Yarborough's call to clear the sky.

Lauren set her jaw tight in the blackness of the thick, suffocating
clouds crawling over the island. She pushed the thought of Oliver hurt
or dead from her mind and concentrated on doing what must be done.
In clouds this dark, they'd be easy prey for the stalking statues of the
Seers, or worse. Sounds creaked and moaned in the clouds, sounds
like avalanches, but Torap had no mountains to speak of, only verdant,
mossy hills.

She closed her eyes—no difference in the dark. She thought of wind,
of hurricanes and tornados. She thought of warm fronts and cold fronts
and pressure systems and every other weather principle she'd learned
in science last year. Her fingers twitched, ran in circles. Her wrists and
arms spun with them. She kicked the toe of one foot into the ground
and spun like a music box dancer.

Wind circled around her, pushed out in all directions. The black
clouds pulled into the wind and ran concentrically with the storm
flowing around Lauren. Her skin, inexplicably, began to glow white.
With the stygian darkness of the clouds circling her, she must look like
an inverse black hole.

Another second, and another. A minute of swirling air streams,
and she turned the winds loose toward Torap. As she hoped, he'd not
used the cover of dark to move positions. The black tornado confused
him long enough for Lauren to repeat Oliver's last order. "Get those
foundations out of the ground!"

Yarborough already stood over one. He worked on it, slamming his hammer into the broadside with every ounce of strength he had. Each blow rang with the sound of metal on stone, the sound of Yarborough's brusque war cry.

Uhesdey turned his attention from the tornado to the dwarf. He opened his remaining hand and moved to swat Yarborough. Before the marbled palm struck, Aiden tackled Yarborough. Whatever football skill he had in North Chester hadn't left him here.

Torap opened his throat and bellowed. The cause of the creaking avalanche sounds in the blackness revealed themselves: Marble fangands and beresus. They'd caught her attention when she first arrived on Torap Island, their macabre faces twisted in the attitude of war. Neldohr's warped taste baffled Lauren at first, but now its purpose became clear. Additional defenses.

"Heads up!" Lauren called. Ten fangands and ten beresus stalked toward them, shoulders hunched in the posture of battle. Though not as fast as their living counterparts, the statues possessed a speediness that belied their stonework. She worked the feeling of cold from her torso to her fingertips until giant blocks of ice formed on the feet of the monsters. It worked well, but not fast enough.

Langley moved in and out of the beresus, using the Blood Sword to separate limbs from bodies. He used the concentrated light spell to punch holes through their chests. While his attention on the Seers waned, Uhesdey plucked him up like a mother collecting dirty laundry.

Torap punched the soil near his feet. Green vines sprouted around Aiden and Yarborough, who'd righted themselves and prepared for the onslaught of stone monsters. Aiden moved the dwarvish sword with deft, swift movements, but the sheer number of vines overwhelmed him. They pulled them down, and a vine grew over each of their throats.

Aiden choked. Yarborough's face turned red.

No. It couldn't end like this. They needed something, needed a miracle. *If we die here, we are absolutely dead.*

Lauren backed away from the pressing of the fangands and beresus until her heels dipped into the water of the Harael Sea. Seaweed pressed against her feet. No. Not seaweed. Too hard. Oliver's rognak staff floated in the tide, nudged her foot like a puppy wanting to be petted. She snatched it up quickly, and everything went black.

* * *

A fist closed around Oliver's robe, and he startled awake. The water of the Harael Sea rushed over his face, and panic seared his chest. How long had he been underwater? How long since he'd last taken a breath? Two lights shimmered near the surface, and he allowed himself enough calm to break the surface. The hand pulled him into a narrow, canoe-like boat. Oliver rolled onto his side and coughed, gasped for breath.

"The Seers demand a sacrifice," a thin voice said.

Blood smeared the face of Oliver's rescuer. A war elf, complete with golden helmet and red tunic beneath a golden cuirass. He extracted a dagger from his hip sheath and raised it high in the air.

"They will honor this sacrifice over all others. This will show their superiority to Adonai."

Oliver said nothing, only breathed. He had no staff, no real means of defense, except prayer. But rather than praying for himself, he found himself thinking of his friends, thinking of the massive statues tormenting them, threatening their very lives.

"And after I kill you, I will take your face from your skull. I will lay it at the feet of the Seers for all to see; Adonai is nothing."

The elf brought the dagger down on Oliver's chest, but he felt no sharp pain, felt no metal point on his skin. Instead, the amulet beneath his cloak pressed hard against his sternum. Oliver used the war elf's momentary confusion to grab the knife. With one hand, he wiped the blood out of his eyes while the other twisted the war elf's arm behind its back. "No sacrifices here today," he said. "Adonai will overcome as He always does."

Something in the distance caught his attention—another boat closing toward them fast. The silent woman on board bent toward them. Her long black hair surfed in the air currents. Her narrow eyes gleamed black. Two sword hilts protruded from her shoulders. She wore a red cloth over her nose and mouth, and a tight black wraparound tunic and loose-fitting black pants.

"No," the war elf said. "Not her."

In a flash, the woman hurdled over the boat's edge and, with two steps over the water, leapt toward Oliver's boat. She flashed both blades out. One sank into the belly of the elf. Oliver had only enough time to dodge the tip of the blade as it came through the body of the elf and pull the dagger up to his face in time to block her second blade from decapitating him.

Now standing in the boat, she pushed the dead elf into the sea and held both swords toward Oliver.

"Who are you?" he asked.

She spun in a flourish. He had no time to react. The ruby-tipped hilt of her blade crashed into Oliver's temple. He crumpled into the boat.

* * *

Lauren felt like she swam in milk. Weightless, she saw only white. Even her lungs filled with fluid. But her surprising lack of fear puzzled her more than anything.

She would die again, and after, the judgment. Her vision may have blurred, but her reasoning seemed clear. Here in the vat of milk, she'd reached a moment of clarity unlike any she'd ever experienced.

All sensation ceased. She saw nothing, heard nothing, felt nothing coarse or soft, cold or hot. She smelled nothing, tasted nothing. Her senses had been flipped off, which gave her clarion reason.

Everything Oliver said over the last few years fell into place. All the pictures lined up like a mosaic, a huge picture of something composed entirely of smaller photographs of the same thing. She stepped back now, and the larger image revealed itself to her.

A flash of memory—she was dead, floating in the tub of used motor oil. Something happened. She hadn't remembered it when she came back, but the clarity of the recollection now startled her. Something about the way the photographs lined up in the mosaic.

The photographs composed an image of a massive bird with shimmering feathers and blazing, copper eyes. She understood who it was in that moment—Adonai. The true God of Alrujah—as real as the breath in her lungs. This mosaic bird, composed entirely of photographs from her life, from North Chester and Alrujah, held both her hands and looked at her the way her dad used to, when he still loved her, before he left her and forgot about her. The look made her vulnerable and safe. It crippled her with a sense of inadequacy and guilt and love.

How could anyone love the way this bird loved her—a love that shocked her and humiliated her and lifted her up to the highest reaches of joy? She had no way to comprehend His love, no way of measuring or understanding or labeling it.

I know everything you've ever done, and I love you anyway.

She felt completely unlovable, totally unworthy of His affections.

And yet He loved her with an unconditional love that comforted her, intimidated her, shamed her, and reassured her.

Lauren's tears came slowly, but punched her in her stomach with grief-stricken joy. Half her tears from guilt, the other from joy. Someone spoke in the voice of a love letter. "This is redemption," it said.

"My God." She meant every word. "You are my God."

"And you are my daughter."

* * *

Korodeth pushed Erica away, raised his hand in the air. Ullwen's dagger flashed in his hand, appeared as if pulled from a different dimension. She stepped back, her mind numb, her fingers and toes tingling.

Ullwen moved with a savage quickness, lunged for Korodeth, but the man sidestepped and threw the dagger hard at Ribillius. It soared through the air toward the wizened old king and sunk deep into the man's chest. Surprise spread over his face, and he wheezed as blood flowed from the wound. He tried to stand, but crumpled back to the throne.

Why didn't he scream?

The wheezing—Ribillius didn't deliberately make the sound. The dagger must have punctured his lung, and now air rushed from it like gas hissing from a hot stove.

"Guards!" Korodeth called.

Norby ran to a glass casing and kicked it over. The glass shattered, and he pulled a light rapier from the sparkling debris.

Ullwen did the same, choosing instead a massive broadsword.

Erica grabbed Breniveer's elbow and ran toward the stairs to the upper exit behind the dais.

Silver-clad guards crashed through the doors of the throne room with swords drawn. Their armor gleamed in the waning light of the setting suns and the torches on each column. "They've killed the king!" Korodeth cried.

A ball rose in Erica's throat. This would not end well. She understood then—Norby was right. With Ribillius dead and Lauren so far off, the only one left to take the throne would be Korodeth. But why wait this long? Why not kill him sooner?

He needed a fall guy. Of course. He'd probably known about the dungeon escape long ago, probably been watching them since they came up out of the water. Everything they'd done in Alrujah played directly into Korodeth's plan to take the throne.

Her stomach soured.

The soldiers charged.

Ullwen lunged toward Korodeth, but Korodeth avoided the attack and absconded to the back of the room. Soldiers converged on Ullwen, swords raised high. He leaned back, side-stepped, and deflected both attacks with his blade.

He didn't stand much of a chance against so many soldiers with a sword that was so heavy. He dropped it, moving from spot to spot, dodging and evading until he found an opening in his attackers' defenses. With a well-placed strike, he landed his fist in one soldier's throat.

The man sputtered and staggered back, clutching at his neck.

Ullwen didn't stop, he grabbed the other soldier's wrist, and with a twist, pulled the sword from his hand. Unlike his first blade, this one was smaller and faster.

"Let's go!" Erica said, but the doors at the top of the stairs slammed open, and more soldiers poured into the room.

Not good.

She hurried Breniveer down the stairs and behind the queen's throne. The women danced around it, dodging the broad sweeping arcs of the swords the burly soldier swung at them. "Korodeth killed him," she said, rolling behind Ribillius's throne. But of course, they wouldn't listen.

They didn't slow. They came in waves, an incoming tide of armor and anger.

Ullwen deflected another strike from a soldier, then kicked the armored man in the chest.

"The stairs," Norby said. He used the light blade to parry and thrust, taking quick stabs at the weak spots in the armor. Here, an elbow. There, the back of a knee. And, more than once, at the exposed chins and necks of the soldiers.

Blood stained the tip of his sword. He no longer looked like the scrawny, hunger-thinned prisoner she'd rescued the day before. This was a man of courage and fierce battle prowess. One did not attain the rank of general in Alrujah without being able to defend oneself.

Erica moved on instinct, without thought or consideration, a dance she'd practiced and perfected and performed thousands of times. The soldier lunged at her. She sidestepped, spun around, and kicked the soldier in the back. He stumbled forward and crashed headlong into the back wall between the two sets of stairs. His body slumped, and Erica grabbed his sword. The blade wasn't light, but it'd have to do for now. She lifted it, held it in front of her like a candle on a dark night.

Two more sentries rushed her. Ullwen deflected their outstretched blades with his. Together, they fenced their way backward to the stairs. Breniveer walked slowly, her face strewn in concentration. The soldiers, as they neared her, slowed and stopped. They looked at her, puzzled, as if they'd gone from one room to the other looking for something, but could no longer remember what it was.

Erica reached out with her mind, searching for animals to call to their aid, but couldn't concentrate. Too many soldiers rushed her, and it took every ounce of concentration to anticipate their unyielding strikes. She scaled the stairs backward, swinging the sword with the little strength remaining in her arms.

She wasn't a soldier. She was a caller. This was not her style of fighting, and her body protested each movement. Every clang of the sword shivered her arms. The shock of the blows made her elbows and shoulders and back tingle. "More will come from the top entrance," she said, pulling from some foggy memory.

Ullwen hit the oncoming swords so hard Erica thought they might shatter. "Go," he said. "Run."

"I'm not leaving you."

Korodeth stood up and wiped the blood from his lips. "Kill the usurpers."

Erica thought her head would explode. "Oh no you didn't," she whispered. She shouted, "You're gonna pay, Korodeth! By Adonai, you're going to get what's coming to you!"

Breniveer joined them on the stairs. She slipped between them and moved up the flight quickly.

Erica wrestled fear from her mind. If she wanted help, she'd have to concentrate, which meant she'd have to work on muscle memory to defend herself, and trust that her body remembered how to use a sword.

She reached out with her mind, ignoring the blades rushing toward her. Immediately, she sensed the souls of what had to be every animal, every beast in Alrujah, shining like torches, like suns. The rest of the world dimmed, and bright, orange stars ignited the darkness. Her golden Ma'at'tall bracelets burned on her arm. "Buy me time," she told Ullwen.

She turned around, rushed to the top of the stairs, and stood in the door atop the balcony. Behind her stretched a long hall with tall windows on either side. She had to do this in waves; she had to call enough to create distractions nearly everywhere. She had to coordinate everything perfectly.

Ullwen tripped, fell backward on the stairs. A soldier leapt up, his sword raised high in the air.

Erica's heart seized.

The soldier brought the sword down with a wicked vengeance, but Norby crashed headlong into him before the blade touched Ullwen. The soldier toppled down the stairs. In the confusion, Norby opened the man's throat.

Two more soldiers stepped in, one fencing with Norby, the other stabbing at Ullwen.

Breniveer rushed toward them from the top of the stairs. The soldiers slowed their attacks but didn't stop. Korodeth must be fortifying their minds against Breniveer. Still, the distraction gave Ullwen and Norby enough time to gather themselves up the stairs.

A thunder clapping of wings and lightning shrieks of razorbeaks swelled over the clanging swords. They flew in the windows of the hallway behind the balcony, enough to blot out the sun. Erica had never seen so many birds, had never imagined so many existed. They poured like smoke through the hall into the throne room and overwhelmed the soldiers who busied themselves with protecting their exposed eyes. The razorbeaks couldn't penetrate their armor, couldn't deal deathblows, but they provided enough of a distraction for Ullwen and Erica to escape, to pull Norby and Breniveer up the stairs.

Running down the hall, Ullwen said, "Fine work."

"Thanks, but we got more to do."

"You have a plan?" Norby asked in heavy gasps.

"To my room. We can grab our stuff and get out of here."

"How?" Breniveer asked.

"Four horses, a half dozen angry beresus, a couple of sasquatch." They ran through the purple cloud of feathers and beaks toward the opposite end of the hall. "From there." She stopped walking.

Ullwen turned to her. "What's wrong?"

"I can't believe it," she whispered. The birds flapped wildly around her. In the throne room, sentries cursed as they flailed madly around, trying desperately to clear the birds from their faces and necks.

The torchlights of the animals burned bright in her mind, but one burned more hotly than the others. The flames of the soul of one animal caught her attention, one she hadn't expected to find, not here in Alrujah. Her eyes moistened as irrepressible joy welled up in her. She said, "Sparky's here."

* * *

Lauren's eyes snapped open, and, remembering the marble fangands and beresus lumbering toward her, she ducked. A statue flew over the top of her and landed with a loud splash in the middle of the Harael Sea. Armed with her new understanding of Adonai, of His love for her, she readied herself to protect her friends. He loved them as much as He loved her, and His power swelled in her, ran hot in Oliver's rognak staff.

Is this what he felt when he held the staff, when he prayed in the Ancient Language? A sense of unyielding, unrelenting love and power?

The staff vibrated in her hands. The power in it, in her, awed her. It unlocked something deep within her, as if her heart itself fell open. She stuck the end of the staff under the left arm of a charging beresus. Instantly, it ceased movement. The statue fell face first in the dirt and rolled over into the sea.

Aiden. Yarborough. Side stepping another attack, Lauren rushed toward her two companions. She stretched out the staff toward them but did nothing else. Any spell might hurt them as much as the vines. She needed help. "Adonai, please," she said.

In the distance of the sky, something silver gleamed. It soared toward them, trading its hoary sheen for a hot red streak.

She moved through the statue warriors, avoiding the massive footfalls of Torap, and raced toward Aiden. His face turned blue. She grabbed his sword and hacked at the vines.

A shrieking shot across the sky. Lauren's ears hurt, but the distraction allowed her to cut the vines and free Aiden and Yarborough. They choked and rolled over, grabbed their weapons. "What was that?" Aiden gasped.

"I don't know," Lauren said. She checked the skies again, and the streak of red and silver grew closer until she made out the shape. An angel. "Bailey?"

CHAPTER TWENTY-THREE

They will ride down from the North. They will fall on Alrujah like water.
Their fury will not be satiated. Woe to all who stand in their way.
—The Book of Things to Come

ULLWELL KICKED IN THE door of Erica's room. It swung back with surprising force and nearly shattered when it slammed into the stone wall. Erica flew into the room and dropped to her knees. Sparky leapt up and slapped both front paws on her shoulders. She hugged him harder than she'd hugged anyone before. His hair tickled her cheeks, her nose, but she didn't care.

"We must hurry," Ullwen said.

Erica stood up again. "Mom, Dad. This is Sparky."

"That's a big dog," Norby said.

"Wolf," Erica said.

Ullwen handed Erica her dagger, a quiver of arrows, and a bow. Norby took a soldier's sword and a shield, and Breniveer took two daggers.

They moved back into the hall, into the cloud of razorbeaks. Erica made a fast left and led them down the narrow corridor. Purple feathers blanketed the floor. The dark hall carried the sounds of soldiers' battle cries, of steel swords clanging on stone walls, of birds shrieking and flapping, a thunderous storm of war sounds.

Without so much as a word, Ullwen pushed past her and charged down the stairs. Erica hung an arrow on her string and proceeded down the stairs cautiously, but quickly, her parents' steps behind her. She kept the feathers of the arrow pulled back to her cheek. The tension of the bowstring made her arm ache. Her heart pounded like birds' wings in her chest.

"All these razorbeaks," Breniveer said, surprise clear in her voice. "You did all of this, Lakia?"

"Wait and see what I have planned next," she said.

"They're coming," Norby whispered. "I hear them."

Erica narrowed her eyes, squinted through the mass of birds. Something silver glinted in front of Ullwen. She released the bowstring. The arrow whooshed, and with a slurk, sank into its target. Erica's stomach welled up in her.

Breniveer squeezed her hand. "Good shot," she said.

Erica didn't want to look, but she forced herself. Her stomach cramped.

Ullwen pressed on beyond the felled soldier, the limp body slid down the stairs, arrow sticking up from his eye. The armor scraped the cold stone floor, sounding like a sled on icy snow. Erica nocked another arrow and followed Ullwen.

Birds flapped up the stairs and down the stairs, around them and between them. Their caws echoed in the narrow spiral staircase. More than calls, the birds carried messages. Erica relayed them to Norby. "More coming. Both sides. Three past the stairs. More beyond them, but their hands are full with my beresus."

Norby nodded. "We go slow. Erica, put an arrow in the throat of the closest soldier. They'll find us soon after. I'll handle the other two."

Sparky growled.

"Easy, boy. Now's not the time for marking territory. You stay close and get out of this alive."

Breniveer put a shaky hand on Erica's hip and followed her every step. At the foot of the stairs, Erica loosed the arrow. In the stillness, the near silence, the soft sound of flesh splitting open echoed.

The other two soldiers charged their position. Ullwen ducked the first, who bled from the side of his neck—she'd missed.

The first soldier, heavy and thick with muscle, brought a resounding attack down on Ullwen. Though he blocked it, the force of the blow buckled his knees. He grimaced, tried to stand, but a second soldier kicked him down. In a flash, Norby had slit the third soldier's neck.

The distracting scream allowed Erica to ready another arrow. Her hand shook, and tears blurred her aim. If nothing else, the arrow should distract one of them long enough for Ullwen to recover. She let loose. The arrow clanged off his helmet. He turned his attention for a second, and Ullwen brought the hilt of his sword under the man's chin. The blow knocked the soldier out, and Ullwen spun to engage the second.

Mid-swing, the last remaining soldier screamed. He dropped his sword and ran.

"What happened?" Erica asked.

The soldier clutched at his armor, threw his helmet off, pulled at the leather straps securing his breast piece. "He thinks his armor is burning him," Breniveer said.

"What gave him that idea?" Ullwen asked, righting himself and steadying his hands.

Breniveer said, "I did."

* * *

Bailey Renee folded her wings and streaked toward the shorter of the two statues. The one-handed monstrosity had something in his hand, probably a human. Lauren? Bailey didn't care.

The statue turned its head, watched her with its one eye. It pulled its hand back and threw the person toward her. The body hurtled toward her. Clearly, it wanted to knock Bailey out of the sky, but it inadvertently made it easier to rescue the person.

Or rather, the elf. The size and pointiness of the ears became clear as it closed the distance.

She twisted slightly and caught the body. Its weight pulled her downward, and she had to strain to right herself again. Her wings spread wide, beat down with startling force, the mechanical brace whirring like a toy helicopter.

The elf, to his credit, didn't say a thing, only stared at her.

Langley.

A long, obsidian bladed sword hung from his hip. She smiled. "Told you."

"Bring me back to the battle," he said.

Beneath her, hundreds of elves scattered across Torap Island, fleeing from the stomping monstrosities. Their dilapidated homes provided little defense against blood-hungry statues. The marble fangands and beresus made no distinction between elf and human, dwarf and angel.

From this height, the entirety of the island spread out beneath her, the decrepit homes, the small booths set up in the market square, the fear etched on the faces of the elves.

This wasn't their war. Their worship of the Seers did not stem from a genuine love or affection for the half-abominations, but because Neldohr demanded it of them, likely at sword-point.

She thought of Adonai, of His patient love for His people, His desire for true worship—a worship of the heart and the mind, a worship of love, not of fear.

She swooped low to the ground and released Langley. He hit the ground, somersaulted, and sprang to his feet in perfect stride. He unsheathed the sword and used it to focus an intense beam of light toward the one-handed statue.

Bailey loosed her fire blade and arced toward the taller of the two statues, the one with both hands intact. It seemed to be using the nature of the island to tie up those who fought against it. She recognized them from the descriptions she'd read in *The Book of Things to Come*. The knight, still in his gleaming armor, wielding the golden dwarf sword and shield, must be Aiden. The dwarf, though, baffled her. Yarborough, the Nameless Heir? It must be. And the princess in the long green dress near the shores must be Lauren.

The one-handed statue swiped at her, and she adjusted her path to carry herself up and over the towering statue. She had a new plan.

* * *

An angel. More than an angel. Bailey.

Lauren put a hand over her mouth, tried to keep her eyes from clouding with tears. "Bailey?"

"Later," the angel said with a smile. "We'll get all caught up once we smash up the baddies. You going to use that stick or hold it for Oliver?"

She'd prayed for a miracle, and in flew Bailey. Adonai—God—kept His word. She shouldn't be surprised, but shock still numbed her.

The staff vibrated in her hand, and something in her swelled with power—a level up on steroids. She had no idea how deep her supply of magic would be now, but it would be enough to do what she had in mind. "I know what to do," she told Bailey. "Can you get your sword in their chests?"

"I'm on it," she said, and with a beat of her wings, leapt from the ground in an impressive backflip, and soared toward Aiden.

The cold water of the sea lapped at Lauren's heels. She let the cold run through her, clutched the staff with both hands, bowed her head, and prayed. She'd heard Oliver do it enough, and now she mimicked him, repeated the same words and phrases he had. She'd prayed before, but this time proved different. Something within her, something strangely familiar and otherworldly, spoke in a voice like Bailey's angelic fire-crackling voice. If water could speak, if vast, endless oceans suddenly ended their silence, they would speak with this voice. *I hear you, and I love you,* it said.

Power swelled in her like an overfilled water balloon. With a few words, she conjured the cold in her heart and sent it hurtling toward Torap. Ice formed between his fingers, between his toes. The crystals joined together, creating a crystalline structure that refracted the light of the suns, split it into rainbows.

A marble beresus charged her, but before it reached her, Yarborough's hammer smashed it with the force of a jetliner. Cracks splintered up from under its arm. Chips of marble sprayed past Lauren's face. Yarborough hit it again, smashing its head into small chunks of pearly rubble.

She turned her attention back to Torap, who studied his hands and feet. The ice ran up his ankles and wrists. It invaded the microscopic fissures, cracks, and holes in the statue, filled them with frozen moisture, which began to expand.

Torap moaned. Uhesdey turned to Torap. Instead of helping his brother, he balled up his remaining fist and punched Torap hard in the chest. The force of the blow, combined with the ever expanding ice crystals, shattered Torap into an explosion of marble and dust.

Aiden rushed toward Lauren holding his shield high, deflecting the debris from her path.

Lauren didn't stop. She turned the spell on Uhesdey. By now, her magic reserves should be exhausted, but power sprang from the staff and replenished her.

Uhesdey found ice between his toes, his fingers. He shouted in some arcane language to the remaining marble statues, commanded them toward Lauren. But Langley had taken the position to her left while Yarborough guarded her right, and Aiden steadied himself in front of her.

Though his blade did little, Aiden made the most of his shield. He moved quickly, smashing faces and deflecting one statue's attacks into another's. Langley twisted the Blood Sword with horrifyingly terminal results. He cut down statue after statue with little more than flicks of his wrist. Yarborough battered the marble monstrosities with the steel head of his war hammer.

Lauren blocked out the rattling ringing of metal on stone, concentrating all the more on the ice growing within Uhesdey, deep into his core.

Come on, Bailey. Come on.

* * *

Bailey Renee had seldom flown this high. The air thinned, and breathing came with stabs of cold pain. How high must she go? She only had one shot. Each minute past brought another marble statue toward her friends.

The mechanical brace whirred as she folded her wings back, extending only the tips, and only enough to guide her fall. Loud, angry air pressed against her face. She pointed her sword forward, tilted slightly to the left, aimed at the back of the one-handed statue. Faster. So fast, she thought she might rip herself in half.

Her sword plowed deep between his shoulder blades. He exploded. The resounding concussion knocked her backward. Feathers singed, she spiraled down to the soft ground, landing only feet from the marble stairs of the capitol building. When she opened her eyes, shards of pearly white stone embedded themselves in the building, in the soil, and in the tree line of the small woods behind the capitol. She sat up, every muscle bruised. Her wings ached, and the pain shot up her spine. She fisted both hands, and despite the pain, righted herself. Her legs shook, her teeth ached, her ears rang.

She put a hand on her head, steadied her vision, and surveyed the battlefield. The beresus and fangand statues lay immobile, stiff as mannequins. Lauren knelt huddled under Aiden's arm and shield. Yarborough stood, face bloodied, a shard of stone in his shoulder. Langley, the elf, lay motionless.

The ringing in her ears subsided, and a sound wrested her attention behind her. The stone shavings vibrated within the buildings and soil.

"No. Way."

Rubble, pebbles, knife-like daggers of marble shook, hummed with vibrations. They flew together, swirled in the air like water down a bath drain until they reformed into a massive two-headed monstrosity. Pieces of Torap and Uhesdey melded together. The resulting abomination walked with four legs and lashed out with four arms.

"You have got to be kidding me." She leapt into the air and soared to her friends.

Lauren shouted, "The foundation stones! Something's under them."

"Take me," Yarborough said. His shoulder bled from where the stone had stabbed him.

Bailey touched down. "You're injured."

"I need but one arm."

Langley sat up. He drew the Blood Sword and growled. "These are my people now," he said. "I'll not let them be slaughtered by deceivers like these."

"We need a distraction," Aiden said. "Bailey, you take Yarborough to Torap's foundation stone. I'll handle Uhesdey's. Make sure, after you drop Yarborough off, to get in their faces. We want them as far from the foundation stones as possible."

"I'm on it," Bailey said. She grabbed the dwarf, who, for being four-foot-nothing, must have weighed about three hundred pounds. He grimaced when she took him under his shoulder but set his jaw.

"Go," he said.

Bailey frowned, grunted with the effort, flapped her wings and ascended. On the ground, Aiden rushed toward the monstrosity. He rolled between hammering fists and massive footfalls. He moved as if his silver armor weighed nothing at all, fast and light as an elf. Lauren hurled fireballs toward Torap's head, which inexplicably grew out of Uhesdey's chest, and fashioned ice around each of its limbs. Instead of trying to blow up the statue again, she concentrated on slowing it down until they could find a more permanent solution to the problem.

Langley shot beams of light. They chipped portions of Torap's chin and Uhesdey's shoulder, but little else. Still, the frontal assault allowed Aiden and Yarborough to make it to the foundation stones on opposite sides of the capitol building.

With his good arm, Yarborough swung his hammer with all his might. The steel head cracked the stone, rang over the clamor of battle. Blood gushed from his shoulder. He dropped to a knee, then stood. With a bellow, he smashed the hammer into the stone again. It budged.

He needed Oliver. They all needed Oliver. Without his prayers, their wounds went unhealed, their exhaustion overwhelmed them. Even with his staff, Lauren's new powers waned.

Aiden's once fluid, graceful movements grew sluggish. He rammed his shield into the foundation stone, dug his heels into the soil, pushed with all his might. "I need help," he yelled.

His voice sounded strange, sounded desperate, drained of life. Anger and frustration quavered it. Ducking behind the capitol building, he used the pointed tip of his shield to dig around the stone.

That'd take way too long. The staff. It'd smashed the enchanted glass casing protecting *The Book of Things to Come* so it might do the same to the foundation stone. It seemed unlikely, but she had to try. "Bailey! Cover me!"

Lauren launched several fireballs toward the terrifying statue and ran toward Aiden.

"It's in the stone!" Yarborough yelled.

The Seers smashed a fist in front of Lauren. She yelped and stumbled backward. Another fist. She lost her footing, fell on her back. The Seers raised a foot above Lauren.

A streak of gold flashed overhead—Bailey, carrying Aiden's shield. She smashed into the raised foot, knocking it a foot away from Lauren. The foot crashed into the earth beside her. The resounding force sent Lauren shooting into the air. She screamed, flailed her arms, and remembered floating in Alrujah castle. She'd been happy, eager to meet Jaurru—Aiden. She harnessed that joy and the new joy she had in finally trusting God.

Her descent slowed.

"The eye!" Yarborough shouted, holding up a crushed orb in his bloody fist.

A shriek of inhuman pain startled her. Torap groaned like the metal hull of a ship ripping open. Lauren's feet touched the ground. She sprinted past the Seers, rolled past the shattering stone. Two of the four arms crumbled and fell from the massively wide torso, as did two of the legs. Torap's neck shattered, and the head rolled down the incline of the island toward the Harael Sea.

* * *

Outside Castle Alrujah, bodies riddled the gardens and the streets. The memory Erica had of the place—the irises and honeysuckles, the deep red roses growing near wild around the edges of the silvery pond, purple Nymphaea on the lily pads—all seemed shadowed in a reddish hue of chaos and destruction. She longed for the days of her childhood, sitting with the queen and laughing with Indigo.

Ullwen, Erica, and her parents stood near the door through which they'd exited the castle. An entire platoon of soldiers lay unconscious or crippled around a lumbering beresus. The bleeding beast heaved, stumbled forward, groaned in a surprisingly human tone. Her heart went out to it. She wanted to catch it, to bandage its wounds and lead it safely to a bed of leaves in the Cerulean Forest, but the damage extended beyond her help. Instead, her eyes met its sad eyes, and she said, "Thank you."

It reached a hand toward her, touched her face with a gentleness she'd seldom felt from human hands. The long hair of its knuckles tickled her cheek. The beast that had terrified her so long ago, on her first night in Alrujah, demonstrated its capacity for kindness and love. She understood their defense of their territory, of their homes, how they would fight any threat to their families. None of her past parents had been as human as this animal.

Sparky howled with her sadness.

A bell rang, and more soldiers poured from various towers. On a balcony overlooking the courtyard, crown still snug on his scalp, Korodeth shouted orders. By some miracle of acoustics or magic, his voice carried over the chaos.

"We need horses," Ullwen said. An arrow zipped past his head, and he flinched. He covered his ear with one hand, pulled it back. Blood pooled in his palm. He tackled Erica roughly, told her to stay down, Breniveer and Norby huddled into a corner.

More arrows split the air between them. Norby knelt in the dirt and lifted his shield in front of him. "We're pinned from all angles. If we move forward, we'll be shot for sure. Our best chance is to stay small against the walls."

"Forget that," Erica said.

The arrows slowed, their screams replaced by the terrified shrieks of men. Ullwen peeked around his shield. A sasquatch moved through the squadron of archers, smashing and throwing guards with apparent disinterest. Archers on the towers ceased their assault as they defended themselves from an onslaught of bats.

Two sasquatch finished with the soldiers on the ground, but more sentries rushed from the city gates. Hundreds poured in, and the guards closed the gates after the wave of new bodies.

"Horses won't do us much good at this point," Erica said. Hiding behind the shield, she tuned out the sound of arrows clanging against steel, against rock. She had to think of a way out of here. "Can you do something, Mom?"

"I can help with a few of them, but not with all of them."

"I wish Lauren were here," she said.

"I wish Aiden were here," Ullwen said.

"Oliver," she said. "He'd know how to get us out of this. Probably say something about Adonai."

"Adonai, help us," Norby said.

The door opened behind them. Ullwen spun around, but the figure in the doorway stood nearly seven feet tall. It held a flaming sword in its right hand, and in its left, a seven-foot stave.

Erica's jaw fell open. The man's stature frightened her, but more so, his back. Two wings spread out behind him. He leapt into the air, soared toward the mass of soldiers, and, with a flick of his right wrist, sent a flood of flames sweeping over the armed soldiers.

CHAPTER TWENTY-FOUR

He will cut down the trees of the Cerulean Forest. He will smash the walls of My monastery. He shall spill the blood of my chosen priests. And for this, My wrath will burn against him.
—The Book of Things to Come

BAILEY ARCED TOWARD YARBOROUGH. She flapped her wings hard, flew faster than she'd ever flown. She sheathed her sword and reached out her hand. As she neared, the dwarf lifted his hammer high in the air. She snatched it out of his hand.

The other foundation stone shielded Uhesdey's eye, his final link to life. Moments before half the monstrosity crumbled, Yarborough pulled Torap's eye out and smashed it in his fist. But, without a hammer, Aiden had little chance of cracking the stone. She spiraled up into the air until her keen vision struggled to pick out the tiny people moving among statues. Aiden and Lauren shrank, the dwarf diminished to a pebble and the elf to a twig. When the air thinned and her skin broke into goose bumps, she tilted downward. Holding the hammer behind her back, she plummeted. The ground raced toward her. Yards from the soil, she opened her wings enough to catch a current and level out. She swung the hammer with all the force of her descent and swung with all her might. The foundation stone exploded like a tree in a forest fire.

She took three steps and launched herself back in the air, and with a wide arc, brought the head of the hammer into the back of Uhesdey's skull. The fractured statue stumbled forward and turned on her in a violent rage. She didn't care. She'd keep it busy long enough for Aiden and Lauren to take care of the second eye.

* * *

The massive angel spiraled back toward Ullwen, Erica, and her parents. Landing in front of them, he said, "I can take two at a time."

Blood splattered his wings. "Take my parents first. Ullwen and I can take care of ourselves. Can you get the front gate open? If so, we can ride out of here."

"Ride?" Ullwen asked.

Erica neighed, and two horses reared up, kicking their riders from their backs. The armored horses galloped toward them. The angel spun around and, with a wave of his sword, set the nearest city gates ablaze.

Erica leapt on a horse, Ullwen on the other. Sparky leapt onto the neck of the horse and lay low. "We'll meet you at the nar'esh cave. Wait for us," Erica said.

The angel nodded. He stowed his sword on his hip belt and the staff on his back, then took Norby and Breniveer, spread his massive wings, and fled in the air. A volley of arrows chased after him.

Erica kicked the horse, and she and Ullwen hurdled toward the flaming city gate. They kept their heads low, snug against the armored necks of the steeds, to avoid the arrows racing at them. God help us, she thought.

Her skin twitched with heat as she neared the flaming gates. Black smoke stung her eyes, but she lay low and urged her horse on.

Don't stop now.

With a crash, the horses leapt through the gates. The sounds of battle faded until only the commanding voice of Korodeth rang in her ears.

Korodeth would pay for his actions, and pay dearly.

* * *

Lauren spent most of her life resenting Bailey Renee—for being thin and popular, smart and athletic, for being everything Lauren wasn't in North Chester. But when Bailey smashed the second foundation stone, Lauren swelled with a sisterly pride.

Aiden punched his hand into the small hollowed section of the stone and snatched Uhesdey's eye. He pulled the white orange-sized orb from the stone and stared at it. "This is what gives it its power?"

"Must hold its spirit. Spirit demands flesh," Lauren said.

Aiden's chest heaved with deep, ragged breaths. He took the eyeball and drove his dwarvish sword through the pupil. Immediately, the blade lit with fire. The eye sizzled as the golden flaming blade passed through it.

The statue moaned and covered its head with its hands. It collapsed to a knee and crumbled. Ankle separated from foot, foot from toes, legs from knees. Hand fell from wrist, wrist from arm, arm from elbow until only the head, shoulders, and torso remained intact.

Langley staggered from out of the rubble of the fallen statue, bruised and bloody, but okay. Yarborough limped over, his hand on his still bleeding shoulder. His face had little color, and his legs wobbled. Aiden's heavy breaths carried over the surprisingly incongruous sound of a gentle sea breeze.

Overhead, the scattered clouds united into a dense, black, undulating mass. Crimson flickers webbed through the rippling shade.

"Finally," Lauren whispered.

A blistering ruby light bolted from the cloud and snatched the remnants of the stone Seers into oblivion.

Lauren's skin prickled with electricity, with a reluctant relief.

Bailey landed near her. Without a word, she grabbed her sister and pulled her into a rib-cracking hug. "I love you so much, Lauren. I should have said it before. I should have said it every day and never stopped saying it. I promise you, I'll never stop saying it from now on. I'll tell you every day how much I love you."

Lauren hardly felt her sister's hug. The adrenaline had let down, and her head spun. Everything sounded funny—different as if she watched the events on a screen rather than experiencing them.

Soon, when the reality of the situation settled in, she wrapped her arms around her sister. "Bailey?"

Tears and sweat streaked Bailey's face. Lauren's cheek grew damp with it. Bailey's angelic body began to shake in Lauren's embrace, and Lauren's followed.

"Where's Oliver?" Yarborough asked.

Lauren looked out over the sea and shook harder.

END

Look for the third book in the series, *The Book of Sealed Magic*, coming soon. In the meantime, enjoy an excerpt from another Brimstone fiction book, *The Breeding Tree*, by J. Andersen.

THE BREEDING TREE

J. Andersen

THE ANNUAL PARADE AND OTHER REVOLTING PRACTICES

Code of Conduct and Ethics: The Institute—Sector 4, USA
Section 9 Article 3.8: Community celebrations must be attended by all indi-
viduals, regardless of age, gender, or physical capacity.

THE PARADE OF VALUES is my best friend Taryn Black's favorite event of the year, and every August 2nd she shows up at my door bubbling with energy, dressed in something fabulous; strawberry blonde hair waving in the breeze, and ready to nag me into leaving early.

Too bad I detest this day with my whole being.

For her, it's a holiday. For me, it's duty. Even if we were allowed to miss the event, I wouldn't, because no matter how much I hate it, I go to support Gran. At least there will be one person there who knows the truth.

Taryn knocks at my door with an hour to spare, wearing a white sundress.

"Why aren't you dressed yet?" she shrieks at me in her breaking soprano.

"We don't have to be there for another hour, Taryn. Chill, would you?" I pull myself out of the recliner and shuffle my fuzzy pink slippers across the tile floor to the sink.

"Katherine Dennard! Get your butt upstairs and put on something presentable this instant! We need to leave in five minutes to get a good view." She stomps her foot like an angry child.

I clink my cereal bowl against the porcelain sink and sulk my way upstairs. "Yes, Mother," I tease. Every year she forgets about my preferred seating ... having family involved and all.

We leave twenty minutes later, and by the time we make it to the main attraction, a mob of people cover the lawn of The Institute. I flash my ID badge to the guard posted at the edge of the preferred seating and worm my way a little closer to the stage, bypassing the common seats. Taryn follows.

We find two seats in the fourth row and settle ourselves. Mom and Dad are already seated a few rows ahead, having arrived early. The tension in Dad's neck is visible from where I sit.

At precisely 5:00 p.m., Dr. Fishgold, head of The Institute and leader of the eastern sectors, steps to the lone microphone at center stage. Normally, having the leader of the entire eastern sectors speaking in front of you should be a big deal, but since he chooses to live and work in Sector 4, his presence here is nothing new. He doesn't even have to call attention to the crowd. Instead, he stands in front and straightens his suit coat. The people feel his presence, and a hush works its way to the far corners of the crowd.

"Welcome to the 56th annual Parade of Values."

Cheers well up from the multitude, but he quiets them with a single motion of his hand.

It's the same each year: a history of our medical advances and how everything is hunky dory now and how one day we'll bring the perfected races together again to form the flawless human race. I try to let my mind wander a bit, but sitting so close requires me to at least pretend like I'm paying attention.

"It is my duty and honor to officiate this year's celebration of our community. Nearly a century ago, the races segregated themselves into the sectors we know now in order to wipe out maladies specific to each race. Breakthroughs in medical science allowed our people to eradicate many diseases of the past. The introduction of the first Microchip Implant for Health helped destroy illnesses such as cancer and heart disease, all the while increasing the longevity and quality of the lives of our people. One day, we will once again join together to create the most perfect human race in the history of mankind.

"It is these advances in technology and medicine that we celebrate today."

I lean into Taryn. "Think he'll add anything new to the speech this year?"

She shrugs. "Probably …"

Suddenly, Dr. Fishgold raises his hand in the air, and the crowd follows with the same gesture. "Success and health for all," we chant.

He cuts us off. "Do not forget how frail our bodies were in ages past. Without the evolution of our medical practices, you would be like the last generation of Natural Born, whose bodies and minds are left to chance as they age, deteriorating to mere nothingness. It's the natural development of life without advances like the MIH."

My stomach twists. It's my great-gran he's talking about.

"Today, we present them to you as a reminder of what once was and of the blessings we now have of superior mental and physical health." He makes a sweeping gesture and steps back. "This could have been your fate."

"Here they come." Taryn points offstage to the line of silver-haired people. Only three of the ten can still walk by themselves, aided only with canes; the others are pushed toward the stage in wheelchairs. One of them is my gran.

My fists clench the sides of my chair. Every morsel of my body hates that they parade Gran and her friends before the masses like a circus sideshow. I have to restrain myself from running toward the stage to stop them.

Dr. Fishgold may have told part of our story, but he left out the most important detail—that they killed thousands of Natural Born when

Gen 1 took over, and then tried to finish the job when the rebellion took place.

My great grandmother and the few others standing beside her are the last of the final generation of Natural Born allowed to live in our society.

Taryn must notice the look on my face because she says, "Kate, it's no big deal, you know."

I nod. "I know." But Taryn can't understand. She doesn't have a Natural Born relative being paraded in front of the entire community, much less one who's entirely lucid. And I can't tell her about Gran. No one can know about her clear mind or about what she's told me.

Dr. Fishgold steps to the microphone again. Just seeing the movement makes my blood boil, and I brace myself for his next announcement.

He gestures to the row of people in front of him. Three of them are drooling, and almost in unison, assistants reach around with rags to wipe the saliva from their chins. One woman stares into the clouds with a blank expression. And Gran's friend, Henry, keeps shaking his head and saying, "No, you're wrong," over and over.

I wonder who he's talking about.

Gran allows her chin to drop and her eyes to glaze over. Years of practice allowed her to perfect the look of dementia.

"This, my fellow citizens, would have been your fate had our scientists not chosen to make the sacrifices they did for the good of our society. But now, you all benefit from the MIH."

In unison, the crowd calls, "Success and health for all."

"Not all." Fishgold's sharp voice stops the people's chants. "Not all."

I look at Taryn, who has the same confused expression I do. She shakes her head and shrugs her shoulders at my silent question. Everyone around me is looking to their neighbors for an explanation. No one knows what's going on, so we turn our attention back to Dr. Fishgold for clarification.

"There is one group of people that will not benefit from our successes. Those who work to destroy the progress mankind has made. From the raids of years ago until now, there is one group that seeks to undermine further growth and development for our people: the Natural Born Rebels."

Whispers rise through the crowd and soon turn to gasps. From the far corner of the stage, Institute workers carrying weapons emerge. Two in front, two in back and between them a young man in handcuffs and ankle chains. The soldiers lead him onstage next to Fishgold where a folding chair awaits. One soldier forces the man to sit while another withdraws hair clippers and presses them to the man's scalp. There's silence as the soldier shaves the man's head, revealing to the crowd the community identification tattoo at the base of his neck. (A barcode with identification numbers.) It looks the same as the rest that come with the MIH we all receive at birth. But it's not.

"This man tried to infiltrate our society. He was caught attempting to upload a virus into the latest batch of MIHs. Tried and failed." Fishgold then withdraws a scalpel from his pocket, letting it glint in the August sun. He snaps rubber gloves around his hands and holds the knife with expert precision.

"Let this be a warning to any of those who dare to join the rebellion. You will be caught. Treason such as this will not go unpunished."

He turns toward the man as the soldiers step forward and grab the rebel by the arms, forcing him to stand.

"Any last words?" Fishgold asks as a soldier holds the microphone in front of the man.

"Long live the rebelli—"

His cry is replaced with a shriek of pain that echoes through the silent multitude as Fishgold presses the scalpel against the man's neck. In a few swipes, he's removed the thin layer of skin where the tattoo was. The man tries to pull his head away from the knife, but his chains and the soldiers restrain him. Fishgold makes one more cut, fully removing the tattooed section of the man's neck.

From my seat, I see the blood run down the back of his neck, soaking into his shirt. Taryn clenches her eyes shut. I wish I could, but I can't stop staring. This can only mean one thing. The man is a Natural Born. His tattoo is a fake, and he'll most likely die for his cause.

Made in the USA
San Bernardino, CA
08 June 2017